MW00943680

Let The Dead Stay Buried

Robert R Glendon

authorHOUSE®

AuthorHouse™
1663 Liberty Drive
Bloomington, IN 47403
www.authorhouse.com
Phone: 1-800-839-8640

First published by AuthorHouse 6/29/2009

ISBN: 978-1-4389-1064-2 (sc)

*Printed in the United States of America
Bloomington, Indiana*

This book is printed on acid-free paper.

Dedication

To My Children Who Sustain Me

Previous Titles by Robert R. Glendon

Faith Of Our Fathers
Case Day One

The Cast

Nick James
His father, Michael, died suspiciously in 1940.

Gene Petersen
He didn't tell Nick what saw until 1993.

Matt Jackson
Nick's best pal has a secret of his own.

W.D. and Red
Nick's brothers point him in the right direction.

Frank Dowling
He recalled the night Michael James died.

Oscar Swensen
Deceased local cop investigated all the deaths.

Duster Grimes
Charlie Cole's #2 knew plenty but didn't tell.

Ellen Mann
Nick's ex wife who he still adores.

Jessica Landes
Her May complicates Nick's December.

Mamie Esterhaus
Nick's aged teacher prays to die.

Mae Belle Foster
WWII captain, loyalty is her strong suit.

The Suicides

Charlie Cole
Bootlegger shot himself in 1951. Or did he?

Clara Reece
How did Crazy Clara obtain cyanide in 1953?

Duster Grimes
Nick found him at home an apparent suicide.

The Extras

Sarah Petersen
Gene's mother refused to let him talk. Why?

Ann
Nick's niece possesses a vital clue.

Pete Benson
He saw Duster the night Charlie Cole shot himself.

Icky
State Hospital Director claims he knows nothing.

Mary Lou Johnson
Jessica's mother's concern is Nick and her daughter.

Lt. Dawson
Local copper is uncooperative.

Scott Mansfield
Retired state hospital nurse recalls Crazy Clara's death.

Dolph Sterns
Funeral director knows where the bodies are buried.

Aggie Blaine
Her mother knew secrets long buried.

Ace McNally
One of Charlie Cole's bootlegging gang and The Children of God

The Settings

The East End
Where the Mississippi runs east to west

Mercerville, Il
Notional central Illinois town

Armstadt, Il
Notional southern Illinois town

FOREWORD

I slid down the wall clutching my chest, blood seeping through my shirt and fingers as I tried to hold onto whatever was left of my life. I had been shot. Jesus Christ I had been shot and I was bleeding and my mind was playing tricks on me. My butt hit the floor but my hands still clung tight to my chest. As if that would help. I didn't feel anything, nothing hurt but that damn blood kept seeping. My back was up against the wall, my legs dug into the carpet keeping my body from falling over. It was important that I not fall over. Why that was so I hadn't the foggiest. The shooting must be a mistake intended for somebody else. Nonsense. I knew damn well it was intended for me.

But I hadn't seen it coming. Me, Nick James, a homicide detective all my working life had never been shot. Psychopaths, drug dealers, even non-custodial parents had me in their sights but missed. I had thirty plus years pushing the envelop in the high crime area of Raymond, Texas and never was shot. Nightriders never got me. I craved action, hitting the door first always expecting but never getting. Close a few times, but close doesn't count.

I tried to focus on the pale, gray eyes, those damn faded gray eyes but all was a blur. I couldn't get a fix on the figure in the chair. I focused on the gun, kinda wavy like, still pointing at me. It was an old time shooter. The make escaped me. I had taken a round under the heart and I was wasting what little time I had left trying to figure out the make of the damned weapon.

Where was that corpsman that saved my life in Korea? He was zipping up my body bag when he saw my ring finger move. What was I thinking about? Oh, I know. I hadn't been shot. I was concussed and in a body bag that was it. Even the Chicoms couldn't shoot me. Tough Marine. I was dreaming up nonsense. I needed more than a corpsman now. Doctor more like it. And fast.

I didn't know why. Not all of it. I knew who shot me but didn't know why. Surface reasoning wasn't enough – not to die for anyway. Please, Lord, don't let me die without knowing. This was maddening. I was about to check out and I, a chief of detectives, didn't know why. I had come home to the neighborhood of my youth for my sister's funeral and now was about to join her. Everything was fading, my eyelids drooping like a slow curtain *ending the scene. I couldn't see. Then I heard another shot. The round must have hit me but I didn't feel anything.*

It was all black. Just black.

OCTOBER 1993

SUNDAY

My sister lay in a silver casket against the far wall of the funeral parlor. Soft lighting respected the departed in the hushed room. A table holding black and white and color photographs stood just past the flower arrangements surrounding the casket. Tripods displaying wreaths lined the walls. Chairs filled with mourners were grouped in rows fronting the casket. The overflow stood in the back talking in lowered tones. The over-sweet aroma of flowers brought back my parent's deaths, clutching my heart with a grip from which there was no relief.

I had been in the reception line since late afternoon with my niece, Ann, a clone of Sis, and my brothers, W.D. and Red. Another hour speaking the words of remembrance, smiling a cramped smile, nodding at the right times, awaited me. I recalled many of the oldies, most of whom I had

1

tossed the daily paper to some fifty years ago. But for the most part the attendees were younger church going friends of Sis that I had no recollection.

My sister was ten years my senior. She was my second mother and I loved her dearly. She coddled me as a kid, tended the skinned knees and puffed up face that cropped up during my childhood misadventures. She wrote phony excuses to the high school admissions secretary on those occasions when I had skipped classes in favor of the pool hall. She never told my mother, or if she did, I never knew about it.

My dad had died when I was a kid of eight or so and my mother was the rock that held us together, Sis, W.D. Red and me. Among the photographs on the table was a black and white one of my mother and us standing arm in arm in the back yard, laughing. What we were so happy about I couldn't say but seeing us all together filled me love and loss. She died the week after I graduated from high school. I immediately joined the Marine Corps and what with college and marriage, for all intents and purposes never returned to live in my growing up neighborhood again.

Often when I listened to Ann speak and laugh the image of my sister came to life. My eyes misted.

"You okay?"

I turned and saw my lifelong pal, Mathias Jackson. We embraced, and stood back looking at each other. My childhood buddy's face had fleshed out and had a reddish tinge either from booze or high blood pressure. Maybe both. His sky blue eyes still held a glitter that said a lot about Matt Jackson. Full of it up to his eyebrows as a kid and had never changed.

"Still the high sheriff?"

Matt swiped his hand through his blond hair as if boasting that he had yet to find a gray strand. "This is it, partner. My last election."

"Locals got your number?" I had heard rumors about my pal, things like encouraging prisoners to do the odd jobs around his home lest they find an extra six months tacked onto their sentences. Political trash I told myself.

"Nah. This old geezer is too smart to corral. What about you?"

"What any retired copper does that doesn't want to play golf every day. I'm in private business conducting interviews for law firms defending clients charged with homicide."

Matt said not too nicely, "Working the other side of the street."

I had yet to meet the copper that liked private investigators, especially me, a homicide cop now involved in defending the shits he used to prosecute. "If you say so."

Matt laughed. He motioned toward my brothers. W.D. stood quietly beside Red watching him play his tune on the locals. The curtain never dropped for Red, on-stage as long as there were bodies ready to listen to his line. Matt shook his head, admiring Red work the room. "How does W.D. stand it?"

Matt had a clue all right. If ever brothers were opposite W.D. and Red fit the pattern. A year plus apart in age W.D., the eldest, carried himself erect, tall and slim, a tailor's dream layered in a navy blue suit and white-on-white shirt appropriate for the somber occasion. Red had a problem with poundage; he draped his girth in brown, suit to shoes, belly to the west wind. His eyes, like Matt's, were starlit. He knew everybody, everybody knew him. When they were catting around at night after skirts I was still a kid.

"Listen, Nick, I gotta go but how about getting together later."

Absolutely."

"When?"

"Eight-thirty, I think, is closing time."

"The old watering hole?"

I nodded and watching him work his way through the crowd, shaking hands, dropping a word or two as the occasion warranted. He had the sincerity of a politician slicing baloney as he made his way to the exit. But it was excusable. He did say he was running for sheriff again.

The day had been wearing, and I was drained. I made my way through a side door into the alleyway that tomorrow would be the scene of limos and cars lined up for Sis's last ride. I lighted a cigarette and

4

sucked in deeply. Evening began earlier this time of year and security lights shadowed the alley. It was chilly, but maybe it was simply relief from the warmth of the funeral parlor.

"Junior?"

At first I couldn't make out the figure, but as he shuffled closer I remembered him. Gene Petersen a schoolmate from my growing up days. He had on levis and a denim jacket, and his straw blond mop hung to his eyes. I glanced down and saw his boots were untied. Gene's shoes were never tied. He clomped along to school always behind the rest of us guys. Gene was slow in more than just his walk, and kinda sad. He lived down the street from me in a shack between the river road that bordered the Mississippi river and the Rock Island railroad tracks.

Junior? Is that what he called me? I hadn't heard that since I was a youngster. Back then everybody called me Junior. Except for adults who, out of deference to my mother, used my given name, Nicholas. None of that Junior stuff for my mother.

"I wanted to tell you how sorry I was to hear your sister had died." The words came out haltingly as if Gene had memorized the lines. Proper respect, I thought, for Gene was a measured effort.

"And, I wanted to apologize for not attending your mother's funeral." Gene paused, frowning. There was more to his speech. "She was a very good woman."

I couldn't quite understand Gene dipping into the past because my mother had died in 1949. But, as I said, Gene was slow. "Thanks, Gene. I appreciate you could come."

Pointing towards the streetlight, he said, "That's my pickup, the red one."

It was a flat bed, the type you see in rural areas. The wheels and truck bed were covered with mud, its age indeterminate.

"Looks nice," I lied.

"I call 'er Red Boy." Words said with pride.

"Do you farm?" With Red Boy in my sights it wasn't much of a guess.

"Used to, but I injured my back."

"How is your mother?"

"Oh, she died long time ago."

Sarah Petersen came to mind, a frail lady who always wore a big floppy hat that covered her face. She whispered in a flat, nasal tone that left you nodding yes but not understanding a damn word she had said. Happily I never saw too much of her.

"I'm sorry about that. And your Dad?"

"He died, too. Heart attack." Again the words came out like a record repeating a familiar passage on the gramophone.

"I'm truly sorry. I liked your Dad." Richard Petersen was one of those hard luck guys that couldn't find nor keep a job. I surmised that was why they lived in a shack. I lighted another cigarette, wondering what to say to this man who shared my youth. He had had a difficult time in school, and after dropping out of high school became a non-person in my life. I don't even recall seeing him since high school.

"You shouldn't smoke. It's bad for you."

I inhaled, considered the advice. Ignored it as usual. "Where are you living now?"

"I got a place out on the river. It was my grandpa's farm."

"Which river?"

Gene shuffled his feet as if figuring out what to say. I sensed my question was unwelcome, that he had answered only to be polite. Why that was so I was unwilling to pursue.

Before I could respond he said, "I saw yer Pa standing on the railroad tracks that night he died."

"What!" My dad died in 1940. My God, that was fifty-three years ago and now Gene comes up with a man on the tracks with him. If I remembered right no one saw him die. For the moment I just stared at Gene, unable to speak.

"There was another man in a long coat and big hat waving his arms at yer Pa. I swear that's what I saw, Nick. I'd never lie to you. You were my best friend."

I was momentarily numbed. Was Gene inventing this story or did he actually see my father and another man? Gene was simple but I never knew him to lie. I nearly yelled at him, but calmed myself. I said, softly, "Did the other man do anything to my dad?"

"I couldn't tell because Mr. Dowling's freight came between me and the tracks. I was so scared I ran back home."

"Why didn't you tell me when we were kids?"

Gene stammered, "I was scared."

I lit another smoke. His answer was what I might expect out of Gene. My fingers were shaking. "How come you happened to see it?"

"I had to go to the outhouse. That's when I saw your dad and the man. I didn't see what happened, but I knew something bad happened because fire came from the train wheels for a long time before Mr. Dowling stopped it. I didn't know until the next day that your dad had died."

I nodded. We had been only eight years old, Gene and I. Oscar Swensen, the local copper who lived on our street, told my mom and us kids that my dad had apparently fallen and struck his head on the rails, then had crawled off the rails before Frank Dowling's freight passed. It was common knowledge that my dad took a walk of an evening. He was often seen either going to or coming from the river, but on that faithful night no neighbor had seen him. Oscar said that without witnesses he could only conclude that it was an accident. As to the rumors that my dad was a drunkard the neighbors testified en masse that such was a nasty lie. I sure remember that.

It had taken me a long time to realize that he was really gone. My mother and Sis comforted me, but the worst hurt of all was that I never had a father. I cried myself to sleep trying to understand why God had taken him from me.

"Who was the man?" I asked Gene, "Did you know him?"

"I don't know."

"Didn't your folks know what you had seen?"

Gene was laboring, almost in tears. "I told my Mom."

"Didn't she tell Oscar Swensen?"

"She said not to tell anyone. Please, Nick, you're scaring me."

Gene was visibly shaking and he looked at Red Boy longingly as his means of escape. I felt sorry for him. The fact was I always felt sorry for Gene. I asked, "Why are you telling me this now?"

Gene didn't answer me, probably didn't know why. He said, "Your sister was a mighty fine woman." Then he made off across the street, shuffling as he did when we walked to school. He got in the truck and drove off, never once looking back.

I puffed away, smoking as if the act gave me respite from an unavoidable truth. In my mind's eye I saw a little boy sitting on the back porch swing waiting for his dad to came home from work. He'd wait there every night and run to the garage while his dad parked the car, and then walk back to the house with him. Sometimes they didn't even talk much, it was enough just to be with him. After he died the boy still waited on the back porch swing as if his dad would somehow magically appear. Mom or Sis or W.D. or Red would sit with him. What they said was lost in time. Then one day, it was winter, and he didn't sit on the swing any more. He knew his dad had died. That wasn't why he waited. He couldn't explain himself, not to Mom or Sis, or his brothers.

I broke myself free of the past. The canister was filled up with my cigarette butts, but I still lit up. Gene had brought my father back to life, rather back from death. Why was my dad on the tracks that night? And who was he with? Who was the man in the long coat waving his arms? That was fifty-three years ago. Who could I confide in now? my brothers certainly, but not yet. Matt had been the Police Chief before running for sheriff and could, I was certain, obtain old police records. But I was getting ahead of myself. I decided to walk softly until I knew more. If Gene was right the possibility existed that my dad's death was not accidental. It could it have been an assault or even murder. The memory of him demanded that I act. Dig up who and the why. And give a measure of relief to little boy who cried himself to sleep asking God why.

I doused out my cigarette in the sand canister, took a deep breath, and opened the door to the funeral parlor.

The crowd was dwindling. Stalwarts from Sis's church drifted out promising to return for the services and burial tomorrow. Then, as if a magician's wand had cleared the room, I joined Ann and W.D. and Red before the casket. I put an arm around Ann, praying silently. "Please God, accept my sister."

We walked out, our goodbyes muted, not a whole lot to say.

"Be here at ten, Unk," Ann said to me. As a little tyke she had shortchanged uncle to, "Unk," but she never shortchanged her affection for me. Nor I for her. I could have stayed with Ann in Sis's home, my mother's home, the home I had been raised in, but I wanted rest and solitude. I had booked a room in the downtown hotel, but having promised Matt I would meet him for a drink I fired up my rental and headed for our old watering hole. I debated all the way what to tell him.

Matt

I walked through the small package liquor store into Hagen's Tavern needing a drink badly. A sepia glow descended sluggishly from overhead neons yellowed with the residue from cigarettes, cigars, and the lethal emissions from old man Hagen's Turkish shag tobacco. Ceiling fans rotating at ought miles per filtered the smell of hops and malt that, like the once cream, now brown paint job, clung to the walls. Blind Pew could have sniffed

11

his way into Hagens and known exactly where he was. Atmosphere was everything.

During my high school years, Hagens was a sure fire stop. That was when Jimmy watched the till. On his good days he didn't cuss you when you walked in. I remembered it well.

I scanned the room but didn't see Matt. Spotting an empty booth, I weaved my way through a line of checker cloth tables and sat down.

"Whatcha having, hon?"

I caught the image of the quick talker staring down at me. Blond hair neatly combed, small frame. Had a bit of age on her, but had that perky sass that wears well on a half pint. She had, as they used to say down at the railroad yard, circled the round house more than a few times.

"Name's not Nellie is it?" I grinned.

"Stella. And don't be a wise guy." Returned the smile. Quick on and off like flicking a light switch to see if the electric bill had been paid.

"How about a shot of VO, draft chaser. Just none of that light stuff."

"Heavy hitter, huh." Stella dropped a napkin on the table, added, "Expecting anyone else?"

"Yeah, an old buddy."

Dropping another napkin, she tittered, "Listen hon, at your age they're all old."

"Thanks."

"Don't mention it."

Stella danced away, tiny rump moving fast tempo time, stopping to clear a table. When she returned she said, "I know a guy that orders the same thing, VO and beer chaser. This some kind of ritual"

Unwilling to discuss my youthful drinking habits, I said, "Must be a coincidence." I watched her swivel away, but my thoughts were on Gene Petersen and what, if anything, I was going to tell Matt. We had shared secrets as kids and mutually trusted one another. So, I asked myself, "What's the problem?" I didn't have an answer.

Then I saw Matt at the bar, tapping some old geezer on the back, giving out with happy talk to the old timers. When Stella reached the bar Matt broke away from the 1930s crowd and put his arm around her, grin strobe bright. She didn't seem too thrilled. Looking over Stella's shoulder Matt caught my eye. He turned the waitress around, nodding in my direction, said something that upset her. She removed his arm, acting like a woman put out for putting out.

Matt eased his way through the crowd, grunted his way into the booth gut first.

"Friend of yours?" I said.

"Gotta make 'em happy." Then, frowning, he said, "How did it go?"

"Compared to what?" I said.

"You know."

"Yeah. Sorry. The minister asked me to say something tomorrow at the grave site, but I knew I couldn't do it."

"Like tonight?"

I paused, the image of my sister smiling down at me. It was her first job and she gave me a quarter, said it was my allowance. I never had an allowance before. Jesus, how much could she have earned a week back then? I breathed hard, forcing back the emotion. "You okay?"

I took down the shot of VO, waved the empty glass to Stella. "The mood in the mortuary lightened up, people remembering all the things Sis did for the oldies. She made a regular run to the hospital and nursing home."

"And you?"

"Like the pit of my stomach was filled with ice. I was glad to leave."

Stella dropped a pitcher of beer and two shot glasses on the table, said to me as if I had suddenly contacted a case of leprosy. "Why didn't you tell me who you were waiting for?"

"And be tossed out?"

"Wouldn't be the first time." Matt grunted as if bringing back the times old man Hagen showed us the door.

To the disgusted tone of, "You men," Stella pranced her way back to the bar.

Hoisting a shot, Matt said, "Here's to Sis."

Clicking his glass, I said softly, "Here's to Sis."

"So, Nick, what's new?" Proforma question, asked as if he was afraid of the answer.

"Still single, retirement is a dead end street."

"Have you seen Ellen?"

Only my childhood best friend could approach the forbidden region of my feelings. It had been nearly fifteen years since our divorce, or should I say her divorce. I refused to ask him if he had seen her. Being reminded of her, especially now, didn't help.

"My god that was a long time ago." It was not precisely an answer but how I did or did not feel about my ex-wife wasn't on the table. I drained my glass. Damn Stella had given us a pitcher of lite. I hated lite beer.

"Well, Nick, don't take any offense, but I got you figured for a brooder." Matt picked up another shot glass. "I see Ellen around and about. Her husband died of cancer three, four years ago. Guess she figured twice was enough, but she has plenty of chasers."

I said," Brooder? You're a hell of a psychologist, Matt. How's the sheriffing?"

"Get to that in a second. Don't tell me you been celibate all these years?"

My temperature raised a tad. "What do you think I am, a priest? For your information I was married once. Once, got it? Like a virus shot that didn't take, the divorce didn't cure me of Ellen. The others didn't measure up. Drop it, Matt, for Christ's sake."

Matt said, "You don't have to get huffy about it, I was just asking."

Drop the attitude, Nick. I said, "So you're running again?"

"Yeah. But after twenty plus years in the PD, six as chief, and nearly eight as sheriff, I'm about burned out."

Common complaint. A lifetime of law enforcement has a way of beating the crap out of a guy. Or maybe it was Matt's home life. I said, "How's the family?"

"The wife gave me my exit notice, my son ditched college in favor of surfing and screwing in Maui, and my chief deputy's been indicted for looking south when the gamblers dropped a hundred grand on his door step. The papers are after my ass claiming I'm too old for the job. Otherwise, everything is right as rain."

Stella dropped two more shots on the table, nodding toward the bar. Matt waved to the bartender.

I eyed him through my shot glass. His face, like his personal life, came out contorted. "Stella part of your problem?"

"Yeah. I figured she met the profile."

"Profile?"

"You know, half your age plus ten."

I produced a blank stare, waiting.

"Jesus, you're thick. The ripe ones got their juices running too fast for this old geezer, and the old ones had their bread in the oven too long. Like I said half your age plus ten."

"And Stella fits the profile?"

Matt grinned like Tarzan ogling Jane. "Thought so, Nick. Now that the wife chased me out Stella thinks we ought to get hitched."

I chased the shot down. Damn, I forgot to tell Stella to bring us real beer. "Gene showed up tonight."

"Gene?"

"Gene Petersen."

"Gene Petersen who shadowed us when we were kids?"

"Right."

"The buster who never talked?"

"The same."

"I haven't seen or thought of him for years."

"Neither had I. He cornered me outside the funeral home. Told me he was sorry about my sister's death."

"Wonder what brought that on?"

"I haven't the foggiest. Gene said he is living in his grandfather's farm out on the river."

"Lots of rivers, which one was it?"

"Didn't say, and I didn't ask."

Matt said, "Never knew what happened to Gene. He was a strange one."

"Tell me about it," I said. "Did I ever tell you about the time I took him to the state hospital?"

Matt's orbs flickered. "The loony bin?"

"I was making a few bucks driving this old International newspaper truck from downtown through the East End all the way to the state hospital."

Matt interrupted. "I don't remember that."

"You were too busy starring in football and basketball. Big man the girls went gaga over."

Matt sighed caught up in the memory. "Best time of my life. Had the pick of the litter."

"I'm sure you did. Anyway, some of us had to work. There was a shortage of drivers during WWII and I lied about my age. I didn't even have a license, maybe sixteen or so. Anyway, Gene used to go with me tossing off the bundles to the paperboys. He liked the ride I guess."

Matt signaled Stella who promptly returned with two more shots.

"Put it on my tab."

"The one you never pay?" Stella, still huffy, waltzed away.

I took a sip, sighed. A lover's quarrel I didn't need. "This one night was as cold as a well driller's ass, the wind was up, trees stretched out in the wind. It was November or December and the sun decided to quit for the day. There were only five papers to deliver and Gene got a kick when he handed the bundle to the inmate who every night

18

gave out with a smile and the words, 'thank you, oink, oink.'"

"Oink, oink!"

"Every night, thank you oink, oink."

"Did the guy think he was a pig?"

"Sure, doctor. I sat him down for a session every night. When sir, did you first notice that you were a pig? How the hell should I know why he said oink, oink? Pat was his name, a middle-aged inmate, tall, nicely dressed, but living in gaga land.

"Anyway, the truck died. I grind away, but the son of a gun wouldn't start. So we start walking to the administration office that was a couple of blocks away. Full moon, like the time we saw the nutty doctor and his number one digging up the monster's body from the graveyard."

Matt said, "That movie scared the crap out of me."

"Me too. So on the way to the office we hear this God awful screaming. I looked up and there with her arms outspread against the bars was Clara Reece screeching like a banshee. Damn near peed my pants. We took off like a pair of missiles, feet never hitting the sidewalk. First time I ever saw Gene cross the finish line in first place."

"This the same Clara Reece who harassed the hell out of us for stealing apples from her orchard?"

"Same old bat. When we get to the office I grab the phone and call the paper. I inform the night man, you remember Uncle Tom, the truck won't start. He says everybody's gone home and why don't I go back to the truck because I probably flooded it. I allow as to how I'm not too thrilled with that advice because the inmates are on the loose it being a full moon and all, and I am a bit shy on starting flooded vehicles. Uncle Tom gives me a tsk, tsk, and hangs up."

Matt savors his shot, downs it with a flourish. "So the monster pops out and hands you and Gene your heads."

"You want to hear this or not?"

"Sorry."

I paused, a bit ticked off, hated interruptions when I had the floor. "No, the monster does not pop up. The night guard tells me the screamer is only Clara Reece. I tell him I already know who it is, and, given the chance, she'll tear us to bits with her bare hands. He says she is absolutely locked up tight. He agrees with Uncle Tom that all I've done is flood the engine.

"I look at Gene who is shaking like an aspen, and his face has a greenish tinge to it. Like a dimwit I ask him if he's okay, and he backs away as if I ought to be confined with the rest of the nut bars. I start out but he doesn't want to go. So I grab him by the arm and once more we set the hundred-yard dash record. Clara is still plastered up against the bars, screaming crazy words, something about I see you children I see you children. It's all a blur.

"When I stick the key in I hold down the gas pedal and pray. And that old International pops off. I skid around the corner and down the hill. Tell you, there wasn't a copper fast enough to catch me that night."

Matt's laughing and pouring beer, slopping excess on the table. "Gene ever go with you again?"

I watched Matt soak up the spill with a few napkins. When he had finished I said, "Come to think of it, I don't remember ever seeing Gene again."

"You mean not until tonight?" Eyebrows up like a raccoon under the spot light.

"Not that I remember." I paused, lit a smoke, fingering my Zippo lighter that had been a part of my life since Korea. It had the Marine Corps logo on it. I was temporizing.

Matt said, "You wanted to say something?"

"It's about Gene. Tonight he told me that he had seen my father on the railroad tracks the night he died."

Matt bummed one of my cigarettes and lit up. He didn't say anything. Like a good cop he knew when not to talk.

"You remember he lived in that shack between the tracks and river road. According to Gene he was going to the outhouse when he saw a man waving his arms at my dad. And then Mr. Dowling's freight passed between him and my dad and the other man. He didn't actually see what happened to my dad, nor does he know who the man was."

Matt said, "I remember my folks talking about your dad, but I really remember wondering what to say to you. Hell, we were just kids. Do you believe Gene?"

"Gene was no liar. If this occurred as Gene recalls it is likely a repressed memory. But if that is so what triggered it? At the time it must have been traumatic for him. He said he told his mother, but what I can't understand is why Sarah Petersen didn't tell Oscar Swensen. What possible motive could she have had?"

Matt said, "Knowing Gene's mother she was probably as scared as he was. As I remember she was spacey."

I countered. "Yeah she was that, but Mr. Petersen was a fair man. Why didn't he say something?"

Matt doused out his cigarette. "Hate coffin nails."

"So?"

"I don't know why Mr. Petersen didn't tell Oscar. My first job was with the Springfield PD and when I got on here with the Moline PD Oscar was a detective. We used to share a beer or two up at Casey's, and he'd go on about his best cases. To relieve your mind he never mentioned your dad or the night he was killed."

"Never?"

"Oh, he talked about you sometimes. He couldn't understand why you were wasting your time with a Texas PD when you could have come back here. Oscar said the PD would have opened a position for you even if none existed. Almost being zipped up tight in a body bag in Korea when you were still alive made quite a splash in the papers, and made a big impression on Oscar. But no, he never spoke about the night your dad was killed."

I said, "And everybody who would know is dead."

"Not really. Frank Dowling is still alive. He's hanging on, bad ticker I understand. He has caregivers every day. The only time I see him is when I want his vote. That makes me some kind of shit because Frank is one of the good guys. He took it hard when your dad died. He and Oscar and your dad were fast friends."

"I have to know."

Matt said, "You need to locate Gene and talk to him again."

"I know but not yet. Sis's funeral is tomorrow, and I promised Ann I'd help her clear out the house."

"Sorry, I didn't mean to press."

I said, "But I don't want Gene's story to get around."

Matt pushed back his shot glass, and gave it a once over as if disbelieving it was empty. "You shouldn't have to say that to me."

"Forgive me, this has really upset me."

Matt said, "See Frank. After the funeral if you can."

"I gotta hit the head." I walked to the restroom. When I returned Matt had left.

Stella waved me over. "Himself got a call. Said to tell you he'd be in touch."

"Thanks. Tell you what, bring me a cup of coffee, black."

"Looks like a pot would do you better."

The room was almost empty, quiet was exactly what I wanted. I sipped and smoked, got lost in self-pity. After Ellen divorced me I lost myself in the Job and booze. Which was the problem to start with. Melancholy clung to me like barnacles hugging a rusty ship's hull.

When I was a student pilot fighting the cross winds on my final approach, my instructor would snarl, "Landing's gone to shit, Nick." That's what my life was like, a bad landing, gone to shit. Shaking off the VO, I approached Stella, said, "What's the tab?"

"Himself paid for it."

"Leave a tip?"

"That's the only thing he's left me lately."

The evening had a washed chill to it as if a great hand had scrubbed the sky. Stars and a nearly full moon ruled over the fall night. I motored though the downtown slowly, taking in the present, thinking about what once was. At ten p.m. there wasn't much to offer, a few closed stores that, like deserters, had fled to the malls of plenty. But the two major banks still clung to main drag, life support systems providing a flow of greens to businesses on the edge.

I dropped down to the river road to take a look at the new convention center. It had replaced blocks of farm equipment industries that once fueled the life of the town. As I considered the concrete rotunda and the expansive parking lots I didn't much appreciate it. Then again, I was acting like an old poop. If it was good enough for the Boston Pops who was I to say nay? The city had to do something to stop its death rattle.

I parked in a lot behind the hotel, got out and sat on a bench where the railroad station had claimed the lion's share of travelers to the city of big shoulders. My first train trip to Chicago started right here. In the dining car I had the first sandwich of my young life not home made. My mother dipped in deep for that treat. God, she was good to us.

I sat on the bench, my eyes misting. My mother died over forty years ago, and her dear face is as clear to me now as it was when I was a child. We were boarding the train, right here, and she was smiling at me, letting me sit by the window so I could wave as we passed through our neighborhood in the East End. Ever after, my visions took me someplace beyond the horizon.

I got up and walked around to the hotel. It still towered over downtown. Having been refurbished, it returned the center core of the city to a semblance of its past vitality. Until the lure of gambling had infected the locals with visions of quick riches the hotel had lain dormant. But with tax revenues rolling in from the riverboats and the need to house the out of town risk takers, the shabby hotel came to life once more.

I strolled into the lounge and scanned the interior. It had been done in the fashion of its original theme that, I decided, was kind of neat - red leather booths, soft music, a seeing-eye dog required to navigate a path to the bar. I passed a table of losers talking loudly about the woman from Muscatine who had cashed in on the BIG BONAZA. I wondered if, in their fever-ridden eyes, they had forgotten Uncle Sam who, demanding his immediate cut, marched to the same greedy tune as they did. Again, I felt like an old poop.

I placed my rear on a red leather stool and ordered Wild Turkey, light on the rocks. Should have picked up a bottle at Hagen's, but like most of my good ideas, they arrived after the stage had left. I sipped the smoky bourbon, listened half-heartedly as Roger, the bartender, cut up the riverboat oldies that had last left a tip during WWII. I ordered bagels and lox and a Corona to be sent to my room, signed the bar bill and carried a double shot to the elevators. The losers were still in an upbeat mood, planning to give the riverboat hell tomorrow.

I took the elevator up to the eighth floor, got off and wandered down the hallway. My room overlooked the Mississippi; directly below ran the mainline tracks. The room was generous, ceiling high enough for a game of hoops, wainscoting painted cream set off framed prints of the city of yesteryear, beige drapes and matching valance skirted huge windows. Bob and Carol, and Ted and Alice could have rumbled comfortably in the large four-poster. Didn't fancy Bob and Ted, but Carol and Alice was a thought.

I draped my suit jacket and tie on a chair, kicked off my Texas boots and pulled a chair up to the window overlooking the train tracks and the Mississippi. I flipped on the TV for the noise content, couldn't stand silence. I sat down, wearily. A cigarette came naturally into my fingers. I smoked and finished the Wild Turkey. Room service delivered my bagels and lox. I uncapped the Corona, ate and watching the river.

I heard the sound of a train horn, the diesel kind. It didn't have that same waa, waaa, waaaa of the steam engines that put me to sleep as a kid, imagining places and people yet to be seen. I sat there for the longest time, smoking, dipping into my memory bank.

It was the week after my dad had died. I had been absent from classes for the past week and I dreaded going back to school. I was up on the bluff under my favorite oak, a good place to avoid my pals.

It was a hot Saturday day, and I took in the Mississippi imagining myself on one of the barges chugging up and down the river. Gene struggled up from the street below, puffing with the climb.

"I'm awful sorry about yer Pa."

"He weren't any drunk like they been saying."

"That's the pure truth. Yer Pa was a right fine man. He didn't kill hisself either."

"What? How do you know, Gene?"

"What do you mean? How do I know?"

"Were you there?"

"No."

"Well?"

"I just know."

"You're confusing me, Gene."

"We still friends, Nick?"

"Sure. Friends what I got now."

"I'm scared, Nick. I cain't tell."

MONDAY

The sun warmed my back yet a cool breeze brushed through the pines and trees. Leaves painted red and gold and yellow set off a cloudless sky with a pale blue hue, one of Sis's favorite colors. A procession of cars filled the cemetery lanes. Sheriff deputies, parade ground sharp, stood attentively at the front gates. I spotted Matt but he kept well back of the mourners who were lined ten deep at the gravesite. I sat in a folding chair next to Ann. W.D. and Red flanked us. Sis was poised to lie by her husband, a grand guy who was my hero when I was a kid. The choir sang Amazing Grace.

I hardly heard the words of praise, nor the singing. My eyes were trained on Sis's casket resting on the straps above the hole that would seal her remains forever. I resisted the finality of the moment. Ann had her hands folded, back straight, eyes directed at the minister, at the speakers, missing nothing. I dimly heard W.D.'s choking sounds. The tough guy wasn't so tough after all. Red kept his feelings off stage. My mother and father, I was sure, were watching.

The minister gave us each a long-stemmed rose that, one by one, we placed on the casket.

The service was over.

"You are coming to the church."

I put my arms around Ann, whispered into her ear. "I thought I'd stay for a while if that's okay with you."

"Sure, Unk."

I saw my brothers standing along side Red's Jaguar. "Tell the boys I'll see them later."

"Sure, Unk."

I strolled across the cemetery. Up ahead a familiar figure was waiting for me.

Matt said, "I suspect you don't want a ride."

"I just thought I'd pay my respect to my parents."

"I don't want to break your mood, but I remembered something about what you told me last night."

"Last night?"

"Yeah, about when Clara Reece scared you and Gene at the state hospital."

"So?"

"Clara was Gene's aunt."

"Gene's aunt?" I mumbled.

"Yer talking to yourself, Nick."

"It's a habit of mine. I suspect there's something more."

Matt said, "Clara reportedly committed suicide about the same time when the Chinks invaded Korea. "

I never saw so many Chinese in my life. They came at us in waves. Matt was with the Army X Corps, me with the 1st Marine Division. How we lived through the carnage is a wonder. I was damn near zipped up in a body bag still alive. It was a subject I chose to ignore. I mean the war. So did Matt.

"Oscar Swensen told me the facts of her suicide made public didn't make sense. Oscar said his attempts to talk to the hospital staff were rebuffed."

"So?" Why the neighborhood copper was interested in Clara's Reece's death didn't interest me.

Matt shrugged. "Sorry. I know this is a bad time."

I lit a cigarette, eyeing my pal. "Forget it. I didn't mean to be an ass."

Matt forced a grin, started to walk away.

"Hey, aren't you gonna tell me about Crazy Clara?"

Matt turned, neon lights replacing his faded blue eyes. "Oscar said he found out Sarah Petersen was Clara's sister when he stuck his nose into Clara's death."

"You mean all those years nobody knew Sarah Petersen and Clara Reece were sisters?"

"If Oscar didn't know it, nobody in the neighborhood knew it." I said, "I thought we two knew everything that went on in the old neighborhood."

"Just goes to show you. A couple of nosy kids weren't as smart as they thought they were."

"Speaking of noses, what did you mean about Oscar sticking his nose into Clara's death? Didn't he investigate it?"

"Not officially. The state hospital is in county territory. Being on the local PD Oscar had no jurisdiction, but he said he had a few words with the sheriff. Sheriff told him to go blow smoke."

Oscar Swensen's giant frame came to mind. When he told us kids to stop nutsin' around we said yes sir and went quietly. I said, "Have to be mighty brave to tell Oscar to get lost."

"Seems Oscar had lipped off more than once about the sheriff allowing whore houses and gambling operating in the county."

Sounded just like Oscar Swensen. "So Oscar thought there was something more to Clara's death than a suicide?"

Matt said, "According to Oscar the word was that she was found dead of unknown causes. But shortly after her death the guard of the violent ward was let go. This red flagged Oscar. He tried to talk to him but he moved to parts unknown."

Matt squinted, one eye half closed. Same look he had when he was a kid without answers to a difficult test question. "Sorry I got so wrapped up in Oscar. You got other things to think about."

I said, "You have access to county records. Dig out the coroner's hearing of my dad's death will you? Michael James. He died September 16, 1940."

He nodded. I followed his broad back to the sheriff's wheels. Then I made my way across the cemetery to my parent's graves.

Their gravesite overlooked the East End and the Mississippi.

I kneeled and prayed, seeing Ma and Sis, W.D. and Red, in my mind's eye. For years every Sunday we trooped up to the cemetery to pray before my dad's grave. My dad, Michael, died 9-10-1940, as I had told Matt. My mother, Georgina died 6-15-1949. Their deaths etched in my mind happened a lifetime ago, my lifetime.

My thoughts were still revolving around unanswered questions over my dad's death. Why was he on the railroad tracks that night? Who was the man with him? Was it an accident or his death of more sinister consequences? Possibly the coroner's report would tell me something, but I doubted it would answer the questions Gene's account raised.

The flowers in the gravesite silver urns were a bit bedraggled. I pulled out some crab grass and picked up a few twigs. Autumn leaves were scattered about, dancing to the tune of a soft breeze. Sis had taken care of their graves. Now the task would fall to W.D. and Red. Task? Honor was more like it.

Ellen

I felt a hand on my arm and turned.She was wearing a wide brimmed hat and a tan cashmere coat. A paisley silk scarf surrounded her throat. Her eyes captured mine, but only for the moment. Classy dame in a fashionable hat, my former wife.

I muttered, "Ellen."

"How are you, Nick? An almost smile brushed her lips. "That's a dumb question considering the occasion. I know how much Sis meant to you."

She was my life once. But she couldn't or wouldn't accept the uncertainties of a cop's life that, in my case, was tinged with the image of me in another body bag. I didn't understand how much she hated the Gulf coast heat and my job. My drinking didn't help. "It's either the Job or me, Nick." I really didn't believe she would leave me.

God, the years had been kind to her. I wondered if she had any feelings for a retired, beat up chief of detectives. Dreamer.

"Frank Dowling wants to see you."

"Is he still alive?" The words were out before I could get my foot out of my mouth. Flunked tact.

I also forgot that Matt had told me he was alive. Memory was going to shit.

"Alive and kicking. Well, not much kicking. He was sorry he couldn't get to your sister's wake, but Frank doesn't go out much anymore. He sure remembers you."

From a signboard across the avenue from Mr. Dowling's house Matt and I used climb up the girders to spy on Clara Reece and whoever else drifted into our sights. "How is he?"

"In a wheel chair, but his mind is sharp as ever. I fill in when the care giver takes her days off."

I reached out to touch her. She stepped back avoiding my gesture. A cloud crossed her face. The moment held a message that I sensed meant hands off. I was embarrassed, felt like a damn fool. I recovered, said, "I'll get down after I stop by church."

"Do that, Nick. You'll make an old man happy."

Not you'll make me happy.

She said, "You remember where Mr. Charles lived?"

"Sure, down by the river."

"Frank lives there now."

I watched her walk toward a Buick and drive off. She still had a classy stride. The old guys basking in the park eyeing that stride used to refer to her as a looker. And some young guys, too.

Down below the cemetery trees and undergrowth blocked my view of the avenue, but the river, my river, captured my eyes. A huge red and white paddle wheeler loaded with gamblers plied a new sort of river trade. The cool breeze and touch of fall massaged my tired body with a mother's caress. I should have gone to the church but the river beckoned me.

Up the berms and over the railroad tracks but not with the same abandon I had when, during the winter's days of snow and ice, I passed papers to old Jep's shack and the few nice houses fronting the river. The river road was now paved and a tree-lined concrete walkway followed the sweep of the Mississippi. The smell of Jep's smoke house had surrendered to the venting of a modern riverside restaurant. I watched a tug pushing coal barges down the river so all was not lost. I lit a cigarette, scanning the surroundings lest my habit, like the odor of Jep's catfish, was forbidden. Foolish thought. Nothing was ever the same.

A copse of bushes covered the ground where the Petersen shack accompanied by their outhouse had hung low to the ground between the tracks and the river road. It was here Gene said he saw my father with another man standing by the tracks. I couldn't get it out of my thoughts that neither he nor his parents had told Oscar Swensen what Gene had seen. I paused for a while unable to bring back my childhood to focus on the reality of my dad's death. I walked on.

Frank

Standing before the veranda of a home once owned by Mr. Charles I imagined the arc of my paper as it settled softly on the front porch. The times I had hit the big front window were, along with the shouts and glares, erased from my memory recorder.

"Nick."

Ellen was on the front porch waving to me. I must have looked like a nut grinning foolishly at empty atmosphere.

"Frank is waiting."

She wore a navy blue skirt and white blouse. A tan cardigan draped over her shoulders. Her ash blonde hair, shorter than I remembered it, was, I thought, perfect. Except for a slash of pale lipstick she wore no makeup. Ellen walked me into a den fronting the river. Lord, what a stride.

Pine paneling, oil paintings of river scenes, a TV set, book cases. The room was clinically clean and had an aroma of wax. Frank Dowling, back to me, sat in a wheel chair looking out of the picture window, a lap robe across his legs. White hair slipping around his ears hid the stems of his glasses.

"Frank," loud voice from Ellen, "Nick is here."

He turned, smiled. "This is a real pleasure." Nothing timorous about his words, but faded eyes behind the lens were lined with moisture. His skin fell in folds like a Beagle hound.

Ellen said, "How about a cup of coffee?"

"That," I said, "would suit me just fine."

Before Ellen left she whispered, "You'll have to speak up."

"I heard that." Frank Dowling brushed his lips with a smile, said to me, "Sit down. Here close to me."

I raised my tone an octave. "Thanks, Mr. Dowling."

"Jesus, no need to shout." Again the soft smile. "And call me Frank. You aren't a younger any more."

That, I thought, was an understatement. I said, "When did you move into Mr. Charles's house?"

Frank made a feeble wave, said, "Long time ago. The traffic on the main drag got the best of me."

I pointed to the oil paintings. "Those yours?"

"Yes. Did them in my good days." He held up his hands. They were knotted with arthritis. "Can't paint anymore." An edge of disappointment curled what once was, I presumed, his passion.

"I see you painted Old Jep and his smoke house, and your steam engine highballing it through the East End."

Frank shrugged as if taking the subject off the agenda. "So how are you, Nick?"

"Pretty good, Mr. Dowling." Couldn't bring myself to call him Frank. "You know about Sis." No question here.

"I was awfully sorry I couldn't attend the funeral, but Ellen went in my place. Your sister helped me many times. She was good to us oldies. What is Ann going to do about the house?"

"Sell it, I believe."

"You ought to come home. Get back to your roots."

I paused, giving the impression I was considering his suggestion. But that would have been a lie. "Been away too long, Mr. Dowling. I don't think I could handle the house."

"You mean living in it don't you?" Frank Dowling's head fell forward, his words losing their volume.

"Yes sir, living in it."

"Suppose you're right."

Ellen came in with a tray holding a silver coffee pot, brimming china cups, buttered scones, lace-trimmed napkins. She placed the tray on a table between us. "This ought to hold you."

Frank came back to life, head erect, his voice perking up. "Pretty fancy, don't you think?"

Ellen laughed. "I'll just leave you men alone."

Frank Dowling's gratitude and love followed her out.

He said, "You weren't too smart, Nick."

What to say? I accepted that he was an old man who was to be cut some slack. "If it's any consolation our breaking up was entirely my fault."

"Not my consolation you should be concerned about."

Drop it old man. "I really don't know what to say."

"Say? It's a case of doing not saying, if you get my meaning."

Frank's presumption of age was getting a bit thin. "Bet you didn't know I was still alive."

I mumbled through the scone. "No sir."

"Pushing ninety-two." Hint of pride there as if avoiding the Grim Reaper deserved the blue ribbon. He ate the scone slowly, managing the chore with difficulty. It took both of his damaged hands to lift the cup to his lips. Finished, he patted his lips primly and folded the napkin corner to corner. His movements were an effort. I suspected had I not been present Ellen assisted him. Dignity was important to the aged railroad engineer.

"Well, Nick, what are you up to?"

"Retired mostly."

Frank's head lowered as if he was about to nod off. I shook a cigarette from my pack, put it back.

"You can smoke if you like." Wet eyes, somber smile. He shifted his wheel chair, offered me an ashtray from an end table.

"Thanks." I lit up wondering what to say. The only thing I had in common with Frank Dowling was the past. I said, "Gene Petersen came to the wake."

"Gene? I haven't seen nor heard of him for years."

"Neither had I." There was no way for me to prettify this. Or make it easier for the old man. Frank Dowling drove the freight that nearly ran over my father.

"He told me that he saw my dad standing on the tracks with another man the night he died."

Frank's head came up sharply. What?"

"Exactly what I said to Gene. I couldn't believe it either. I asked Gene why he hadn't told me at the time and he said he was scared."

"My God, if Oscar only had known." Frank's dismay paled his face, and his fingers danced to a tune of his own making. "We were all friends of your dad. It was common for your dad to take an evening stroll often down by the river so him being found lying by the tracks wasn't an odd place for him to be."

"I'm sorry if this upsets you Mr. Dowling, but I have to know what you know."

"Not to worry about me, but I'll have to say this is a real shocker. The problem is I don't know much of anything. As you may or may not know we always slowed down passing through residential areas, especially when approaching downtown.

My attention was on my speed but I spotted a body lying by the tracks. In fact, it was laying along side the tracks passing our street. At the time I didn't know it was your father nor did I know the man was dead. I finally got the freight stopped at the main station downtown and called Oscar. I was headed for Denver so I didn't know it was your dad until the next day when I called Oscar. I had to sit down when Oscar told me it was your dad. I never saw anybody else by the body. Who was it, did Gene know?"

"A man in a big hat and wearing a long coat. Gene says he didn't know him. He also said he told his mother but she told him not to tell anybody."

"So Sarah Petersen knew?"

I nodded.

"And Richard Petersen must have known too."

I said, "I would say so."

"Oscar told me he had talked to them, but they claimed they were sleep."

"The reason Gene saw my dad was because he had to pee and was on the way to the outhouse."

"But they both knew what Gene saw. Why didn't they tell Oscar?"

"I don't know."

Frank's eyes were in that far away mode struggling with his own memories. "Oscar testified at the coroner's hearing. There was a rumor that your dad had been drinking. There was an empty whiskey bottle found some way down the tracks. Oscar testified whiskey bottles found along the rail lines was common, and he cleared your father's name of that charge. The coroner ruled accidental death.

"Oscar and me talked over everything. My wife and his wife were sisters so it was kind of like keeping confidences in the family. He felt badly that he couldn't come to the truth of your dad's death. He didn't believe he committed suicide. The facts suggested that it was an accident but Oscar didn't think so. Oh, I know he testified that he had no proof of wrongdoing but in his heart he didn't believe it was an accident. There was no way he could prove his suspicions, and that never left him. Ever"

I said, "If it wasn't an accident who did he suspect?"

"Charlie Cole, who else?" Frank Dowling stopped suddenly as if as if his mind had hit overload.

Charlie Cole was a bootlegger who had a house up on the bluff. When we were kids we used to spy on Charlie and the thugs that ran with him. I asked, "Why Charlie?"

Frank shook his head. "Won't come back."

Was he telling me all of it? Or was it simply memory loss. I said, "Sorry, Mr. Dowling. I didn't mean to press."

He smiled, sad smile. "Sometimes it comes and goes, Nick. Tough when you get my age."

Give the old man a break, Nick. I stretched the facts about Gene and me getting scared shitless by Clara Reece at the state hospital. Frank laughed which was an improvement over his sad smile. Then I gave him a sneaks-eye view of Matt and me spying on him and Officer Swensen from behind the signboard on the main drag.

He laughed again. "Do you think we didn't know you and that rascal Matt Jackson weren't perched up behind the sign? Clara was an old witch, forever ranting and raving about something or somebody. Only time she was halfway pleasant was when she was boozed up. She committed suicide out at the state hospital. Crazy as a loon."

"Matt told me Oscar found out that Clara was Gene's aunt."

The old man shifted in his wheel chair, misty eyes trained on me as if questioning my intent. He said, "Seems to me you know a lot."

"Not really."

Frank turned his head toward the river, ignoring me. Again, I waited. Finally, the words came out. "Lots of graft during the war. Sheriff built himself a new house, buzzed around town in a big old Cadillac. Oscar called him on it. They weren't exactly friends so finding out anything official about Clara's death was out of the question. Somehow Oscar found out that when Clara died,

Sarah Petersen claimed the body. When Oscar confronted Sarah she admitted Clara was her sister."

Interesting, but Clara Reece's suicide was not exactly in my sights. Patience, I told myself, let the old man talk. I asked, "But he had no idea they were sisters before that?"

"Maybe, maybe not."

"I don't understand."

Frank said, "Oscar always had a feeling there was something more to Sarah and Clara than just neighbors. He couldn't figure out why Clara was so interested in Gene, Sarah's boy, but when he found out Clara was Gene's aunt that explained Clara's behavior. And there was something else."

I gave Frank an encouraging look. As a homicide detective I found that encouraging looks nudged the story along. Not all the time, but the old man was no hard ass case.

"Just came back to me. After your dad died, Sarah took Gene to live with her father. Richard stayed in the shack. The next summer she moved back."

I said, "Nothing sinister about that."

"But instead of the beat up shack down by the river she settled into the Reimers's place. Of course, Richard went with his wife and son."

"That wasn't much of a place."

"It was a sight better than that shack."

"Yes," I said, "But there could be a number of reasons why Sarah Petersen moved into the Reimer's place."

Frank wiped away spittle on his lower lip. He said, "Oscar said that the Reimers's place was owned by Charlie Cole."

"I didn't know that."

"Nobody else did either. Oscar checked the records."

"Why did he check the records?"

"Like I said. When he found out Sarah was Clara's sister he dug into anything that might have linked them."

"Did Sarah buy it or rent it?"

"How in tarnation should I know that?"

Frank is about out of gas, Nick. Back off. "Sorry."

He waved his grotesque fingers in the air as if erasing the black board. "No offense taken, Nick. It's just that sometimes it's so hard to remember. Go ahead, ask me whatever."

"Did Oscar think Charlie had something to do with Clara's death?"

"Not Clara's." Frank peered at me as if I was slow on the uptake. He said, "Charlie couldn't have been mixed up in Clara's death. He was dead when they found Clara. Put a gun to his head one night up there on the bluff."

How the hell many dead bodies did Oscar investigate? I watched Frank Dowling, but his head was bowed, and he had drifted into silence. I waited, poured another cup of coffee, and lighted another cigarette. Then his head lifted once again.

"About Charlie?" I said.

His voice was back nice and strong. "Oscar thought Duster Grimes knew who killed Charlie. Big hero in WWII, but a no account bum if you ask me. Claimed he was in an army hospital when Charlie bought it, and a major confirmed it."

"Is Duster still alive?"

"Oh sure. Inherited his Pa's place just up the block. Pa kicked him out when he was running booze for Charlie, but when his Pa died he moved in when he retired from the army. I don't recollect when that was, but I know he spent a considerable time in the army."

"And Oscar's dead."

"These past twenty years. Wife went two years after."

"Puzzling isn't it?"

"Well, Nick, Oscar was a good friend, but he had a habit worrying his big cases to a frazzle. It's a shame he didn't know then what Gene saw."

"His big cases?"

"The ones here in the East End. Your dad's death and Charlie's and Clara's suicides were the biggest cases he personally investigated."

"When did Charlie and Clara die?"

"During the Korean War, thereabouts."

I said, "He was a big one."

"Lot of the neighbors thought Oscar was just a big lunkhead, but he had a brain on him. And he was the most generous man I ever had the pleasure of knowing."

"He wasn't the only one. I remember you giving me a piece of chocolate as my mother and I waited for the trolley."

Laughter erupted deep in his chest. "You were the apple of your mother's eye. Sister's, too as I recall."

I spotted Ellen in the doorway, concern on her face. She motioned toward the front door and disappeared. I got the hint. I caught Frank's eye and said, "Mr. Dowling I'd appreciate it if you wouldn't say anything about what Gene told me. Until I get my bearings I wouldn't want my dad's death to come up. About Charlie and Clara I don't much care."

Frank nodded. "Can't bring yourself to say Frank can you."

"No sir." I nearly offered my hand, but the sight of his tortured fingers stopped me. Instead, I patted his arm, said goodbye with feeling.

Ellen opened the front door for me. "Come see him again before you leave. By the way, are you staying with Ann?"

"The old house has too many memories. I'm at the hotel downtown. Wasn't the Grimes house up by the school?"

She smiled, took my arm as if leading old Frank to bed, and pointed to an ancient path. "Just follow your paper route over the tracks and up the street. The Grimes house is just shy of the bluff."

I sat down on a river walk bench, lit a cigarette and let the river come to me. I should have asked Ellen to sit with me, but once again I was behind the curve. Damn, she looked terrific. Then again, to me, she always was a looker. How come she remembered my paper route? I delivered papers to her parent's house but back then she was just a skinny little girl hardly worth noticing. Noticing arrived in a brand new package in college. She was a freshman and I was a senior, former Marine, and like John Wayne, I was fast on the draw. To her mother's dismay we eloped.

Did her gesture, any more than my pitiful attempt to touch her, mean anything? Not likely, but what was likely was that she had discussed me with Frank Dowling, or maybe Frank Dowling discussed me with her. I had never discussed her with anyone, including my sister. The fact of the matter was that I had trouble talking about anything personal. Ellen once said that we never had a meaningful conversation. Talk about meaningful. When she left me that was meaningful.

I lit a cigarette and got back to Frank Dowling. Oscar suspected Charlie Cole had something to do with my father's death. Running booze was Charlie Cole's game. But my dad was no boozer.

So what could they have been arguing about? Oscar couldn't understand why Sarah Petersen had moved into a house Charlie Cole owned. If only Oscar had known what Gene had told me he would have had Charlie under the lamp at headquarters. The coppers weren't as noble about civil rights in the old days. But Sarah Petersen hadn't told Oscar what Gene saw. There had to be a connection.

A family connection.

Duster

I got up, moseyed along the old path, crossed the railroad tracks, and followed the creek bed to the main drag. The homes had some age on them but showed a working class concern for upkeep, nicely painted, uniformly white with a variety of window trim, brown, black, and blue. Nothing pastel. When elm disease had wiped out the towering trees the neighborhood showed its blemishes like a teenager with acne. Now leafy oaks and maples were beginning to color the scene enhancing the aged homes, warts and all, with natures paint brush.

I spied a down-at-the-heels scudder sitting on the front porch of a once was house. The house wore a pathetic façade no paint job could cover. Paint was the least of its worries. The eaves hung askew, like a victim hanging on the edge of a cliff gripping with his fingernails that were losing traction. Both the man and the house must have passed seventy on the way to the graveyard.

It was Duster Grimes. Charlie Cole's rumrunner was still a fixture in the neighborhood, an image that must have made the neighbors miserable.

"Duster Grimes?"

"You got it."

I approached, said, "Remember me?"

He stared at me through rummy eyes leaking oil. Rumpled shirt, pants hiked up over bedroom slippers, sans socks. Gray hair needed a sheep shear's, nose could have been used for a stoplight. He said, "Can't say as I do."

"I'm Nick James."

Duster frowned and shifted his rear as if reaching for a thought that was tied up on the off ramp. Blue lines traversed his pearl white legs like rural roads meandering on a road map. Not a pretty sight.

"Red and W.D.s younger brother."

"Oh yeah." Recognition was a fitful accomplishment. "Sit."

His teeth reminded me of a mine disaster, black and full of holes. I looked askance at a lawn chair with some of its plastic strips hanging free and sat down gingerly. It creaked but held.

"How are you doing?"

"Poorly. War wounds."

You never, ever ask an old person how they feel unless you have an overweening interest in

51

the minutia of their medical histories. Duster had an audience of one listening to the years he had suffered. Then came the battles of the Big Red One in WWII, the Chicoms when they overran the Yalu River in Korea, his Bronze Star for bravery and his wounds. He was an army lifer who had given his all for the good old U. S. of A., and nobody gave a rat's ass. Duster Grimes was bitter. Not as bitter as I was for asking him how he was feeling.

"Stay," he ordered. He stumbled into the house, flopping along in his ratty slippers. On the way one fell off and he booted the other into the bushes, cursing, "Ain't worth a shit."

I thought about taking a hike, but the old buzzard might know if Charlie had met my dad that tragic night. Chances were slim he knew or even remembered but I had to ask. He reappeared with a bottle and two glass tumblers. My first instinct was right.

He poured a couple fingers of Old Loud Mouth, licked his lips and shook like a dog begging for table scraps. He pressed a glass into my hand. Stupidly, I took it. "Mud," Duster whispered. The booze slipped down quickly as if he was pumping gas into his tank. Adam's apple didn't even bounce.

I tilted my head back, kept my eyes on the treetops as the rotgut hit bottom. I'm no wimp when it comes to booze, but, Jesus, it was awful.

"Damn good, don't ya think?"

"Yeah," I croaked. It wasn't the voice I was born with.

Duster's gazers never left the bottle. He poured as if decanting a rare wine, precisely, slowly, every drop an experience in high living. Then he eyed the glasses side by side. Decision made he poured the better portion of mine into his glass. Bottle empty, he tossed it into the bushes. Thank God for greed. It was saving my insides.

"Mud." With a magician's sleight of hand the booze disappeared down his maw.

If I didn't drink with Duster I wouldn't get out of the starting gate. I took a deep breath and slugged it down. I ignored the fact that it could be my last breath. It was, after all, a matter of honor.

I watched Duster settle down in his chair. A comfortable haze passed over his face. I waited for the explosion to hit my gut, but all I received was a warm afterglow. Felt damn good as a matter of fact.

"This as good as Charlie Cole's?" I asked.

Duster roared. "Them were the days. Me and the McNally boys delivering for Charlie." He gave me a sneaky look, said, "You were nothing but a kid." The surprised lifted his eyelids. His one thought for the day had arrived. "Hey, you're Junior, ain't ya?"

"That's right, when I was a kid."

"Lived down below Charlie's place."

"Down below Charlie's place," I repeated.

"Your Pa was tough one. No disrespect intended."

I grinned, said, "None taken."

"Brother W.D.?"

"That's right."

"Tough guy." Disrespect intended.

I tested Duster's recall, wondering if I should take him back through the time W.D. had nailed him with a right cross. "W.D. didn't take kindly to anybody questioning the family."

Duster grunted, shutting out the memory when W.D. beat the shit out of him. He must have had W.D. by a couple of years and good twenty pounds. Deciding it was healthier to remember a couple of kids he said, "You were up in the tree spying on us."

He gave me a nasty stare, all that was left of an old man's anger. "You and that bastard Matt Jackson."

"Right"

"He's a cop," as in the enemy. "Sheriff now. Wouldn't vote for the son of a bitch if ya paid me."

Duster hated cops, but maybe he'd cotton to an ex-Marine that had also won a medal. I buffed up my Bronze Star, lied about what a hero I had been. Nasty stare went west with the 205 headed for Denver. Old Duster even smiled when he said, "Body bag, huh?"

Back on sound turf, I said, "Remember the guy who sold the elixir?"

"Hell yes. We called him Dr. Feelgood. Him and Charlie were in cahoots. Charlie'd run off a batch and we'd fill up the bottles with booze and rose water. Jaundice Bitters what they were called. The doc would pick up a load in that old bread truck down on the Edwards River. Scam lasted until Oscar Swensen run him out of town. Then we went back to personal deliveries."

"In the neighborhood?"

Duster shrugged, asked slyly," Got any whiskey with ya?"

"Sorry."

"Shame."

Duster was pulling down the curtain, but I gave it another shot. "Who did you deliver to?"

"Hard to remember. War wounds ya know."

"I could scare up a bottle later. Figure I own you."

Duster licked his lips, pondering me with a suspicious glare. His wheels were assessing not if, but how much of a liar I was. "Clara Reece, old lady Masterson, Kenny Merchin's Pa, ya remember Kenny, the guy who slobbered all the time. No wonder his Pa drank. Anyway, the Delany boys, plenty customers in those days."

Enough of the BS, I said, "Was Charlie delivering to my dad the night he died down by the railroad tracks?"

55

The blank look crossing Duster's face said something, but it was not the something I wished to hear. I repeated, "You remember the night my dad died?"

"Ya questioning me?" Surly response from the top kick.

"Somebody told me that Charlie was with my dad the night he died, and I wanted to check with you. Nothing personal you understand."

Duster's pulled himself out of his slump and muttered into his empty glass. "Sure I remember. But Charlie never had anything to do with yer Pa. Yer Pa didn't even drink." He slumped back, his eyes slipping into a memory mode. "Damn, Charlie had an answer for everything."

I switched tacks. "Mr. Petersen drink?"

"Ya mean get it from us? Nah. Stiff as board temperance man. But I remember his misses attended those revival meetings in the empty lot down on Main Street."

I said, "That was where the doctor sold Charlie's booze as a magic elixir wasn't it?"

Duster grinned. Teeth were still bad. "Yeah. Minister one night, Dr. Feelgood the next. Clara Reece and Sarah Petersen perched on a bench ears up listening to hell and damnation, and the next week Clara buying a case of the doctor's elixir. Same tent different messages." Duster gave out with a boozers laugh, throaty phlegm ending up with a cougher's hack.

"I understand Charlie committed suicide."

"So I heard."

"Blew his brains out what I heard."

Silence.

I said, "Were you here when he died?"

"You're getting to be a pain in the ass."

Pumping Duster wasn't the problem. Keeping him awake was. A little digging wouldn't hurt. I didn't know a damn thing about Charlie's death, but Duster did. I pulled myself up, said in the fashion one drunk addresses his benefactor. "I'm deeply sorry. Especially when you offered me your hospitality." Sorry, my ass.

"Aah, that's okay."

Duster was fighting his eyes, and sucking in air as if it was the last yawn of his miserable life. I took a wild shot at keeping him with me. "Way I heard it Charlie wasn't a suicide."

Duster's eyelids fluttered. "That bastard Oscar Swensen tried to nail me for it, but I didn't kill him. Not me."

His chest was beating time to his snores, up, pause, down, pause, ripping the shingles off the roof. I'd get no more from Duster. Even with a load on Duster was a damn good liar. He saw something when Charlie Cole blew his brains out. I'd bet on that. Was he telling the truth when he said Charlie had nothing to do with my dad? As to Charlie being on the tracks with my dad I was less certain. And Sarah sitting with Clara at the revival meetings only proved what I already knew. They were sisters.

The Boys and Ann

My rental was parked behind Sis's garage where I had left it before going to the cemetery. Red's first car, a used Model A, had fit comfortably in the garage, but now even a mid-sized car would have a tight squeeze. As a kid I hid my secret stuff in the garage, prized possessions like the beat up baseball I saved from my first home run swat.

The back porch had been glassed in and the elm tree that had graced the back yard had been replaced by an oak that, given twenty years or so, would shade the house. The house was newly painted, a sort of greenish hue I didn't care for. It was a neat old bungalow, old for sure. My father had built it long before I arrived on the scene, but Sis and my brothers would remember. I opened the back door and shouted, "I'm home." The words came out as if I was still ten years old. My mother was always up the few steps in the kitchen or in the living room slaving away on the sewing machine waiting expectantly for a smooch. Coming or going, we gave her a hug and kiss. Now, as I thought about it, those smooches must have gotten her through the day.

"Come on in," returned Ann.

W.D. and Red commonly referred to as The Boys by irate neighbors sat at the kitchen table in their old familiar places. Ann sat where Sis had sat. I faced the window, back to the stove, looking out towards the bluff. The chair next to me where Ma sat was empty. Like I felt.

I bent over and kissed Ann. "How you doing?"

"Phew. What have you been drinking?"

"Duster Grimes made me drink his hooch. I didn't want to do it, but he would have been offended had I refused." A lie, it is said, will suffice until the truth arrives. Or so I reasoned.

Red, who had researched the insides of the county's numerous taverns as one might ruminate the meaning of life itself said, "You can do better than that, Junior."

I ignored him.

I had a soft spot for Ann. She was a lot like Sis, slim, sharp, nifty looker. Had a lot on the ball, or as my mother would say, "No flies on that one."

The table offered a coffee cake leftover from the church luncheon. W.D. lifted a forkful towards his mouth, nodding to me as he tucked away the goodies. W.D. didn't nuts around when the table offered a bounty. Still tall and slim he burned off his calories with intense energy. Only now were streaks of gray climbing upwards from his sideburns.

Red had a cigar going, inspecting the ash with the flair of a connoisseur, part of his ex-Marine persona. The bright red hair of his youth was now burnished bronze, and his added pounds drifted south towards his mid-section.

Ann motioned to the cake. "Want some?"

I shook my head no.

"Coffee?"

I shrugged. Not quite a yes, but close.

"Where have you been?" Bit of a reprimand from Ann.

I should have gone to the church, but what could I say? I wasn't in the mood? I said, "I got talking with Mr. Dowling."

I decided not to mention Ellen. My ex-wife was best left out of the equation. Ann clucking about what a shame it was we had divorced, I didn't need.

"How is he?" said Ann.

"Not so good. His hands are awful looking, big knots from arthritis. He must be the only one alive from the old neighborhood."

Ann nodded. "Mom used to visit him." She went to the stove, took hold of the coffee pot and poured a cup for me. That done, she sat down. "But Mr. Dowling isn't the only one alive. I got a call from Mamie Esterhaus expressing her condolences."

Red said in disbelief. "Mamie Esterhaus? Good Lord, how old is she?"

Ann's smile was a clone of my sister's. She said, "Ninety, a hundred, who knows? She's been at The Manor for years and years. Mom called her a tortured soul waiting to die."

"What do you mean? 'tortured soul.'" I said.

"Mom never said. It was just that when Mom talked about Mamie she, I don't know, spoke as if Mamie had tragedy in her life. Mamie asked to be remembered to you, Unk. You ought to see her."

I thought I might just do that. Mamie Esterhaus lived in the neighborhood and was my teacher in grade school and again in high school. She was a stiff, old-maid teacher who ran her classroom with a ruler that was quick to the mark.

I said, "Sis was a saint to the oldies."

"You're right, Unk. Mom not only carted them to doctors, but she cared for them when they were sick. And she sent them birthday and Christmas cards without fail. Her address book is filled up with seniors. She must have spent a fortune in stamps."

W.D. said, "What happened to it?"

Ann said, "In the dining room desk, I think."

I lit a cigarette, said to Ann, "What are you going to do with the house?"

"Sell it. Unless any of you want it."

The house and the coinage of our youth were so intertwined it was impossible to think of one without the other. Each succeeding year the assessed valuation of our pasts increased a hundred fold so that by now our youth returned to us pure gold wrapped in a silver lining. To give up the house meant the end of something precious to each of us. The house was family.

First my mother then Sis was the acknowledged head of the family. It was here that Ann, too, had grown up, but I understood her position. She had her own life downstate, taught school, and never married.

Both W.D. and Red had married and raised their own families. Except for visits, I hadn't lived here since I left for a stretch in the Marine Corps and then college. I was the only one in the family who had wandering feet, but it was always a treat to come home. Greener pastures didn't seem so green on those visits. Sadly, there was no longer a head of the family, no longer a reason to come home.

"Need help clearing it out?" I said.

"Tomorrow, if you're free. Ann got up, again went to the stove. "Anybody want more coffee?"

"Coffee?" Red shuddered. "There must be a touch of cough medicine someplace."

Ann patted him on the back as if reassuring a petulant child who had received horse poop instead of a pony for Christmas. "No hard liquor in this house. You know my mother."

Red said, "I always told Sis she'd feel a whole lot better if she took a shooter now and then. Erase the cobwebs, buck up the spirit."

Unspoken memories, as if by agreement, silenced us. I could feel my mother's presence, especially in the kitchen. Red was busy relighting his cigar, W.D. eying another nosh, Ann staring at her coffee cup. From the kitchen window I could see the road that ran from our alley up between the twin halves of the bluff. In the dead of winter I climbed up the bluff to deliver the paper to Charlie Cole. I fiddled with my coffee, lit a cigarette said, "Frank Dowling told me that Charlie committed suicide."

Ann asked, "Who is Charlie?"

I said, "Before your time. A bootlegger and gambler who lived on top of the bluff."

"Lemme get this in first." Red waved his stogie as if instruction time had come. "Charlie hauled moonshine in a 38 Ford flathead V-8 with really stiff rear suspensions. It held upwards 80 gallons of white lightening. The word was that Charlie could outrun the coppers even when he had a load of bootleg booze in the trunk." I broke in. "Where did Charlie get his booze?"

Red eyed me as if I was shy of a load. " As if the Junior here didn't know. Charlie had a still on the Edwards River down in Mendon County."

Ann interrupted, nodding my way. "I never understood why you were called Junior. W.D. is the eldest."

Red shrugged. "I don't really know. He was always nosing around the camp, asking dumb questions like what's Ma's brandy taste like."

I broke Red's spell, said to Ann. "Dumb is right. I caught the dimwits sipping Ma's Christmas cake brandy and darn near didn't make it to the ripe old age of ten."

W.D. paused munching long enough to smile. I turned to Red, said, "What do you mean as if I didn't know. If anybody knew anything about Charlie Cole's business it had to be you and W.D."

Red put a match to the stub of his cigar, took in a load of tar, said, "Not me, you. Remember W.D.? Junior comes home and tells Ma that Charlie has a still on the Edwards River. He wants to know what a still was."

"Ma was fit to be tied." Pushing away his plate, W.D said, "Don't you remember?"

I shook my head no, but after my conversations with Frank Dowling and Duster Grimes I had a hazy notion he was right. I said, "Yeah, sort of."

"Yeah. Sort of." Disgusted tone from Red. "Ma cross examined you right where you sit now. That's how we found out Charlie's still was in Mendon County."

"By the way, Mr. Dowling told me today that Charlie blew his brains out right up there on the bluff. When did it happen?"

"Early fifties, thereabouts, best I recall." W.D. produced a quizzical frown. "I can't believe you didn't know Charlie committed suicide. It made headlines in the paper. Oscar Swensen testified there was some question about the suicide weapon, but nothing that changed the verdict of suicide."

I said, "I was in Korea. I remember getting all the news, but I don't recall Sis sending me any clipping about Charlie."

Red said, "She probably didn't want to interrupt you chasing those South Sea beauties." This from the Marine who spent WWII on the island of Maui.

Ann's laughter brought me back to the present. I said, "Frank Dowling told me that Oscar Swensen did not believe Charlie committed suicide."

"The papers said it was a suicide. I don't recall anything about murder, do you W.D.?" said Red.

W.D. shook his head no.

Red twirled the butt end of his cigar, a satisfied customer in the prime of life. "What with all the boozing up on the bluff and the gang of no accounts that ran with him, Ma considered calling in J. Edgar. One day after Charlie and his boys had a snoot full, Charlie's dog started yelping, head up to the moon, making a hell of a racket. What was that dog's name?"

"Dodger," I replied wondering how I knew it.

"Anyway, Charlie reached for his rifle and started firing. For the moment the pooch was lucky because Charlie was so drunk he couldn't hit his rear end with both hands. Then he yelled to the rummies on the porch. 'Get off your duff and get rid of this critter. Driving me crazy.' Duster Grimes tries to explain that the mongrel is Charlie's favorite, but Charlie was too far-gone to get the message. So Duster grabs the rifle and lets one go. The dog leaps in the air, gives his last yip, and settles to earth. Charlie staggers over to

65

his best friend who is lying there with vacant eyes trained on a bone he can't rightly reach. Charlie finally gets it that the dear departed is bound for dog heaven."

Red is on a roll, waving that damn cigar around as if sending a message to Garcia up on the bluff. "Charlie grunts a few times, then picks up the rifle and starts shooting at the gang. Bullets are flying, as are Duster and the McNally boys. Jesus, did those guys disappear."

W.D. has his mitts holding his stomach that by this time is stretched taut from the Ladies Aid coffee cake. "Charlie," he gasped, "was a runt of a guy, but he had a temper. I saw him beat the crap out of Duster Grimes who was about twice Charlie."

Red stretched and yawned as if regretting the afternoon nap he had missed. "Got to get home," he said.

I said, "I should have told you before, but last night I was having a smoke in the ally outside the funeral home and Gene Petersen came up to me."

"Gene Petersen? The kid that lived in the shack down by the river?" Always hanging around with you and Matt Jackson?" Questions from Red.

I said, "That's him. Gene said there was a man on the tracks waving his arms at our dad the night he died."

W.D. didn't shout but it was voice I hadn't heard since I was a child. "He WHAT! Oscar

Swensen told Mom his investigation didn't turn up anybody that had seen dad the night he died." Why W.D. had suddenly developed an attitude was beyond me.

"You got the wrong guy in your sights, W.D. What Gene said upsets me as much as it does you guys." I filled them in on Gene's story and gave them what Frank Dowling and Duster Grimes remembered.

Red damped out his cigar and gave me a look that spelled disbelief. "Why now? Gene says he didn't tell you back then because he was scared. But why tell you now?"

"I don't know."

"Duster told you Charlie had nothing to do with dad. Isn't that enough for you?" W.D. still with the attitude. My brothers had eight and nine years on me. Growing up, they were as close to a father as I would have. Unless I missed the pitch they were telling me to forget what Gene said.

I said, "What Gene told me raises the possibility that dad's death wasn't a self inflicted accident, rather his fall on the tracks may have been initiated by an Unsub, sorry, Unknown Subject. You have to ask yourselves what dad would expect done, not what you expect done."

Ann broke the impasse. "Listen Unks I have to meet the Ladies Aid about clearing out the house, so I'll be leaving now. I never knew my grandfather, but Mom spoke of him often and told me grandma didn't believe his death was an accident." She gave me a hug and a kiss, then transferred her love to my brothers.

Ann touched my arm. "Want to stay here tonight, Unk."

"Thanks, but no. I think I'll grab a quick bite at the hotel and hit the hay. I'll see you tomorrow morning. What about you guys? Little work tomorrow?"

My brothers shrugged their shoulders in unison, edging towards the door as if reacting to the times Mom told them to stick around because there was work to do.

I grinned, mimicking Mom. "Boys, If I Could Do It, I'd Do It Myself." They laughed and left.

I drove back to the hotel wondering if I hadn't seen my old neighborhood through a distorted lens. Even with my dad's accident I thought nothing ever changed in the East End, same neighbors in the same houses, same school with the same teachers, same pals nutsin' around, same old same old. And I was mistaking seeing my brothers through a lens distorted by time. Maybe W.D. was right. Duster claimed Charlie had nothing to do with my dad. And Red raised the question, why now?"

But Ann recited my mother's belief that dad's death wasn't an accident. Her belief was my belief, to hell with my brothers.

I lit up and glimpsed the smoke curling out of the window. It got dark early now, about the same time fifty-three years ago September when my dad took his fatal walk. I'm going to find out what happened that night.

Learning of the suicides of Charlie Cole and Clara Reece made me wonder if there was a more sinister force at work. Oscar knew that Clara Reece was locked up tight. Hell, even I knew that. I could still see her plastered up against the bars, raving like a maniac, scaring the crap out of Gene and me. Nobody would question Clara was a suicide. But Oscar suspected her death was not as reported.

I lit another cigarette trying to get into Oscar Swensen's mindset. What was it that made Oscar Swensen believe Charlie Cole had been on the tracks with my dad? He knew something. What was it? And Oscar believed Charlie's suicide wasn't a suicide. Maybe the problem was simply Oscar. I knew coppers that worried the hell out of a bone that was bare of meat. I never knew him as an investigator so speculating about his mindset not only was unfair to him but pathetic on my part.

I chucked the butt out of the window, and checked the rear view mirror, saw sparks light up the pavement. Why didn't Gene tell me what he saw when we were kids? He said he was scared, he said, "*I cain't tell ya.*" I was tormented with thoughts of my dad.

I missed my sister. So damn much it hurt. I remembered her giving me my first allowance. I was just a little guy sitting on the floor glued to the radio when she handed me a quarter. I had never had an entire quarter before, didn't even know what an allowance was. "Here," Sis said, "this is for you." Memories.

It was one of those fall dusky dark evenings with a black backdrop when stars shimmered aloft announcing their nightly show. I was tired, needed a drink, maybe two and dinner. I hadn't eaten since Ellen prepared tea and scones for Frank and me. I was empty in more ways than I cared to consider. I parked behind the hotel and entered the lounge. They still hadn't paid Edison's bill.

Ellen

The lounge had an intimate aura about it. Sort of a weekday hush absent the gambling crowd. It was hard to tell what with the meager wattage, but I wasn't necessarily looking. I was about to capture a stool at the bar when the barkeep said, "Mr. James," he nodded toward a table in the gloom, "there is a lady waiting for you."

I stepped between the tables to where she sat. "Ellen!" Surprise and anticipation were in my voice. I sat down. She wore a navy peacoat over a soft blue sweater. A locket on a gold chain fell in an area I once knew so well. I sucked in a breath there was nothing sometime about that memory.

"You're not much of a detective, Nick." A slight smile brushed her lips. She knew that her gibe, although innocent of intent, would get to me.

The barkeep placed a glass of Wild Turkey in front of me, said, "Not much ice. Right?"

"Right, Roger."

He turned to Ellen. "Your wine okay, Ma'am?" She nodded. He disappeared behind the bar.

"I see you are well acquainted."

She didn't say it nastily but anything said about my drinking habits, past or present, was not on the board. "I can read a nametag you know." Thank God she hadn't pulled out an eye chart. I wouldn't have been able to see the big E in the dim glow much less a nametag marked Roger.

"What do you mean not much of a detective?" I took out a pack of cigarettes and motioned to Ellen if smoking was on the menu. She nodded.

"What I meant was the Nick James I knew would have scanned the room as he walked in. What did you call it? Casing the joint? You didn't even see me."

"That's because I'm no longer on the job. I've retired." I played with my lighter, an unlit cigarette between my lips. Ellen took a cigarette from my pack and my lighter, lit our cigarettes. "Still with that beat up Marine Corps Zippo lighter. And I see you still wear your Marine Corps cuff links." She eyed me, said, "I always thought you should have gone back into the Corps."

"Last thing I remember was a horde of Chinks, sorry, Chinese, bearing down on us. I wasn't too enthused thinking about wearing a body bag a second time. Besides it was time for college."

"Oh, you would have rationalized the glory of it all, Nick, if you really wanted to. I finally figured out you lived for danger, for the rush it gave you. And what fooled me is that you don't look the part. Or act the part. This nice, quiet spoken, sort of beat up guy really lives for the raid, lots of guns, the arrest, the whatever."

"Beat up guy?" I raised it an octave. "Beat up guy?"

Ellen laughed, stubbed out her cigarette, signaled Roger for another wine. She wasn't much of a drinker. Two was her absolute limit. She said, "I'm joking. You were the best-dressed copper in Texas. Which may or may not be a compliment."

Seeing as I had on my Brooks Brothers navy blue suit, white on white shirt, and red and blue tie, I took it as a compliment. I said, "Want an autograph?"

Roger appeared with her wine and another one for me. "I'll run a tab, Mr. James."

Again she laughed, throaty and if caught right, sexy. "And a great sense of humor. Even my mother loved you. What kind of pie can I bake for you, Nick? What would you like for dinner, Nick? God, you should have married her."

Is this why she was here? Reliving the times we came home to visit good old Mom? I took her shot and laughed it off. "How the hell did I know

72

you couldn't cook? When I asked for French toast you said we didn't have a toaster." An old joke she had heard a thousand times. "Speaking of food would you care to join a beat up guy for dinner? I understand the chef is first rate."

Ellen slipped my question as if occurring a sudden hearing loss. "The reason I'm here is that Frank asked me to tell you that Pete Benson knew something about Charlie Cole's suicide. You ought to see Pete."

"As I said, I'm retired, no longer on the job."

"You're fooling yourself, Nick. You've only been back a few days and you're worrying Frank and that disgusting Duster Grimes and god knows whom else about long dead suicides. Don't misunderstand me. I know how much Sis meant to you but you just can't help yourself."

She took a sip of wine, doused the cigarette and returned her attention to me. "It was what, forty years ago? Oscar Swensen is dead and the cases are closed. But not for you, Nick James is on the Job with a capital J, Nick James will solve the suicides of Charlie Cole and Clara Reece."

Didn't Frank tell her what Gene Petersen had told me?

She never raised her voice, hell she *never* raised her voice. No wonder she got her masters in psychology. But the edge was there. Curse you Black Bart you have wronged me. The damn job was the lodestone that justified her dumping me.

The kicker was when her mother told her she was a damn fool.

I told myself to talk softly. "I don't think I deserve that, Ellen."

"You're right, Nick, you don't." She took one of my cigarettes and held my hand, as I lighted it for her. "I have you to thank for finishing college."

"No thanks necessary."

I meant it but my response was unfeeling. I owed it to her. She had given up her education to marry me. She was just a freshman when we eloped.

I was walking on the quad when she approached me. "Hi, you don't remember me but I'm Ellen Mann from the neighborhood." I had served my tour in the Corps and was then a college senior, big man on campus. The only Ellen Mann I recalled was so high and had braces on her teeth. Her glasses were perched on the point of her nose and she was carrying a couple of books under one arm, big books as I recall. Couldn't tell you how she was dressed, but she had all the parts in the right places. I carried her books, big tough Marine reduced to putty. We went to Bennies, a student hangout of uncertain vintage. And talked. Or I listened and she talked. Talk about falling. You could have heard the thud in Chicago.

"Where have you been, Nick?"

"Oh, I was just rummaging around my attic seeking some lost books." She looked puzzled but let it pass. I said, "And you, Ellen? I was sorry to hear your husband died. He was your age wasn't he?"

"We were in the same high school class, and we both taught at the local junior college. Herb Jensen was a kind man. Good to me."

I'd hate to have, "He Was A Kind Man," etched on my tombstone.

Like saying he drove an Edsel. I didn't want to consider what she'd say about me. Probably, "the SOB never got it."

I listened to Ellen talk about her life after Nick James. I took it in but I was still back at Bennies drinking a beer, a coke for her, and falling into those eyes. Smoky eyes. I wanted to say I love you but she'd reply you only think you love me. Jesus, I know the difference between I love you and you only think you love me.

She got up, said, "You really aren't beat up, Nick, but I think I'd better skip dinner."

I couldn't think of a thing to say. I sat mute like a dummy whose master had lost his voice. I watched her leave and pondered for the hundredth time how I could have screwed up our marriage. When she left me she said if I had taken up with another woman she would have fought for me, but the Job was beyond her. It was a love she couldn't deal with. So she said.

Etched in stone. "The SOB Never Got It."

I got up and went to the bar. Roger said the chef was featuring fresh grouper but I declined, and then he asked if I wanted room service and I told him I wasn't hungry and to send up what was left in the bottle of Wild Turkey and ice. It seemed as if he wanted to say something about Ellen but was wise enough to drop it. I paid the tab and made Roger happy with the tip.

I had no sooner removed my jacket and tie than the bellhop delivered the booze and a generous dish of mixed nuts that he said were on the house. I tipped him too much, a surprise gift coming from a cop who didn't know the meaning of the word.

I pushed my chair and small table in front of the window and once again stared at the river, smoking and sipping my bourbon. I cursed myself for expecting a response out of Ellen that just wasn't in the cards. But why had she come to see me? She could have called the hotel and given me Frank's message. And she could have had dinner. What the hell was wrong with that? After our divorce I tried to repair the damage but she wouldn't have any of it. I mean me. Then when she married Herb whatever the hell his name was, I finally got the picture. I disappeared from her life permanently.

Then it came to me. Matt had called her, told her I wanted to see Frank Dowling and would she be so kind as to make the arrangement. Meet Frank Dowling my Aunt Martha. Meet Ellen was more like it. I still didn't understand why she wouldn't stay for dinner. The thought arrived that I was more than a little bit dense.

I drank some more, had a few cashews, and lighted up the nail coffins with my trusty Zippo. Red's story about Charlie Cole's dog was right down to the ground only Matt and me and Gene were the ones that actually saw it. Red wasn't even in the picture. That I remembered Charlie's dog's name amazed me.

I unlaced my shoes and tipped them on the floor, slid back in the chair, remembering. We were up in this huge elm on top of the bluff spying on Charlie's house. It used to be a pastime of ours when things were a bit slow in the neighborhood:

Charlie

Charlie and Duster were shooting at targets nailed to trees in the woods behind Charlie's house. It must have been a contest because both fired their rifles bent for hell and missing. They quit and went to the front porch. Matt pointed to Charlie passing the bottle to the McNally brothers and Duster lolling around the porch. We couldn't hear them but their bodies said a lot. Boozed up for certain.

"My Pa said Charlie had the fastest Ford in the county and that the McNally boys kept the engine in top notch condition."

"Yeah. He brings up the hooch from Mendon County. He's got a still down there."

"What's a still?"

"It's where he makes the hooch. On the Edwards River."

"Wow. Pa said he never got caught."

I nodded wisely. "What's up with old Dodger? Won't stop barking."

Matt shrugged. "Charlie's sure mad. Slapping his leg with that old hat, and yelling at Dodger. Charlie is drunker a skunk."

"So's Duster and the McNally's."

"Holy smokers, Charlie is shooting at Dodger."

"He's so liquered up he'll never hit him."

"Now he's waving at Duster. Did ya see that? Duster shot old Dodger. Dodger's dead."

We watched Charlie kneel down by Dodger. Then he looked up at the sky and shook his fist. Couldn't hear what he was yelling but it musta been some first class cussing. Duster dropped his rifle and took off. Charlie picked up the rifle and started shooting. The McNally boys raced after Duster into the woods.

Matt said, "We better get the hell outta here."

"Ya. Come on, Gene, Ma'd kill me if she knew I was here."

The scene came back to me as if I was still up in the elm tree spying with Matt and Gene. Charlie was wearing a Stetson hat that sort of hid his face, and long coat like the kind the cowboys wore when they were on a cattle drive.

The man with my father on the railroad tracks had on a big hat and was wearing a long coat. That's what Gene told me at my sister's wake. Recollecting us kids spying on Charlie Cole and his gang I was certain now that the unknown man was Charlie. But Gene must have known that back then. He was up there on the bluff with Matt and me. *"I cain't tell ya."* Damn right he couldn't. Mama told him to shut his mouth. What did she say to Charlie? Let us live in the Reimer's place and I won't tell Oscar Swensen? That is probably how it happened, but threatening the local bootlegger was not in Sarah Petersen's persona, somebody's persona for certain. There was something more in this equation. Of that, I was positive.

TUESDAY

I stood beside my sister's grave now covered with green screening that I presumed contained grass seed. I chatted with her about this and that, private talk. I then walked to my parent's graves and talked some more. I still had a headache, probably due to the empty bottle and quashed cigarette pack that were mute testament to a sadder but not wiser Nick James. I wore a navy blue sport coat, blue button down shirt and gray pants. A coppers out of uniform uniform, but no tie, casual chief of detectives in a pricey sport coat.

I left the cemetery in a dour mood wondering if anyone would say a few words about me when I was planted away. No wife, no kids, nobody. Here lies nobody. His name was Nick James. Nobody remembers him. As I drove to the home of my youth on this crisp, bright fall morning the reds, yellows, and burnished browns fluttering to earth tugged at my spirits. The sky was clear, and the sun promised to generate a warm day. Hopefully, it promised to wipe clean the slate stained with my melancholy.

On the way to Ann's I planned the day. Pete Benson definitely. I was anxious to listen to his account of Charlie Cole's suicide. Hopefully, he was not slipping in and out like Frank Dowling. I was amazed so many oldies were still alive in the neighborhood. It must be the water.

And I wanted to see Frank again, but the thought of Ellen being there put a damper on that plan. If she wouldn't have dinner with me the expectation of tea and scones went out with last weeks trash. Then there was Duster Grimes. He was holding back. I had one of those brilliant ideas reserved for coppers on the make. I stopped at a liquor store and bought two pints of rye and plastic glasses. It would make Duster Grimes' day, and maybe mine. I put the package on the floor.

I parked in the alley.

Ann

"Anybody home?" I called. Ann's voice from the basement answered, "Down here."

I walked down the narrow steps, and saw a basement I didn't know. In my childhood a huge coal-burning furnace filled the cellar, but now a three by six gas burner gave it a whole new dimension. The basement was neat and clean, not at all like the old days when soot escaped from the enclosed coal room, and residue from the clinkers, not to mention the noxious fumes, permeated the basement. How any of us had any lungs left was a miracle.

"Hi Unk."

I found Ann in the fruit room immediately to the left of the steps. Store bought can goods lined the shelves that once held over a hundred Mason jars filled with my mother's garden vegetables. Ann sat on the floor sorting through boxes of family whatevers. Her face was wrapped in a frown contemplating what to keep and what to toss out. Indecision marked her face as she pawed through boxes and aged trunks.

I bent over and kissed her. "Problem?"

Ann shook her head in disgust, waved at the boxes. "I don't know what to do with all this stuff."

I laughed. "Wouldn't have been a problem for your mother."

"Don't I know, Mom would have backed up the truck and shoveled it out the door."

What I saw was Sis's face and her laugh, but Ann had a softer, laid back manner. She was, I suspected, a wonderful teacher. The fruit room was much smaller than I remembered, but then so was the entire house. Sis was good at tossing out whatever she considered to be worthless. When the mood struck her, which was quite often, she'd clear out any object not deemed useful with a determination that seemed to delight her sense of rightness. I peeked behind the can goods but the object I sought wasn't there. It was stupid of me to think it still existed. Sis hadn't had much humor when it came to hard liquor.

I said, "One day when I was a squirt I caught W.D. and Red with a funnel dripping water carefully into the Ma's brandy bottle. W.D. jumped as if he'd stuck his finger in a light socket, darn near dropping the bottle. Red attempted to cover it up saying all they were doing was measuring the contents to see how much had evaporated over the summer."

"And you believed him?" Skeptical grin, lips upturned.

"No way. They were sampling the brandy that Ma used in her Christmas fruitcakes. Anyway, the scene was slightly tense. I decided it would be better for my future if I suddenly got amnesia."

"What devils," Ann declared.

"Ma used to say, 'divels.'"

My eyes were on the far corner of the cellar, staring, transfixed, "We were down at the river."

"Who?"

"Me and Gene Petersen. He lived down by the river."

I spoke to Ann but I had the notion I was really talking to myself. "W.D.'s diving bell sat there in the far corner for years. He had made it out of an old water heater. Anyway, W.D. enlists Red and

83

Robert R Glendon

Swede to man the bicycle pump up in the rowboat while he's inspecting the Mississippi bottom. The idea is to keep the air flowing through a long piece of hose."

"And he trusted Red?"

"Even as a shaver I knew W.D. was in trouble. They cart the diving bell in my wagon down to the river. Mr. Jepson lent his rowboat to W.D. Gene Petersen and me watched them row out.

"W.D. straps on the diving bell, gives a thumbs up and goes over the side. I'll tell you, Ann, I was darned impressed. Red and Swede didn't seem to be doing much pumping, then all of a sudden W.D. shoots up like a Polaris missile, all blue and gasping for breath. He yelled out something about what the hell were Red and Swede doing while he's drowning. Red said he didn't see any bubbles.

"W.D. gasps out, 'YOU DIDN'T SEE ANY BUBBLES,' and collapses in the row boat."

"Did W.D. ever go diving again?" Ann said.

"Never. But there was something else. It wouldn't mean anything to you, but Clara Reece, the neighborhood witch, appeared from no place and grabbed Gene's hand. Said in a nasty voice the river was no place for him to be. Which is dumb because Gene's parents lived across the road from the river."

Ann said, "Maybe Clara was afraid Gene would fall in." "Hardly. We played along the riverbank all the time. I didn't know what to make out of Clara

84

grabbing Gene. Nor why Gene went with her. Back then nobody knew Clara Reece and Gene's mother were sisters."

"Well," Ann said, "that explains it."

"Maybe. But what I don't understand is why Clara and Sarah never told anybody they were related. What, for heaven's sake, was the secret?" There were, I decided, more mysteries in the East End than Clara and Sarah Petersen being sisters.

"How are things, Unk?" Eyes serious now.

What was I to say? "Okay," I said.

"I understand you saw Ellen yesterday. Have you ever considered remarrying?"

Left unsaid was remarrying Ellen. Like everything else that was emotionally difficult I hid my feelings in work. "That's a two-parter, the answer is yes and no."

"My mother really liked Ellen."

There was a rebuke in there somewhere. Smoke signals from Sis ordering Ann to watch over me now that she was gone. I said, "Is this going anywhere?"

Ann went back to the boxes. "Just wondered. Grab a box, Unk."

I sat down on the floor and opened up a box of books. Garage sale stuff nobody bought. The stuff tire kickers fingered over, and, preserving their coins, looked for better stuff.

Ann produced a book and handed it to me. "This one has your name in it."

A washed out green cover bore the title, *SUNBEAMS,* in gold lettering. Inside was the inscription, *"To Nicholas James. Miss Mamie Esterhaus."* I flipped through the pages, poems, and more poems. On the inside back cover I traced a parched 3 x 5 blank space that suggested a photograph had been pasted on it. I couldn't recall when Mamie Esterhaus gave it to me, but the thought lingered that I had misbehaved in some way.

Ann said, "I never figured you for poetry, Unk."

"Me neither, kiddo. My interests as a kid never got farther than a ball and bat, and comic books." I showed her the back cover. "I know you wouldn't know whose photo was here but if you run across one of Mamie save it for me."

"You ought to visit Miss Esterhaus." This was the second time Ann had urged me to see my aged schoolteacher. What was it Sis told Ann? Something about Mamie Esterhaus being a troubled soul. Yes, I thought, I would see Mamie.

"Oh, I forgot to tell you that your sainted brothers and the sheriff will meet you for lunch at Hagens. And," she shook her finger at me and smiled, "no drinking my good man."

As Ann opened another box, she squealed, "Here's Grandma's address book." She handed my mother's book to me.

Her familiar pen filled the pages of the tiny address book. In it was the births and deaths of the family from Scotland to the new world. "Let me ask you, Ann. Did Sis really tell you that my mother believed my father's death wasn't an accident?"

"No."

I looked at her quizzically. Ann said, "It wasn't your fault Gene told you what he saw. I think W.D. and Red are afraid of what you may find out if you keep asking questions. That's about it."

I didn't know what to say. I watched her as she fingered through the pages of Sis's albums. She suddenly started sobbing. "I don't know what to do."

I put my arm around her, and held her tight to my chest. Was it always like this? Photographs trimmed in black?

My eyes focused on the dust moats riding in the rays filtering through the basement windows. Ann's sobs eased into whimpers. I gave her my handkerchief and she wiped her eyes then passed the handkerchief across my lapel. "Your jacket is spoiled."

"You couldn't spoil anything, kiddo. Do you mind if I take a walk?"

"Sure, Unk."

"I'll stay if you like."

"No, no. That's all right."

"Sure"

"Go." She didn't have to add, "for heaven's sake."

Pete

I tossed *SUNBEAMS* on the front seat, drove the few blocks and parked in front of Pete Benson's house. Climbing the steps to the porch I noticed a swing dangling all its lonesome in the morning breeze. These were homes of front porches and swings, of garages and alleys, where neighbors gathered or helped out tuning up the old Model A, the homes of lifetime friends that saw each other through difficult times. My condo in Texas was one of those low level bricks with a two-car attached garage that had no swing much less a front porch. It had about as much warmth as a dentist's office. I was building up to a black mood again and the day had hardly started.

I pressed the doorbell and Pete Benson responded as if on command. "Come in, Nick."

I was slightly taken aback as somehow Pete had managed to skip twenty years of aging. His hair was steel gray and his face wrinkle free, none of that pinched eye bit, and stood upright sans cane, or walker. He was maybe three inches shy of my six feet and twenty pounds under my one-eighty, a forty regular with a firm grip. And he hadn't sent away for a set of store bought teeth. The pearly whites were his.

"Let's sit in the kitchen. I have some fresh brewed coffee and a sweet roll if you are so interested. I'm sure sorry about Sis. She was one of the good ones."

I nodded. We were silent for a bit respecting our absent loved ones. We sat in an attractive nook. The table had the gleam of hand-waxed oak as were the chairs. He noticed me pass my hand across the wood and said, "I made this table and the chairs. Woodworking became my hobby after I retired, and when the misses passed on it was my salvation." Pete poured coffee and put a bottle of brandy on the table. "I'm partial to a splash of brandy in my coffee. Call it morning dew." He laughed. "How about you?"

I nodded, took a sip. After a bout with the bottle last night, and losing, the coffee had a mellow flavor that suited me right down to the ground. I took another sip. My mood lifted. The brandy was good. I said, "How's Zach?"

"Got his own construction company, married, two kids."

Pete's son was not quite a boyhood pal being three years my junior. A good kid. I liked him.

Pete said, "I appreciated what you done for him."

"I don't remember doing anything for Zach."

"Kept him out of jail, that's what. You hid him under a tarp in Wedman's garage when the coppers were chasing you kids. You and Matt Jackson were caught and to think you both turned out to be law enforcement officers." His baritone laugh hid no censure.

I said, "Seems the cops were a bit riled. We were only engaged in Halloween pranks, not WWII."

"Riled? One of the cops failed to jump the creek when they were after you. They were riled enough to toss you in the slammer."

I had had enough of my youthful misdeeds. I said, "Frank Dowling said that you knew something about Charlie Cole's suicide."

Pete set an ashtray on the table between us and lit up a cigarette. He inhaled deeply, a living testament that not every smoker dies of cancer. I didn't quite believe that, but I paused before pulling out the old Zippo, following his lead.

Pete said, "Seems like a long time ago to be chasing a dead man. I don't mean to be nosy but what is your interest, Nick, at this late date?"

So Frank Dowling had kept his word and had not told Pete about Gene Petersen's memory recall. I inhaled deeply and said, "It's important that what I say not be mentioned around. You were a friend of my father's so you will understand my reasoning."

I walked him through Gene Petersen's story and Oscar Swensen's belief that Charlie Cole had something to do with my father's death. I left out my own memory of spying on Charlie Cole. I didn't want anything to color Pete's recollections.

Pete was a good listener. He didn't interrupt me, just inhaled and drank his coffee fix.

I said, "This doesn't mean that Charlie deliberately shoved my dad and he hit his head on the rails, or whether it was an accident, or whether my dad tripped without Charlie's assistance. I don't know why Oscar Swensen suspected him, but he didn't know then what I do now."

Pete said, "I'm sorry to hear this. Your dad was my friend and none of us could understand what he was doing on the tracks that night. This won't make you feel any better about his tragic death but I can say for certain that Mike James was not a boozer. He wasn't a teetotaler but absolutely not a drunkard. But why he was on the tracks remains a mystery."

"Thanks, Mr. Benson."

"I knew Oscar suspected Charlie but he said that he had no proof. But even if he knew Charlie had been on the tracks would he have come to any different conclusions than you just did? I'm not taking Charlie's defense, but all Charlie would have had to say was that your dad tripped and fell on the tracks. Which brings up an interesting thought. If he fell on the tracks how did he get alongside the rails? Either he was still alive and crawled off or someone pulled him off before Frank's freight was upon him."

I said, "If Charlie was present why didn't he tell Oscar?"

"Knowing Charlie, he was scared and ran."

I said, "Why he was there is the key question. Why would my dad have even met Charlie Cole?"

"And given the times," Pete inhaled and took his time exhaling, "Charlie would probably have met his own accident, if you get my meaning."

I said, "Which brings us up to Charlie's suicide. In fact, when did it happen?"

"More coffee? No. Another splash of brandy? No. Had to be the spring of 50, or was it 51? The Korean War was on, but the reason I remember is that I had just made yardmaster. On the night Charlie bought it I was working a three to eleven at the main Rock Island switching yards. Besides my regular shift I worked overtime many nights.

"I got in the habit of making a regular stop at Vic and Sue's tavern after I signed off. Vic extended closing time whenever us railroad men were late. This was one of those late nights. I got to the tavern about one o'clock. George Hibler, who had also worked overtime, was with me. Anyway, if you remember Vic and Sue's, from the front door the bar was on the right and curved around the back so if you sat at the back you had a line of sight to the front door. Got it?"

I never figured Pete Benson for a drinker, but him being a railroad man I should have known better. "Got it."

"It wasn't ten minutes after I got there that Duster Grimes entered. More like staggered in, but when he took sight of me he didn't let the door hit him in the ass on the way out. I asked George if he had seen him but he hadn't. Neither had Vic. Which was a shame."

"How so?"

"I'll get to it. Well sir, the problem was that I was working nights and even though I had read the papers about Charlie putting a gun to his head – they even had a photo of the death scene – I didn't connect Duster to his death."

I said, "You knew that Duster was his right hand man."

"Everybody knew that." Slightly peeved response. "Everybody also knew that Duster was back in the Army hospital in Chicago for another operation. Never liked Duster, worthless, no good bastard, but he got shot up in Korea after serving in the big War, and that means something regardless how I feel about him.

"Anyway, the coroner's hearing concluded Charlie had committed suicide, and I simply forgot all about Duster. One summer day, it was a couple of months later, Oscar and me were sitting on Frank's front porch watching the river pass by, talking about this and that and I mentioned that I had seen Duster Grimes at Vic and Sue's the night Charlie bought it. Oscar nearly had a fit. I never seen him so excited. He grilled me good I'll tell you. Wanted to know if Vic or George had seen him, the circumstances, that kind of stuff. I felt like a nickel having let Oscar down."

Pete lit up again. I noticed he smoked regulars, saw him eye my filtered brand as if I was wearing a skirt. "Guess that makes two of us that should have told Oscar what we knew. Gene Petersen had an excuse being a kid and all, but I was a grown man and just didn't put two and two together."

I said, "You understand why I'm interested."

"You mean making it up to Oscar?"

"That and finding out what actually happened to my dad."

"I'll tell you, Nick, Frank knows more about this than I do. He's slipping some but if you get him on the right day he'll be able to explain away some of your questions. Oscar spent a lot of time with Frank."

"Thanks Mr. Benson."

"Can't say Pete can you?You're a good boy, Nicholas." He drew out Nicholas as if admonishing a ten year old. Pete was still smiling when I left.

Frank

I told myself that maybe Frank was having a day of slippage, but the truth of it was that I did not want to confront Ellen. Confront was the wrong word, see her is better. I did not have enough invested in our relationship, whatever that amounted to, to confront her. But walking out on me last night had the taste of a wormy apple that Eve pawned off on Adam. But there was no use seeing Duster until I had checked in with the old man. This might be an up day for him.

I parked in a small lot fronting the river, got out and approached Frank Dowling's house. Ellen answered the door, waved me to the sunroom. Not exactly the honored guest but she welcomed me with a smile. "Himself is waiting you." I mumbled something inane.

The old codger sat deep in his wheel chair still staring at the river he could see only through his mind's eye. He was a bit more sunken in his chair, but wore a tattered smile, and through moist eyes greeted me with a friendly cock of his head. His tortured arthritic hands lay in his lap.

"Thought you'd be back." Said like an old fox watching the dogs pass by.

I grinned, said, "I'm sure you did."

Ellen appeared magically with two mugs, and coffee pot. Piled high on the tray were my favorite shortbread cookies. She poured then backed off. "I'll leave you men to the past."

Frank stirred sugar into his cup, adding cream slowly. It was painful to watch. What passed for a sly grin covered his words. "I was thinking about the furnace we put in for your mother."

I had learned early on as a detective that rushing a witness rarely got what I wanted to know. As a Yankee working east Texas I'd sit on a rocker at a country store, sip a cola, share a cigarette, and talk of this and that before getting down to cases. The locals refused to be hurried. Like swinging a golf club, tempo was everything. If Frank Dowling wanted to talk about the con artists who had invaded our neighborhood so be it.

"What I recall," Frank laughed, "is that those two twisters who came to your back door caught your mother when she was ripe for a sales pitch. She had been complaining about all the trouble she had with the furnace the previous winter. First thing out their mouths was that a first class cleaning would solve all of her problems. But when they called her down to the basement the furnace lay in pieces like a jigsaw puzzle.

"The main guy said they couldn't save it. He said she required a new furnace. Your mother picked up a broom and started swinging. She chased the swindlers out the door and half way down the alley."

Frank gave a sort of laugh, chugging along like his old steam engine. "She went straight to Oscar Swensen."

I said, "I don't recall that, but that evening I caught my mother sitting on the basement steps with her head in her hands. Mumbling about whatever would she do."

Frank Dowling pulled himself up, recapturing the moment. "Oscar Swensen found a used furnace in a shop downtown that had gone out of business.

We worked all one weekend putting it in your basement. Your mother had tears in her eyes."

What could I say? I finished Ellen's shortbread caught up in a time when neighbors came to each other's rescue. I lived in a warm house because of these men. No wonder my mother cried.

"Pete said you stopped by."

There had been, I suspected, more than one phone call between Mr. Dowling and Pete Benson. "I told him about Gene Petersen's recall and Oscar's suspicion that Charlie Cole was mixed up with my dad's death. He couldn't understand why my father was on the tracks nor why Oscar suspected Charlie Cole's involvement in the tragedy."

Frank patted his lips with quivering fingers as if a shortbread crumb would destroy his image. I continued, "Pete did say that the night Charlie blew his brains out he saw Duster Grimes in Vic and Sue's tavern."

Frank said, "Of course Oscar wanted a rehearing but the coroner concluded that without other witnesses affirming Pete's sighting of Duster at Vic and Sue's he couldn't reopen the case.

"The coroner even got a letter from the Army administrator in Chicago stating that Duster was hospitalized for a combat related injury, and he was not off site on the night in question."

I said, "But Oscar believed Pete."

"Absolutely."

I said, "I understand why Oscar may have wanted to nail Duster for Charlie's death, but there had to be something more substantial for him to suspect Charlie's death wasn't a suicide. Did he ever say?"

"We were sitting in my living room. You remember my house up there on the corner? Across the alley from crazy Clara Reece?" I nodded. Frank was recreating the scene. "The wives had gone to the movie. We were drinking some of my home brew. Charlie's death was fresh in Oscar's mind, and he was upset. Darn it. I just had it and it slipped away."

I sat mute willing Frank Dowling to remember. Frank was working on it, his lips tightly bound. Seconds seemed like minutes. Finally he said, "When he first got to Charlie's house up on the bluff Charlie was dead and his rifle was standing by the front door, ten feet away from the body. Oscar testified that he then went home, which, as you remember was down the block from your home, to call for backup and the coroner. When the detectives and Charlie returned to Charlie's house the rifle was lying beside the body."

I said, "Surely Oscar brought this out in the coroner's hearing."

"He did, but the backup detectives testified that when they arrived at the scene Charlie's rifle was lying by the body. The coroner was there too, so he knew first hand the detectives were telling the truth. He concluded Oscar testified wrongly about the placement of Charlie's rifle. If the rifle was upright by the front door as Oscar claimed the verdict would have been murder by a person or persons unknown. It was ruled a suicide.

"It wasn't until Pete's story about Duster Grimes being at Vic and Sue's tavern the same night that Oscar had anything to go on. It was common knowledge that Oscar had been after Charlie and his gang for running booze and gambling. The problem was Oscar had no other witnesses other than Pete so the coroner refused to reopen the case. The verdict stood. Suicide. Nobody questioned it."

I said, "I was wondering why Oscar went home to call back up. Didn't Charlie have a phone?"

"The detectives testified that Charlie's phone cord was pulled out of the wall. It was left at that."

I said, "Critical timing I'd say. Who did Oscar think killed Charlie?"

"Oscar never had a real suspect."

"But if he had known Duster Grimes had been in town that night what do you think he would have done?"

"How would I know? The fact is he didn't know anything about Duster being at Vic and Sue's."

I said, "You remember telling me that Oscar suspected Charlie Cole having something to do with my dad's death."

Frank drained his coffee cup and wiped his lips with care. He asked, "Did I say that?"

"Yes sir. I believe so."

"Well, if you say so."

I explained recalling the time Matt, Gene and were me spying on Charlie. "Given Gene's description of the unknown man on the tracks with my dad, I now believe, absolutely believe, that Charlie Cole was that man. And that Gene damn well knew at the time it was Charlie Cole."

"Where does that get you, Nick?" Nothing nasty in Frank Dowling's words, just a statement.

"Good question," I said. "I'm not precisely sure, Mr. Dowling. I sure as hell don't know why my dad would have been on the tracks with the local bootlegger but I have to find out the why of it all. It's important to me to make some meaning out of my dad's unexplained death. Following the trail of Charlie Cole may not the give me an answer, or it might not be an answer I want to know, but Charlie and for some unknown reason Clara Reece are my only leads."

Frank nodded.

I said, "Frank, is it possible Sarah Petersen blackmailed Charlie for the Reimer's house?" I lighted a smoke while Frank cogitated on my question.

"I wouldn't think so. I always thought Sarah was a bit strange but the threatening type, no."

I said, Duster Grimes told me yesterday that Charlie had nothing to do with my dad."

Mr. Dowling leaned over, tapped me on the knee. His hands were grotesque. I tried not to look at them. He grunted in disgust. "Duster Grimes is worthless. Never worked an honest day in his life. Brings up his war wounds as if the government owes him a lifetime on the dole. I don't know how he made it after Charlie died. He was Charlie's number two. Did you know that?"

The old man's words came out slurred spittle drew down from his mouth. Duster obviously wasn't a pleasant subject. Ellen came in and cleared the cups. Picking up the tray and departing she gave me a look that said you've overstayed your visit. Nothing huffy about it, but her meaning was unmistakable.

I glanced at Frank. His eyes followed Ellen and a faint smile rimmed his lips. He said, "I understand you and Ellen got together last night"

My God, what did Ellen tell him? I couldn't admit she walked out on me. But I sure as hell wasn't going to tell him all was coming up roses. I said, "Yes. We talked old times. Very nice."

"That all? Very nice?" Frank wore a disgusted manner like the tout who had lost his last ten bucks betting on a sure thing.

Interrogation over, I said, "You mentioned Charlie's gambling. What was that all about?"

"Charlie owned a road house on Route 6, the Antlers Inn. It had slots, punchboards, all the usual gambling paraphernalia out front, and two rooms in the back where the high rollers gambling took place. You had to be invited to get in those back rooms."

I said, "Before I joined the Marines I drank beer at the Antlers and played the slots, but I never knew Charlie owned the place."

"The problem for Oscar was that it was in county territory and he couldn't do a thing about it. Charlie still pushed illegal booze but it wasn't the big money maker it once was."

"So the sheriff got a payoff."

Frank squinted and grimaced as if I had overloaded his plate with tainted catfish. "You mean bribes?"

"Yes." If Oscar was nosing into Charlie's gambling operation there probably was a tie in to the neighborhood, something or somebody that might give him leverage. I asked Frank if Oscar had mentioned the sheriff.

"Can't remember, could of but I just don't remember." Frank's head dropped, flesh folded into his neck.

From the door Ellen once again she glanced at me with her warning bell eyes that time was up. I got up, patted Frank on the shoulder, avoided touching his arthritic hands. "Thanks, Mr. Dowling."

He produced a crooked smile, said, "Come again, Nick. I really mean it, come again."

Ellen was waiting for me at the front door. Her body language spelled disgusted. Pleased she wasn't. "Really, Nick, I would think you'd be sensitive enough to know when Frank is tired."

I wasn't too keen about her attitude, more like Mom admonishing her wayward kid. "I admit I pushed it, but when was the last time that Frank has been asked his knowledge about anything? For God's sake, Ellen, he's sitting there waiting to die so what if he is tired? What he knows is important. He knows I can't clear up the past without him. When was the last time Frank felt important?"

I left her standing by the door letting the gas out of her balloon and again sat on a bench fronting the river, used my Zippo lighter and inhaled. Here in the East End the Mississippi ran east to west with two interstate highway bridges and another major span running south to north, from Illinois to Iowa. Why anyone would willingly go to Iowa was a mystery. Every four years politicians getting their first ride in a Ford 150, and media by the truckload sought the opinions of hayseeds that to a captive TV audience meant squat. Dallas Town cars, that's what they call pickup trucks in Texas, rushing Mom, Dad and the in-laws to the next caucus. Once the circus was over Iowa returned to its natural state – corn growing, cows mooing and birds tootling – forgotten until the next political cycle.

God, what a mood I was in.

Duster

When I drove up to Duster Grimes' house I found him perched on the front porch waiting for the ship to dock. He wore a faded field jacket and greasy baseball cap, fending off the morning bite. Same ratty house slippers, still no socks, his milky white legs were a grabber. Maybe he only felt the chill from the waist up. The two pints of rye I had purchased ought to cure the old critter's case of the nasties. I was about to make Duster's day.

I tucked the pints in each pocket of my jacket. Two plastic glasses and a bag of pretzels were also part of my loot. These I carried in a brown paper bag. Damned if I was going to drink out of Duster's glasses. I got out and waved at the old cuss, strolled up to the porch.

"How are you this morning?"

Duster canted his head to the side, said, "That you, Junior"

"That's me."

"What ya doing back here?" All the warmth of a prison guard.

I sat down on the steps, handed him the bag. "Thought you might want some company."

Duster dug into the bag, said with a pissed off groan, "Pretzels. Empty glasses. This some kind of joke."

I pulled out a pint and handed it to him. Eyes tell it all, and Duster's rounded out nicely. "Holy shit, we gonna party?"

"Kinda early for a party."

"Shee-it, no such thing as early for a party."

Duster twisted off the cap with surprising strength. Poured four fingers into a glass and took it down with the greed of a thief standing before an open safe. Then he glanced at me. Said a bit flustered like a host who had forgot his manners, "You ready?"

"Bit early for me."

"Wimp, hey."

Respect was what it was all about. For some reason I liked Duster. He was full of crap, but I liked him. I grimaced, said, "Okay."

Duster poured grudgingly, got to a finger and quit. "Here."

I raised my glass, quickly lobbed back the matter of honor. "You quitting?"

"Me!" Duster began coughing, phlegmy rattle erupted from his chest, red faced, he poured himself another four fingers, hit my glass lightly. Watery eyeballs held mine. "Up yours."

I never cottoned to that hair of the dog business, but Pete Benson's brandy/coffee had laid that notion to rest. I sipped slowly, caught Duster eyeing me.

I tossed down the shot. Felt like somebody lit a blowtorch in my gut. Good morning, Nick.

"Did I ever tell you that Charlie was on the railroad tracks with my dad the night he died."

Duster eyed me suspiciously. "Don't believe it."

"I know he was there. Positive. No doubt about it."

"Who told you?"

"Never mind about who. The fact is that he was there. Thought maybe you could tell me why he was there."

Duster pulled out a cruddy handkerchief from his back pocket and wiped his eyes. He inspected the bottle, holding it sideways to the sun. Then with a shrug he filled his glass and tossed the empty bottle into the bushes. "Told you he didn't have any business with your dad, and that's that."

I backed up the horse. "That's okay. You weren't there so how could you know what happened. Sorry if I offended you." He talked about his wars and his injuries, how the government gave him hardly enough for a piss-ant to live on. After thirty years of his giving and giving they didn't give a royal shit what happened to him. I had traveled this road yesterday and it didn't get any better the second time around. Bitterness was Dusters long suit.

I considered asking him what he did for a living, but that was like waving a red cape at a pissed off bull. Usually, honey was better than horseradish.

Well, most of time anyway. "It's a real shame Charlie dying like he did."

Duster said, "Never did find out who did Charlie in. Plenty of customers could have done it."

"Customers?"

Duster said disgustedly, "Not customers lined up at the god damned store. I meant customers like gamblers lined up waiting to take a piece of Charlie."

"Gotcha. Charlie had enemies?"

Duster was no sipper. When he drank, he drank. The golden liquid in his glass disappeared quickly. "Charlie made plenty out at the Antlers Inn, but when the new governor got elected the raids started. Caught Charlie in a bind."

I said, "How so?"

"He lost his protection at a time when he needed it most. He was up to his ass in debt, no money coming in, State breathing down his neck. Then he'd be riding high. Up one day down the next. That was Charlie."

"But you saw who killed Charlie."

"Never saw no such thing. I was in the hospital in Chicago the night Charlie put his gun to his head. The coroner showed me a letter from the Army that said I was in the hospital. Got no right to call me a liar. Bad as Oscar."

I played my trump card. "You were seen in Vic & Sue's the night Charlie bought it.That I can prove. And," I lied, "a Chicago copper friend of mine checked the old Army records and it seems you were in the hospital all right, but on the night Charlie was killed you had signed out and didn't sign back in until early next morning."

I took the second pint out of my pocket, uncapped it, and held it over Duster's glass. Duster shuffled his shoulders like an old fighter recalling the day he whipped Kid Whoozits. He stared at the pint of Old Loud Mouth, tongue licking his lips, torn between the truth and what?

I poured. Duster downed it with relief. "Now tell me. You saw Charlie that night didn't you?"

"I was in the hospital. Told ya that."

I capped the bottle and stuck it back in my jacket pocket, said in a disappointed tone, "That just won't fly." His eyes never left my pocket. "The fact is you saw someone." I took out the pint, again measured a shot into his glass. "After all it happened over forty years ago, 1951 as I recall, so talking about it now won't hurt you at all."

Duster tossed down the warmth, said, "I swear you're on the wrong track. I didn't see nobody."

"It must have been awful." I gave Duster my best shot of empathy, one drunk cozying up to another. I didn't know exactly what I had, but I felt it in my gut. "Where was Charlie's gun?"

His words had the force of train slowing into the station. Maybe I had pulled out the bottle too quickly. He said, "How would I know? Jesus, I told you I wasn't there."

I said, "If the gun was beside Charlie it was suicide. If it was standing at the front door it was murder. The question is who moved the rifle? Do you understand me?"

Silence.

Duster's dance card was nearly full with my questions. I had another shot at him. "Where was Charlie's rifle when Oscar first got there?"

He stared at me through blurry eyes. I said, "Somebody moved the rifle. That's right isn't it?"

Duster struggled to get up, but his eyes never left the pint in my pocket. I reached over and took his glass. "Hell, Duster, that was forty years ago. No harm telling me what happened." I was repeating my line but that's how interrogations go.

"You're a shit, Nick. Who the hell are ya to question me? I oughta knock your block off."

"No sense in being a hard ass about it. Here," I gave him three fingers, "drink up."

Duster sat. Duster gulped. Duster belched.

"You know, Duster, I don't cotton to anybody lying to me. You saw who did it. Might as well tell me about it."

Duster's head fell to his breast. Then his snores shook his frame. Damn. I shook Duster awake. "Who shot Charlie?" Eyelids fluttered across a field of glaze.

"Wha?"

I took hold of Duster's shoulders, pulling him upright, yelled, "WHO SHOT CHARLIE?"

"uhhh . gun . . ."

"WHAT ABOUT THE RIFLE?" I shouted.

Duster's snores echoed off the porch. If any neighbor had caught my act there would be hell to pay. I dropped my hands. Duster slumped down, his body split in the middle, a sack of poundage held together by his belt. I took the pretzels with me, left the remains of the booze for a wake up call.

I sat in the car, staring back at Duster. He looked like a rumpled, unmade bed. I had lied to Duster about the hospital records, but the fact was I believed Pete Benson's eyesight regardless what the Army letter claimed.

Duster hadn't caved in but he was right there. My gut told me that another visit with the appropriate props would do the trick. Duster craved booze.

I could feel Oscar Swensen's ghost prodding me, ham-like hands shaking me to get on with it. Get on with what? suicides that weren't suicides, for god's sake? I told myself that Duster Grimes had seen who shot Charlie Cole. Can you prove it? No judge, but Duster Grimes was tavern hopping and Pete Benson saw him. No, judge nobody else saw him. No judge, even if I can prove Duster was in town I can't prove he was at Charlie's house, or that he moved the rifle, or that he saw who did. That would go over big in a courtroom. Case dismissed.

Take a hike, Nick. You have an audience of one and he is snoring his way to eternity. I drove off.

The Boys and Matt

The guy in Hagens package liquor store gave me a big hello as I walked through to the tavern. I had to buy a bottle before I left. Props. Set the stage and Duster would tell all. Fat chance.

The noontime crowd still held fast to their preferred seats. Same geezers at the bar, same attorneys-at-large swapping lies at the big table, and the same oversized loads in the booths tying into Hagens big bale. My brothers were in a booth, a pitcher of beer and two shot glasses before them. Red was talking, W.D. was laughing. Same brothers, same M.O. Red caught my eye, waved his ever present cigar as if saying hurry up, the story is just getting good.

"Take a seat, Junior."

I sat down next to W.D. Red pushed his shot glass over to me, said, "Taste it."

"Is it poisoned?"

"Kinda poison does a guy good."

I took down the shot, watching Red's eyes widen in disbelief. He said, "Jesus, I said a sip, not the whole shot."

"Bitch, bitch, bitch."

W.D. poured a glass of beer for me offering up his shot glass. I chased down half his shot with a swig of beer. Drinking standards in the East End hadn't changed in a century.

"Taste good?" this from the elder whose knowledge of whiskey wouldn't fit on the head of a pin.

By Duster's standards the VO was capital whiskey. I said, "Passable. Panther Piss, but passable."

W.D. adopted an offended look so I added, "Good, really good."

Stella bounced up to the table, said to W.D. and Red, "So this is your brother?"

"Junior, meet Stella." Red held a match to his cigar, eyes squinting, twirling the cigar in practiced circles, speaking sideways like a big time hood.

"We already know each other." Stella smiled, put her hand on my shoulder as if signaling she had the ball on the one-yard line. For a second I panicked wondering if she and Matt had really called it quits, if I was her chosen replacement.

W.D.'s eyebrows upped a fraction. The elder didn't miss much when it came to skirts. "When did all this take place?"

"Nick is Matt's buddy," Stella answered.

"You and Matt patch things up?" I asked hopefully.

Stella tittered, rubbed my shoulder playfully. "You know it, hon. He'll be here in a few minutes."

"Send him over," I said. "None of that fooling around behind the bar."

"You're a kidder, hon." Stella laughed, asked, "Shots all around?"

"Jesus," Red complained, "I never thought you'd get around to it."

"Hold on to your rear buster, I'm on my way."

It wasn't Red's rear end my brothers watched as Stella swished through the tables. W.D. said with a connoisseur's eye, "Lots of movement there."

"Like a fine Swiss watch," Red grinned.

"You guys been here too long," I said.

I was about to take on my morning sessions when Matt walked in the back door, smoothing the geezers at the counter lest their Xes wandered into the opponent's column. He put his arm around Stella and her orbs slipped into his, true love hinting that the altar was just a step away. Matt turned and gave me a wink. It was Stella, I surmised, that should have been winking. He followed Stella as she swayed her hips to our table carrying a tray filled with shots and another pitcher of beer. It might be a long afternoon.

"You know my brothers."

Matt's grin approached maximum. " The last of the East End's heavy hitters. Sure." He sat down next to Red.

"Set for now?" Stella asked. Her hand strayed to Matt's shoulder. Caresses for me had boarded the westbound express.

Red placed his paw over a shot glass, said, "You're doing a hell of a job, Stella."

She tossed him a grin, then hurried back to the bar.

Matt said to me, "What's up?"

Red broke in and handed across a black and white photograph. "Before you Sherlock's get into any heavy stuff, Ann found this in a box of books. She said it matched the size of the missing picture in that poetry book you got from Mamie Esterhaus."

Four children, all girls, dressed in white, page boy cuts standing in front of a rural church. I said, "I'd guess this was taken in the early 1900s, maybe the 20s. They are not our relatives. Anybody remember the church?" No responses from my brothers. I put the photo in my pocket. I explained the missing photograph in Mamie's poetry book to Matt.

Matt asked, *SUNBEAMS,* you gotta be kidding. Is it important?"

"Not so you would notice."

Red said, "Yesterday when I remembered the time Charlie Cole shot his dog. Damn, forgot that mutt's name again."

"Dodger," I said.

"Right. Dodger. Anyway it got me to thinking about his bootleg whiskey operation and Ace McNally. Remember Ace?"

I never did know Ace's real first name, but he was part of Charlie Cole's McNally crew that reputedly had the collective IQ of a fence post. In the neighborhood he was called Ace because he went around mumbling about World War I aces.

Red again. "Ace got the idea he could fly."

"And," chimes in W.D., "Charlie Cole was dumb enough to listen to him."

Red relit his cigar, blew a wispy web into the updraft. "Ace told Charlie he had a plane he was interested in down in Mendon County and if Charlie was a mind to he'd fly up his booze from Mercerville. Apparently packing his booze in a plane sure beat dodging the coppers down back roads in his souped up Ford. So Charlie agreed."

I put on my innocent face, asked Red, "How come you knew all about this?"

Red nosed down giving me the impression that silence, not mouth, was what he expected. "Because, wise-guy, Swede and me drove Ace down there. Swede's got relatives in Mercerville and since Ace was picking up a plane he only needed a one-way ride. Back then motoring down and back to Mercerville was an all day trip.

"Following Ace's instructions we end up in this farmer's field where sits an ancient biplane. Ace starts walking around this two-seater then this local comes running out. Had on bib overalls and a pair of boots that had a yard of farm on them. Wore a big old straw hat, the kind they advertised in the

Sears catalogue. He informs Ace that it's his plane, and it's for sale."

Stella set a cup of black coffee in front of Matt, put out a huffy tone. "In case a serial killer needs your attention." I held up my hand, said, "One for me, too."

Red oils his chatter with a shot, quick beer chaser. "Ace sizes up the rural sod buster and goes into his act. Tells the geezer that he has a contract flying government mail, but since his own plane is in for repairs he's gotta have a pair of wings right now.

"Well sir," says Ace, "I'll take 'er up for a test flight, and if I'm satisfied, it's a deal."

Red's eyes circle the table as if he has three hostages by the neck. "I got my blinkers on Ace who says to me something about not to worry, that this is a piece of cake. The farmer pulls on the propeller, and after a few misses, the damn thing starts shaking and coughing. Ace taxis onto the grass runway. About this time I figure if Ace crashes the farmer will be all over me and Swede so we rev it up and head for his grandparents in Mercerville."

I took a sip of coffee. Didn't even recall Stella putting it down. Red never missed a beat. "Everything seemed okay, but when Ace didn't return to the field the farmer had the nerve to call the authorities."

"Yeah," Matt laughed, "Authorities can be such a pain in the ass."

Red informs Matt with his orbs that interruptions aren't exactly the approved method of getting out the vote. "Ace flew over to Charlie's still on the Edwards River and then takes a practice run to Charlie's place out on Route 6. Problem was he ran out of gas and had to make an emergency landing at the Moline airport. When he lands the State coppers arrest him for grand theft."

W.D. offers Red his shot glass. Nothing brotherly in the act, more like dumping unwanted heartburn. Red lets it sit.

"The judge doesn't buy Ace's plea that he had simply borrowed the farmers plane. He allows as to how Ace will enjoy the Mendon County's fare and the coppers cart him off. Last I remember Ace was getting his board and room in the Mendon County jail."

Matt deposited a big question mark drifting around the booth. "Did this really happen?"

"According to legend," W.D. answered.

Red relights the nub of his cigar, head canted, eyes squinting off the smoke at me. "Now what was it you wanted to say?"

"Before I get to seeing Pete Benson let me tell you about Charlie shooting Dodger. Matt and Gene and me were actually there, spying from a perch in a tree. What is important is that I remembered how Charlie was dressed – a floppy cowboy hat and a long coat." I paused expecting Red to respond but he was busy with that damn cigar. "Exactly the same description that Gene gave me of the man who was waving his hands at our father the night he died."

W.D. said, "If Gene was with you and Matt why didn't he identify Charlie as the unknown man he saw with dad?"

"I don't know."

He directed his gaze at Matt. "Is Nick right?"

"Yeah. We were spying on him lots of times. Why don't you ask Red? He saw Charlie shoot his dog."

Red said, "Not exactly. I just heard the story."

Matt again to my brothers: "You guys must have seen Charlie plenty of times. Nick's right on. Charlie did wear a long coat and did wear a big hat. Not all the time, but mostly."

I said, "And Frank Dowling said Oscar Swensen thought Charlie had something to do with dad's death. I don't know why our dad met Charlie, but I'm absolutely certain it was, as Oscar suspected, that bastard Cole."

W.D. said, "I'm a little lost here. You told us yesterday what Gene Petersen told you. Gene said he told his mother, but his mother didn't tell Oscar. That it?"

"Correct. According to Frank Oscar never knew what Gene had seen."

"So why did Gene tell you now? Why?" An accusatory tone from my big brother that I didn't exactly appreciate.

"I don't know." It came to me that the carrier of bad news goes into the same pot with the news.

Red added, "You're right, Charlie wore a cowboy Stetson and a long all-weather coat. Were you there when Duster shot Charlie's dog?"

"That's right. Me, Matt and Gene."

Matt nodded.

I said, "Oscar couldn't do anything to that worthless bastard because Sarah Petersen didn't tell him what Gene saw. I was just a kid when dad was killed but I'm not a kid now. I've got to know the truth of our dad's death."

W.D. said, concern shading his attitude, "As I understand it you think because Pete Benson saw Duster the night Charlie died it somehow proves he was murdered not suicide? How does Charlie's suicide or murder give you any answers about dad's death?"

I said, "It doesn't. Not Charlie's suicide or murder especially, but his life for certain. There has to be a reason he was on the tracks with dad. The question is why? There is no easy route to that answer without digging. I want to know why the Petersens moved into the Reimer's, a house Charlie Cole owned. I want to know why Sarah Petersen never acknowledged Clara Reece as her sister."

Red said, "Sisters? Didn't Clara commit suicide in the booby hatch?"

"You got it."

"And," Red hesitated like a student wondering if he could flummox the teacher into a passing grade. "I suppose Oscar thought Clara's suicide wasn't kosher?"

"Yes."

W.D. said. "There are too many ifs here for me to handle, Nick. Let the dead stay buried."

I knew W.D. wasn't being mean about this, more likely he was afraid of what I'd find out. In other words let our dad rest in peace. Red sat mute, making him a tough read. The truth lay far deeper than the six-foot burial plots of Charlie Cole, Clara Reece, and Sarah Petersen. Maybe W.D. couldn't handle the what ifs, but it was just another day on the Job for me.

Matt said, "It could simply have been an accident whether Charlie Cole was there or not." He raised his hand to me. "I know, I know, you believe he was there, but don't tell me you have forgotten the times we slid up and down the berms playing chicken when a fast freight was coming."

"In other words my dad simply tripped when crossing the tracks." I said, "Could be true, but what Oscar did possess was his innate understanding of our dad. For Oscar, dad's accident seemed improbable. Ask yourself, if Oscar knew what

Gene had seen do think the coroner would have ruled dad's death an accident?"

I had the feeling Matt Jackson had me in a photo along side Oscar Swensen. The fact was I knew Charlie was with my dad and he had not been held accountable for what actually happened. I had forgotten that Matt had been on the force in Oscar's later years. "How did Oscar lay it out?"

Matt said, "What do you mean?"

I said, "What, to Oscar's knowledge, happened that night?"

"I'm ashamed to say that Oscar was getting on and us young turks used to make fun of him talking about old cases. As I recall he never talked about your dad's death. Charlie Cole's death was another matter.

"Best I remember he got a call from Larry Hughes, you remember Larry who lived just below the bluff, that he had heard a shot up at Charlie's house. Oscar claimed that when he first entered the living room he saw Charlie lying there in a pool of blood and the rifle was upright by the front door. He tried to call but the phone wire had been pulled out so he went home and called for backup and the coroner. Then he went back to Charlie's and waited outside until they came. When they went inside the rifle was lying beside Charlie's body. Nobody believed Oscar's account of the rifle. The coroner ruled his death a suicide.

I asked, "The phone wire being pulled out didn't raise a question?"

"You're trying too hard, Nick."

Matt's interest had faded. I said, "I had the idea you might want to locate Oscar's police reports for me."

"You're kidding."

"Damn serious."

"I don't even know if they exist. I left the department ten years ago to run for sheriff."

I said, "Left in good standing I'm sure." My brothers laughed and Matt glared at me. What I thought was an innocent remark had an underside suggesting that Matt had departed the PD under a cloud. I said, "Just a favor one copper to another."

"Jesus." Matt handed me an envelope. "Here's the coroner's report you asked me to get on your dad's death."

"And I'd like the sheriff's report on Clara Reece's death."

Matt grunted which I took for a yes.

W.D. said, "You mentioned Clara the other day. I still don't understand what Clara has got to do with this."

I repeated what Frank Dowling had told me. "Oscar found out that Clara Reece and Sarah Peterson were sisters. Oscar believed that the suicides of Charlie and Clara were connected."

W.D. said, "I don't remember Clara's death at all."

Matt said, "Early 50s is what Oscar said. She was locked up in the State Hospital's violent ward. One morning she was found dead, apparently from unexplained causes. Oscar thought there was a cover-up, but the hospital was in county territory so he had no investigative rights. Parker Gould headed the investigation of her death." He turned to me. "You can always go to the hospital and ask."

"Oh sure, and I'm certain whoever is in charge will be happy to turn over a loony patient's records to me. I'm not carrying a badge anymore."

Matt said, "Icky's in charge."

I yipped, "Icky Gould! The wimpy kid?"

"The same. His father, Parker Gould, was the deputy sheriff investigating Clara's death. Icky prefers to be addressed Dr. H. Parker Gould. He is Director of the State Hospital so if you want any information for god's sake don't call him Icky."

Red said, "Why the Icky?"

I said, "Because the poor kid had blotchy skin and peed his pants a lot. Back then he hardly talked to anybody."

W.D. said to Red, "Remember the times we spotted Charlie and Parker Gould together?"

I asked, "So where and why was Parker Gould meeting the local bootlegger?"

Red answered, "They were parked in Gould's car among the trees in Riverside Park late at night. I saw Charlie hand Gould a paper sack, then Charlie got out and Gould drove off. Charlie walked to the edge of the park where his car was stashed and left."

W.D. said, "We figured Gould was getting a supply of whiskey from Charlie and didn't want anybody to know about it."

"Wrong," I said. "More likely Parker Gould was the sheriff's bag man."

W.D. asked, "What's a bag man."

I laughed. "Did this happen on Monday?"

Red shrugged. "How would we know?"

I agreed. "My first encounter with a bag man was when I was a rookie cop. I had become friendly with a deputy who went to our church, a family man, fine, upstanding citizen. Anyway, I learned that he went throughout the county twice a month always on Mondays with his bag collecting payoffs from the roadhouses and gambling joints. I ran in to him one Monday while he was on his run. He even had the gall to invite Ellen and me to their home for dinner."

Red, surprise in his eyes like a raccoon caught rummaging through a garbage can said, "Here we thought Parker Gould was putting the arm on Charlie for free booze."

"Did you see them together more than once?"

W.D. said, "Sure. The park must have been their favorite meeting place."

My eyes took in Matt, a knowing glance that said my brothers were not the only pair that spotted

Parker Gould and Charlie in the park. I said, "For Charlie to get his whiskey from the Edwards River to the East End he had to drive through two counties, Mendon and Rock Island. And to do that he had to pay off sheriff's in both counties. By the way was Charlie into gambling?"

Matt said, "He owned the Antlers Inn and it had a reputation. Remember in high school we went there to drink beer."

"I meant personally. Was he an addicted gambler?"

Matt again. "Could have been but I just don't know."

"I thought maybe Oscar had mentioned it."

Matt shook his head no, said, "Take a hike up to the hospital. See Icky. It's worth a shot."

Red sipped his shot, cogs meshing as he eyed me. "For what it's worth, Mae Belle Foster is still living in Mercerville."

Matt asked, "Who the hell is Mae Belle Foster?"

Red ignored the High Sheriff, said, "You remember I mentioned Swede Larson's relatives farmed down Mercerville way. One weekend we stopped to see Mae Belle. Jeez, what a body. Anyway she takes a shine to W.D. and the next thing we knew she had W.D. in the barn."

W.D. interrupted as if begging the local law for leniency, "It was nothing more than innocent fun."

"Innocent Fun!" Red recaptured his cigar, mouthing the words while attempting to light the stub. "She had W.D. in the barn and from what I saw there was nothing innocent going on. Really ticked me off."

Matt said, "I'll ask again, who is Mae Belle?"

Red grinned, laid his precious cigar in the ashtray. "Swede's cousin." He turned to me, said, "If you want to know all about Mercerville see Mae Belle."

"Drinking is over." Stella slammed hamburger baskets piled high with French fries in front of us.

"Who ordered?"

W.D. grinned. I should have known. W.D. and food were never long parted.

Matt took Stella's hand, said, "Thanks, honey."

"Don't honey me you cheating bastard." Stella stalked away.

Silence.

W.D. dived into his French fries. Red stubbed out his cigar as if laying an old friend to rest. I guess it was up to me. "I thought you two were love birds. What happened?"

"Some shit snitched on me."

"But when you walked in Stella had on that wedding bells smile."

"Damn Gloria must have called her."

"Gloria?"

"Yeah Gloria. She saw me at the Harbor Lights last night."

"And?"

"Gloria's sister was sharing my booth."

Whoever Gloria was. I said, "Tough to patch up. It's going to cost you."

Matt pushed his basket away. Unfinished. "I just remembered Oscar's investigative reports have been destroyed, but I'll check our county files on Clara's suicide." He motioned to Stella exhaling fire at the bar. "This is going to take all night."

I raised my coffee cup. Empty. I nearly signaled Stella but she was still sending up flares. Matt had disappeared.

W.D. said, "You've been a busy boy."

"I left Ann crying her eyes out. I had a couple of hours to kill so in addition to Pete I had another sit down with Frank and Duster."

Red asked, "How come Frank Dowling knows so much?"

"Oscar and Frank married sisters and, living in the same neighborhood, saw a lot of each other. I gathered Oscar used Frank for a sounding board on his tough cases."

"Like our dad's death?"

"Yeah."

W.D. grimaced, said, "How is Duster?"

"I took a couple of pints of Jim Beam along to loosen up his lips."

"Did it work?"

"Almost. He was about to admit that he was in town the night Charlie bought it, as Peter Benson claimed, but the booze killed the conversation."

"The son of a bitch is a liar." W.D.'s eyes carried a bit of flame themselves.

I said, "No question Duster is a liar, but my instincts tell me that he saw someone when Charlie bought it."

"The dickens." This from Red.

Imitating Colombo's sideways mumble, I nodded my head toward Stella, "Speaking of the dickens, I think we ought to sneak out the back way."

"But we haven't got the check."

Had my eldest brother suddenly developed a conscience? I didn't think so. I dropped two twenties on the table and slid out of the booth. "It's every man for himself." I didn't look back.

I stopped in the package store and bought a pint of rye, figured two pints would be too heavy an investment in Duster Grimes. The happy guy behind the counter gave me the obligatory, "Have A Nice Day." Just once I'd like to hear, "Have A Shitty Day," but I guess that wouldn't be good for business.

Red caught up with me in the parking lot. He handed me a slip of paper, said, "This is Mae Belle Foster's address and phone number."

I laughed, said, "And to think you and Swede only went down to Mercerville to see his grandparents."

I watched my brothers drive off. So different, yet as my mother often said, "Struck with the same stick." Same stick hit me too. Heavy on perseverance.

I tossed Duster's pick-me-up, Mae Belle's address, and the photo from Ann in the glove compartment. I took the river road east following the tree lined river walk through the territory that once belonged to Old Jepson's smokehouse and us kids. Jogger's were beating up a paved bicycle path, their gait measured to a stereophonic headset. Sweat bands absorbed their mid afternoon effort. Elderly couples wearing light jackets sat on wayside benches taking in the barge traffic. A speedboat arcing through the water chased the last laps of fall.

The river walk had the look of a neatly trimmed haircut, none of that weedy, ragged scene that had once infested the banks of the great river. Renovated homes with wide verandas and condos with meager porches fronted the river. The shacks were long gone. I pulled into a parking area and got out taking the coroner's report of my dad's death with me. A picnic table beckoned. I sat down, pulled a smoke from the pack, and used my trusty Zippo.

I absorbed the report but it told me little more than Frank Dowling's recollections. He, of course, testified along with Oscar Swensen as the investigating officer. I was heartened that both men, along with various other neighbors verified that my dad was not an alcoholic. Nobody could give a reason why he had been on the tracks that fateful night. Oscar produced the names of people he had interviewed. Included were Richard and Sarah Petersen. Oscar testified they told him they were asleep. They did not appear at the hearing. The name Charlie Cole never surfaced during the hearing.

I promised to let my brothers read it. Especially W.D. It was difficult for me to come to grips with his attitude. Or Red's. Did he and Red know something they thought I shouldn't know? Or dig up? When this tragedy happened they were in their teens, I but a kid of eight. The age difference between us then was huge. Their perspective of what actually occurred might have some grains of difference, but surely was not at odds with the testimony given. They were always my big brothers, and maybe this was the problem. I wasn't Junior any more - investigating was my bread and butter.

As I thought back on those terrible days my mother, Sis and The Boys, focused their grief on relieving mine. It was if by absorbing my tears they were better able to handle their own sadness. I was the kid. I was Junior. We were always a close family, but after dad died ever more so. But aging had closed the gap. I was now an equal with my brothers. I got up from the table a bit sadder, but no wiser.

I drove the back roads to the hospital, spotting along the way the many stops where I dropped off newspaper bundles to waiting paperboys. I was hardly more than a boy myself when I revved up the International paper truck on its afternoon run.

The Icky I remembered was a shrimp of a kid, scared of his own shadow. Couldn't throw, hit or catch a ball. Which among us guys consigned him to the outer limits. One time Icky told me that he was allowed to bring home a guest, a guest mind you, but only one at a time. I was never invited. Even during the summer when I helped him build a model airplane he came to my house. Icky must have had a lonely childhood.

Part of it, I suppose, had to do with his father being a lawman. We sure knew what he looked like. Not a very big guy, slicked, black hair, a joke for a mustache. But his uniform alone was enough to make us scarce. He carried a heater, that's what we called his revolver. None of us hung around Icky.

I turned off the highway and up an inclined road. A new sign marked the entrance to the state hospital. The road circled up and around a steep incline, but the coal pile that had been worked by the inmates was now covered in fall flowers and shrubbery. No more vacant, grinning faces standing idly by with wheelbarrows and shovels to greet me.

The old gray stone buildings seemed smaller, as if time had shrunk their menacing images. Certainly Pat, the middle-aged inmate who delivered the daily paper had not looked crazy, but his daily, "Thank You, Oink, Oink," when he took the bundle from me was a giveaway. Pat and his partner, the little guy who wore paper bags over his ears during the winter, had passed into a time warp of sunny days free of accountability. For all I knew they were still passing papers in the great beyond.

I followed the Administration arrow and pulled into an empty visitors spot. Next to me was a shiny black BMW. The sign in front of the car read, "Reserved, Chief of Staff." Icky Gould had come a long way.

I tucked Mamie Esterhaus's poetry book under my arm and locked the car door. On the way to the main office I scanned across the street to the windows of the gray stone building that once housed Clara Reece. I laughed, but even five plus decades couldn't remove the raw fear I felt when Gene and I set the dash record running away from Clara's frame plastered up against the bars. Her screams still clung to my spine.

The reception area had been modernized. Cream sofa, matching chairs, lamps, a maple table neatly stacked with magazines. A youngish brunette sat behind a desk busily pecking away on a computer.

"I'd like to see Mr. Gould."

Miss Wagner, according to her nameplate, never looked up. "Up the stairs, down the hall. Last door on your left."

I could manage that.

"And it's Dr. Gould." I smiled to the back of a brunette bun and followed her directions.

Icky's office was down a silent hallway. The only sound was my footsteps on the burnished tile floor. I opened the door marked Chief of Staff and walked in. Gray tile became plush pile.

A something thirties face spied me over a pair of outrageous red framed glasses. Chestnut strands, free-falling, to her shoulders set off intelligent eyes and high cheekbones. A white cardigan hugged her shoulders. Lips were splashed in red. Her nameplate read, "Mrs. J. Landes."

"Yes?"

"Is Dr. Gould in?"

"Do you have an appointment?" Her words arrived with a soft caress, the kind that was terrific on the phone, or in person.

"No. I'm a childhood friend of Dr. Gould and I'm in town temporarily."

"And you are?"

"Tell him Nick is here."

She eyed me quizzically, asked, "Just Nick?"

"Just Nick."

"Have a seat."

Mrs. Landes uncoiled slowly and made her way to Icky's door. She glided as if she had just been crowned with a diamond tiara. All her parts seemed to be in working order. Before entering she turned, caught me staring. She smiled.

I waited.

"The doctor will see you now."

Icky

My footfalls were lost in beige pile. The office was airy and sunlit, nearly square, neat, compulsively so. High, slender, double hung windows offered the tops of elms struggling to hold onto their yellow and bronze leaves. An oversized maple desk absolutely clear of paper fronted the windows. It could have been used for a quick game of ping-pong. Icky stood up and held out his hand, smiling. Filtered by the sunrays I made out a thinning pate, thick horn-rimmed glasses, and an immaculately tailored light gray suit that worked on concealing his rather thin frame. I risked a herniated disc reaching over the desk to shake his hand. Wispy grip, small hand. Icky never could grip a bat properly.

"Dr. Gould, I presume." Could have kicked myself. Icky Gould was no Dr. Livingston.

"Nick. It's good to see you." He waved me to a deep-seated chair in the far corner, followed me to its mate. Psychiatric journals were neatly placed on a maple table fronting the chairs. I put Mamie's poetry book on the table.

University diplomas and yards of plaques hanging in religious homage on the walls spoke volumes. Icky must have spent the better part of his life in the ivied halls of academia. I glanced at his arms and laughed inwardly. Carrying all those books hadn't lengthened them at all.

"Matt Jackson told me you were Director, and, as I've been looking up old friends, I decided to drop by." Including Icky as a friend was a stretch, but was as good an opening as any.

"That's kind of you. What is it now, twenty, thirty years since we last saw each other?"

I grinned, said, "At least that." Glancing at the diplomas, I said, "I see you have not wasted the years."

"Hardly. I couldn't get into the service. Eyes you know. The more I studied the less I knew, so I went into private practice. San Francisco, Houston, then back home." Icky laughed as if a bit of self deprecating humor would break down the barrier of time.

"And what about you?" he asked.

"Nothing so grand academically. Marine Corps, Math degree, a cop in Texas for more years than I care to count, homicide squad and chief of detectives before I hung it up. To tell the truth I hate retirement. I miss the Job."

"Ever debrief victims?" Interest showed in Icky's eyes, ever the psychiatrist.

"Many times. I've learned more about survival from victims than I ever did in seminars. And you?"

"I came aboard under Dr. Mason. When he retired, I became chief of staff and director."

"How are your parents?"

Icky shrugged, not in dismissal, but with feeling. Both of his parents were dead. He returned home to care for his mother who suffered from, as he called it, "the Big A." It was evident Icky cared for his father. I was not about to bring up Parker Gould being the bag man for the sheriff. Icky spoke with a genuineness I applauded.

"Are you married?" he asked.

"Divorced."

Icky stared at me, sensing the subject was closed. "And you?" I asked.

"Three times married, three times divorced." Now Icky's laugh was genuine. "No children thank God." He paused as if seeking a way out of a conversation that was going nowhere. He picked up my book of poetry, asked, disbelief marking his tone. "This yours?"

"Don't you remember it?"

Icky noted the inscription. A slowly lit smile turned up the corners of his mouth. "I'll be darned. Sure I remember. You lent it to me after I took a dunking at the Boy Scout meeting."

"As I recall, that was our one and only scout meeting. Not many of the old gang left in the East End." Including Icky in the gang was a concession I made out of kindness. Or was I simply working him for information? Passing his fingers over *SUNBEAMS* Icky said, "When my mother found out I had spent the scout meeting with my head in the toilet she went on a tirade. Don't you remember?"

I said, "Oh yes." Actually, I didn't but Icky was known to blab to his mother whatever our transgressions.

Icky said, "Mamie Esterhaus. I do not recall the reason why she gave it to you, but you were in trouble."

"I spent the winter memorizing poems."

"Me, too. Only it was summer." Icky shrugged, said, "My mother was pleased I had a friend who cared enough to lend me his book. She was strong on improving the mind." And, I thought, protecting her boy from the neighborhood wisenheimers who peed on second base waiting for Icky to slide in.

We sat in one of those painful silences that often happen between people who have no enduring amity. I suspected Icky was looking for a graceful out, but courtesy held him back.

"I wanted to ask you about Clara Reece."

"The crazy old lady who guarded her apple orchard?"

"The same. Clara was institutionalized here, in the violent ward, if that's the correct designation. Oscar Swensen, you remember Oscar, believed there was something odd about her death. I'd like to know when and how she died." That Icky's father investigated her demise was best left unsaid.

A typical administrator's frown divulged Icky's concern. He pursed his lips, said, "Is this official?"

"No, just a personal interest." I related the time Clara had scared the shit out of Gene and me. Only I didn't say shit.

Icky laughed. "Clara Reece. I seem to recall she had been institutionalized, but I have no knowledge about her death." Again the wrinkled brow. "You did say you had retired?"

I had the inkling Icky was making it tough for me. I sighed, said, "Apparently there was an inquiry surrounding her death."

"When did she die?"

"Mid-fifties."

"I was at the University of Michigan. Sorry."

Why do people say sorry when they don't give a rat's ass? "Oscar Swensen thought the hospital's public announcement reporting that she had died of natural causes was in error."

"I am not following you, Nick."

Icky, I decided, was more concerned about a possible investigation into his hospital stewardship than an ages-old death of a crazy inmate. I lightened

138

up, laughed, said, "I'm not too sure I'm following me."

Icky glanced at his watch indicating dismissal time. "I'm sorry Nick, but I have to make my scheduled rounds. But back to your question, all the records prior to twenty-five years have been destroyed." He went to his desk and hit the intercom. "Jessie, will you come in." Order from the COS, not a question.

The door opened and Icky's secretary slipped in. Great pins, eye stoppers. "Yes sir." Only two words but throaty as hell.

"Nick is inquiring about a patient who reportedly committed suicide." He turned to me, asked, "When was it?"

"I'm not positive, but I'd guess sometime in the mid fifties."

"Got that, Jessie, mid fifties. I have to make my rounds, but I would appreciate it if you would explain our procedures." Icky turned to me, said, "I'd certainly like to get together with you to discuss your victim debriefings. When are you going back home?"

"Not for a day or so. I'm helping my niece sift through Sis's effects. After my mother died, Sis bought the old homestead."

"Oh. Sorry about your sister. I did not know. Please accept my condolences." Icky returned to his desk and took a folder out of a drawer. Again glanced at his watch. "Where are you staying?"

"The hotel downtown."

"Jessie will give you my home address and phone number. Don't forget to call me."

I watched Dr. H. Parker Gould hurry out. The inmates had better be standing at attention.

"You were asking?"

I motioned to the companion chair, asked, "Would you like to sit?"

Jessie Landes grimaced, said, "Not in those chairs. It would take a hoist to get me out of them. Better my office."

I followed her to her desk. Any guy dumb enough to walk in front of Jessie required certification. She held onto her desk as she gently sat down. Her regal stride had blinded me to the fact that something was terribly wrong with her legs. I pulled a hard backed chair to the corner of her desk and sat. "Name is Clara Reece. She reportedly died of unexplained circumstances."

"During the Korean war?"

"After, I think."

"Gracious. Dr. Gould had all those old records destroyed."

"There must be something."

She opened a lower drawer, took out a pack of Salem's and an ashtray. She shook out a cigarette, offered the pack to me as if testing my will power. She had the wrong guy. I had no will power. I lighted hers and mine. Peering over the red light rims of her cheaters she smiled, said, "Good man."

We sat silently, dragging in the cancer fumes. Icky, I presumed, had an attitude about smoking.

"Although Dr. Gould expressly ordered all records over twenty-five years old be destroyed, we stored 3 by 5 cards containing basic data on them."

"You are a jewel."

"And you, Nick, are a vamper."

"Vamper? I thought vamp pertained to a sexy woman?"

"Vamp," she purred softly, "applies to anybody who is an unscrupulous flirt." Jesus, I was old enough to be her father. Jessie dubbed out her cigarette nervously, more butt than ash.

What's the name?"

"Clara Reece."

She took the phone spoke to somebody named Hank. "Get me the card on a woman named Clara Reece. R e e c e. On the double."

"So what's the interest?" she asked.

I told her about the time Clara scared the hell out of Gene Petersen and me. Jessie shook with silent laughter. Then, with the perception of a trained interrogator she honed in on me over those god-awful glasses. "You a lawman?"

"Retired."

She waved her hand, dismissing her intended cross-examination. "I can smell a lawman a mile away. No disrespect mind you. I like lawmen."

Jessie rolled out lawman as if sending me a gilded invitation. She had a traveled a few miles, but her voice track had to be heard to be appreciated. She had more sex in howdy do than a nude Marilyn Monroe calendar.

She took another cigarette, fingers steady, eyes on me as I lit it. It didn't take a brain to know who the vamp was.

A white coat walked in, handed her a card. "Anything else?"

"That's all Hank." Jessie held a finger to her lips, whispered, "Nothing to nobody."

Hank turned at the door, grinned, whispered back, "Nothin' to nobody."

Jessie read from the card: "Clara Ann Reece. DOB: June 18th, 1908, Armstadt, Illinois. Committed January 12th, 1943. Diagnosis: Manic depressive. Delusional. Periods of violence. Deceased, May 13, 1953. Cause of death: Self inflicted."

She handed me the card. The space, "Person to be notified in case of death," was blank. Under, "Disposition of body," it listed Coroner/Stern's Mortuary.

I took a folded sheet of lined paper and pen from my jacket pocket and took notes, a lifetime habit of the Job. I asked, "Where is Stern's Mortuary?"

"I never heard of it."

Neither had I. I fingered the card, asked, "Suppose you could check some other names?"

"You're going a long way without a badge. I'm surprised Dr. Gould okayed this check." Smiling all the time, but her eyes carried a bit of flint.

Never listen to an objection, just plow ahead. "You got it. Charles Cole and Sarah Petersen."

Once more she called Hank, gave him the names, held on while he presumably searched the records. "Thanks, Hank. Remember nothing to nobody."

As if imparting a secret, she said, "Nothing in the records."

Jessie, I decided, had a bit of spook in her. All she needed was a trench coat. "Right," I returned, "Nothin' to nobody. Oh yes, where does Dr. Gould live?"

"He has a beautiful home not twenty minutes from here overlooking the river." She wrote down Icky's address and phone number. Then tossing me a knowing smile she wrote down another number, said, "Just in case."

Jessie shook our cigarette butts and ashes into a paper bag, wiped the ashtray with a Kleenex. She sanitized the office with a spray can of deodorizer. Handing me the paper bag she gave me another spook smile. "Here, do something you're good at. Destroy the evidence."

I left with the bag. And her telephone number.

I stopped in to help Ann and found various members of the Ladies Aid busily marking Sis's possessions for the forthcoming sale. I joined Ann in the attic going through more boxes.

"Hi Unk. Wanna help?"

I kissed her and bent to the task. "Where did all this stuff come from?"

"Mainly grandma's. That's her trunk from the old country. Did you see Red and W.D.?"

"For sure."

"At Hagens?"

"For sure."

"Drinking?"

"For sure."

"I'm having a potluck supper at the church with the Ladies Aid. You're welcome."

"I'll pass. But thanks."

"Have you seen Mamie yet?"

"Not yet. Maybe tomorrow morning."

"Morning's a good time. We'll finish tomorrow and have the sale Saturday. Staying over?"

"I expect so."

I kissed her and drove back to the hotel. Icky knew nothing about his father taking bribes, but Parker Gould's investigation into Clara Reece's death nagged at me. I hoped Matt could retrieve the records of the Sheriff's Office but after forty years I was expecting a lot. Had he simply taken a bribe to protect the hospital staff? Or, more likely, bribes were an essential part of his job description. Parker Gould was a moneyman.

The hotel lounge was cluttered with Halloween festivity. Jack-O-Lanterns hanging above the bar cast off a yellowish glow. In the corners above the mirrorfake spiders in their machine spun webs were poised to ensnare imitation flies dangling just out of reach. The mirror had a cloud-like haze. Figures of Dracula and Frankenstein's monster glared at each other from a corner table. Ralph wore a white sheet, his face chalky white with blackened eyebrows and ruby red lips. Hell of a setting to get a load on.

The gambling boat crowd had yet to arrive. I signaled to the get up, said, "Attractive."

Ralph had a few bar miles on him and didn't appreciate the comment. "Same old same old?" came out with a disgusted grunt. I lighted up, contaminating the atmosphere.

He poured Wild Turkey and I sipped. Not long ago I cracked a homicide case because the mutt's eccentric drinking and smoking habits had done him in. I wasn't Sherlock Holmes nor did I have Poirot's little gray cells, but like many an old-timer, I was intuitive and persistent.

Ralph motioned to my glass. "Okay?" Attitude on the up-grade. Open grin showed yellow teeth.

I asked politely, "Early for Halloween isn't it?"

"Yeah." He stood back, spread his arms, asked without expecting an answer, "So why the get up now?"

I sipped the Wild Turkey wondering how quickly Duster Grimes had finished the pint I left him. I had to get down and dirty with Duster about Parker Gould and Charlie Cole. Might be worth the pint I had tucked in the glove compartment.

Ralph answered his own question. "We got gamblers coming in by the boat load. Get it? Boat load?" His stomach shook with laughter. Not a Oliver Hardy jiggle, but close. "Boss thought we ought to get them in the mood."

"Mood for what? I asked.

"Droppin' every dime they got."

"What if they are cleaned out?"

He refilled my glass carefully dropped in an ice cube. "We always got you."

He drifted to the end of the bar. I picked up Mamie's book of poems I had placed on the seat next to me. Strange old thing, Mamie Esterhaus. I fingered the pages, wondering what was fact and what was imagination from my knickered days. I sipped, smoked.

I didn't understand Icky dodging around my questions concerning Clara Reece. I smoked on that one for a while. Icky knew his father had investigated her death, and wanted to protect his image as an honest cop. The simple answer, Nick, is that he had simply destroyed all the old records. I was reaching and I knew it.

Jessie

"Hi sailor. Buy a girl a drink?" Jessie anchored her slender frame onto the stool beside me. Her gross red-rimmed glasses had been jettisoned in favor of slim wire frames, scarlet lipstick toned down to something soft and alluring. Even in the faint lighting her chestnut hair now upswept, glistened.

"How did you know I'd be here?" Smooth, Nick, smooth.

"I guessed," wide mouth grinning, "answer my question."

I signaled the Halloween ghoul, asked Jessie, "What'll you have?"

"What are you drinking?"

"Wild Turkey."

To the bartender she said, "Same."

She wore a pearl necklace, and as I reached to light her cigarette I caught sight of a small pearl earring, and the wisp of a seductive perfume. "You didn't," I mumbled weakly, "answer my question."

"I have my ways." Same throaty voice intoned I'm here aren't I. "That the same book you had today?"

I told her about the time I had lent it to Icky. "Icky?" She laughed. Sweet and low. "Is that what you call Dr. Gould?"

"Well, not now."

147

Jessie twisted her glass. I got the message, said, "Two more Ralph." Watching him pour she said, "The Stern Mortuary is long out of business. It was located in Andover."

"Andover?"

"In Mendon County."

I said, "The county seat."

"Gee, you're a quick study." A Bacall tinge of a smile cornered her mouth. "And Armstadt, Illinois where Clara Reece was born is in Wayne County. That's southern Illinois.

"How about dinner?"

"I thought you would never ask."

I signed the tab, left a generous tip. Ralph's chalky face broke into an oddball grin, said, "If I may, Mr. James, the salmon is highly recommended. Have a nice evening."

Jessie embarked from the stool slowly and slung an oversized handbag over her shoulder. I carried her coat into the restaurant, following her hips as if I had a Soviet agent under surveillance. She wore a slinky green dress. Lord, what a sway.

The hostess, who went by the name Marjorie, walked us to a corner table. The room was partially filled.

"Elegant, isn't it?" Jessie's eyes covered the room.

It was elegant, reproducing its past glory. The centerpiece was a tear-dropped chandelier that cast understated slivers of light throughout. It hung from a domed off-white ceiling with artisan designs. Two tapestries showing full-skirted maidens standing around identical lily ponds abutted a huge sepia mirror encased in cherry wood. Some held fans, others parasols. Crisp white linen graced the tables. Spotless goblets and golden champagne flutes awaited us.

Our waiter approached with a wine bucket containing a bottle of champagne. He uncorked the bottle and filled the flutes. "Compliments of the Manager." He offered small leather bound menus, retreated to a respectful distance.

Unlike show-time menus that engulfed the table, three entrees removed the guesswork, Lamb Chops, Filet Mignon, and Poached Salmon accompanied by seafood bisque and spinach salad. The waiter recommended a dry sauterne. I nodded.

I said to Jessie, "I hear the chef is outstanding. His poached salmon is a work of art."

"I heard the bartender." Eyes lifted.

"You're supposed to be impressed." She laughed. "The truth is I haven't eaten here yet."

She placed the menu down, said, "You order."

Midway through the poached salmon Jessie said, "I made an appointment for you with a woman who worked at the hospital during the nineteen-fifties."

Was there no end to her surprises? "That's terrific. Who is she?"

"Mrs. Johnson. She owns the Johnson and Johnson Insurance Agency just down the block."

"How did you find her?"

Jessie dropped into her spook mode, purred, "Ve have our ways."

"Does she know what happened to Clara Reece?"

"That I do not know. But my advice is not to miss the appointment. Nine sharp."

The waiter cleared the table, returned with a desert menu and coffee. I was a sucker for deserts but declined the lava cake or crème bruele as did Jessie.

The waiter said, "The chef asked if your salmon was up to expectations."

"It was perfection. Please give him my compliments."

"That I will, Mr. James."

Jessie furrowed her brow, asked, "Mr. James, hey. How long have you been here?"

"Three days. Why?"

Jessie laughed. "Champaign from the manager, tips from the bartender. You would never catch Dr. Gould talking to the help."

Dr. Gould? The thought of Jessie with Icky was monstrous. "Are you telling me you broke bread with Icky?"

"Once, between wives two and three. It was one of the most painful experiences of my life."

"I can't imagine you having painful experiences."

"You watched me walking didn't you?" What was she telling me? That I was a dirty old man? I nodded.

"Don't misunderstand. I like you watching me." Jessie stared across the room gaiety giving way to sadness. "In my senior year, actually the night of the senior prom, I was in a horrible accident. It took almost a year of therapy to learn how to walk." She turned quickly to me, smiled ruefully, "So what you get is Miss Stride. Except for getting in and out of chairs which is a bitch." She held up her hand silencing my response.

I asked in a voice not quite mine. "Brandy?"

Jessie smiled. "Later. You're a good guy for a cop, Nick."

"Gee, thanks. When I was a shrimp they called me Junior." What the hell prompted that remark was beyond me.

"Junior." Jessie washed it down with a sip of wine. "Lot of thought in that moniker. Got a room key?"

I fumbled in my coat pocket fit my key card into her palm. Jessie placed the card in her handbag, said, "I know what you're thinking. I'm old enough to be her father. What if . . ." Jessie's words trailed off. I knew damn well how the end of that sentence went. "What's the room number?"

"Eight twenty."

"Give me fifteen minutes. And bring a bottle of brandy."

I helped her up, kept my eyes on her disappearing figure. Was this happening to me? I sat down, smoked, signed the tab, over-tipped received an appreciative thank you and a bow from the waiter. In the bar I repeatedly checked my watch, fifteen times to be exact. Ralph wrapped a bottle of cognac and two snifters for me. As I left he said, "Have a nice evening, Mr. James." He was smart enough not to smirk.

It crossed my mind there wouldn't be anybody on staff who wouldn't know what happened in eight-twenty tonight. I didn't give a damn.

I keyed my way in. Light from the nearly closed bathroom door dimmed the room. The bed was turned down. Jessie stood by the window in some filmy thing that contained nothing but curves. Her hair fell to her shoulders. No glasses, sheen to her eyes. I put the cognac on the table, mumbled, "I got snifters." Dumb, dumb, dumb.

She glided to me, pulled my head down and whispered, "Who needs snifters."

An ancient proverb held that when heaven opened up and a date fell, the wise man opened his mouth.

I opened up.

WEDNESDAY

I awoke to a far away voice booming through a tunnel: "Nick, it's time to get up." I forced my eyelids up. Jessie was at the door, slinging her handbag over her coat. She wore a blue skirt and white blouse. She had come prepared, the minx, which, on hindsight, shouldn't have been any great discovery. "I'm late for work and you have a nine o'clock." She came toward me, brushed her lips across my forehead. "Get up. It's eight-fifteen." Then back to the door. Female fingers waved and out she went.

I pushed myself up slowly. Suddenly, a little man with a hammer began a construction project in my skull. Then the door opened and Jessie's face reappeared. "Forgot to tell you. Mrs. Johnson is my mother. When you talk to her call me Jessica not Jessie." Nice wide smile as if the joke was on me. "Bye."

I went to the bathroom, swallowed three aspirin, shot my eyes with Visine, showered, and shaved, slowly met the world like Punxsutawney Phil. I felt like the aftershock of one of those buildings they blow up on TV. I put on the usual garb I had worn for a zillion years, adding a red striped tie to my blue button down shirt. I upended the cognac bottle. It was empty. No wonder the little man was after me.

I called Ann, told her I would be late to help her clear out Sis's effects. The dumpster, she lamented, would still be there.

I left my laundry at the front desk and ate a continental breakfast in the coffee shop. My watch indicated I had better get moving, so I got moving. The morning air announced that cooler weather was on the horizon. I hadn't brought a topcoat with me, but as I was about to return to Texas a topcoat was the least of my worries.

Mary Lou

The Johnson & Johnson Insurance office was on Main Street. If I remembered correctly the building once was occupied by the city's best men's wear shop. Behind a receptionist, the walls were divided into open cubbyholes from which J & J agents worked their clients. I was directed down a runway to an open doorway. Inside I found Mrs. Johnson. Blue business suit, no lint allowed. Glasses held by a black string formed a perfect V, neck to breast. Short, cropped ashen-silver hair gave away her age.

"Nick, how nice to see you." Files were piled neatly on her desk. To one side shelves of manuals containing the secrets of the insurance game awaited her inspection. Nearly the tonnage of the State of Texas's statues, federal statutes, intelligence memoranda, and inspection guidelines I had once been addicted to. Success measured in pounds.

"My pleasure, Mrs. Johnson."

"You don't remember me do you?" Trace of a frown.

I hated being cornered. I said, "I'm sorry."

"Mary Lou Johnson. We were in school together. From grade school through high school."

I couldn't forget her in grade school. She had her hand up constantly answering questions, actually Mamie Esterhaus's questions. But I lost track of Mary Lou in high school. It was hard not to know about her, she was the class valedictorian, starred in high school plays, a member of all the in scholastic clubs and voted most likely to succeed. I didn't exactly travel in her circles. I hung out in the Uptown pool hall and drove the paper truck.

I nodded, said, "I intend to see Mamie Esterhaus today. I understand she's not doing too well."

"That's too bad." Disinterest bordering on who cares. "She skipped you a grade didn't she?"

Bringing up Mamie Esterhaus wasn't exactly my smartest move. Mary Lou's mother informed the neighbors that my advancement was rightfully Mary Lou's. I said, "Jessica told me you were her mother, but she didn't say anything about me knowing you."

Mary Lou pressed her lips together, said with feeling, "Just like Jessie. She has to play her little games."

My God, Jessie surely wouldn't have told her mother about last night. Not to worry. She was smart enough to warn me not to call her Jessie. Dip your toe in quickly, Nick. I said, "Without Jessica's help at the hospital I wouldn't have known anything about Clara Reece."

"Yes, she told me about your inquiry. What can I do for you?"

"I'd like to know how Clara Reece died. I saw Icky yesterday and he informed me her file had been destroyed. The only existing record showed she died May 13th, 1953."

"Icky? Who is Icky?"

She knew damn well who Icky was. I laughed, but taking in her scowl I knew I had made a mistake. I recovered, hopefully in time, said, "Dr. H. Parker Gould."

"Is this official?"

On the edge of being snotty, but she had the right to ask. My badge was now ensconced on a plaque in my den - like my career. I said, "Nothing official.

No court of inquiry, no testimony required." I was good at placating reluctant witnesses.

"So what I tell you will reside between you and me."

"That's right." My nose was growing longer by the minute. It was important that I know what she knew. Later I'd ask myself why. Mary Lou fiddled with a gold pen, meditating. Then, decision made, she placed it firmly on her desk pad. "I worked part time during the school year in the state hospital's administration office earning money for college. Yes, I recall the incident. Mrs. Reece had been confined to the security ward. I was told that she had committed suicide when I arrived the next day."

"Did they find her in the ward?"

"Yes, where else would she be?" Mary Lou was a pain in the ass as a kid and hadn't outgrown the habit.

"The only hospital record extant shows "self-inflicted" as the cause of death. I wondered what that meant exactly."

She said, "Dr. Jamison tried to put a clamp on the gossip, but you know how that goes. He threatened to fire anyone who talked outside the hospital."

"Which leaves my question dangling."

"Well, Clara Reece died forty years ago, and it's not as if I knew anything personally." Mary Lou paused, fiddled with a file on her desk, making up her mind. If she was only passing me gossip what the hell was the problem?

"It was rumored that she had taken rat poison. I never knew this to be true but what circulated was that it was night guard's fault. He didn't last the month."

"Was he held responsible in some way?"

"That I don't know. But the rumor was that he left the area and retired in Florida."

I said, "Oscar Swensen thought there was a cover-up."

"Oscar Swensen? Our neighborhood police officer? The hospital was in county territory, and the sheriff handled any problems at the hospital."

I said, "Correct. This will interest you I'm sure. Dr. Gould's father, Parker Gould, was the investigator, but his report was never made public."

It must have cost the chief of staff a bundle to keep Clara's death quiet. Then again the sheriff's bagman was not above compromising his authority. "What did the employees think happened?"

"Lots of gossiping. I was only file clerk, but the inmate files were kept separate, under lock and key. But I know Clara Reece's file went to Dr. Jamison. It never came back." Mary Lou canted her head as if deep in thought, continued, "That's not quite correct. It did come back several months later, but some of the psychiatric evaluations were missing."

"How did you know that?"

"Esther Winters, who was in charge of all hospital records, let it be known. The department was staffed with old timers. Not much happened they didn't know about."

"Did she say what was missing?"

"Psychiatric memoranda that related to Mrs. Reece's delusional state. Apparently, I say apparently because I had no direct knowledge. You had to know Esther, she ruled the admin records with a firm hand. She went directly to Dr. Jamison who told her the missing memoranda were being reevaluated."

"For what reason? Clara was dead."

"That's what Esther said. She told one of the ladies in confidence that a month prior to Clara's death she was ranting and raving about the children. It's hazy really, but Clara was really out of it. She attacked the orderlies more than once."

I said, "What I don't understand is how they were able to keep this quiet from the public."

"Given the time it happened it is not to difficult to understand. Clara was not much of a story. I remember the papers only gave it a paragraph and they quoted Dr. Jamison saying she died of natural causes."

I asked, "Were you ever questioned?"

Mary Lou recoiled as if taking on the class dunce. She declared, "No. The fact is none of us were ever talked to."

I plowed ahead. "I suppose Esther is no longer with us."

The eyes staring at me were icy blue. The kind that informs a guy the interview is over. But, to my relief, she continued. "Esther was an old lady then. She died shortly after of pneumonia."

"This is really helpful." Like the reluctant dragon, Mary Lou accepted my compliment with a nod. She said, "Now I remember, Pops Blasingame was the guard's name. Dr. Jamison let it be known it was his fault. He was fired shortly after Clara died."

Blaming the security guard was ridiculous. I said, "The only hospital record extant shows Clara's death was self inflicted. Blaming Blasingame doesn't seem to follow."

"I don't know about that. But to believe Pop was responsible is unthinkable. He was the nicest old man."

I said, "This is touchy and you certainly do not have to answer, but could Parker Gould have possibly filed a false report? That is, do you think Clara took the poison willingly or was her death a more complicated event?"

"If you're implying murder, I don't remember anybody raising the subject." Mary Lou paused, frowned. "It was all so long ago. The people in admin gossiped about everything that happened at the hospital, but, as I said, we had no direct knowledge of anything."

I had run the string on Mary Lou, and to continue to beat the bushes would only further irritate her. She knew more than she was willing to admit, but I was grasping at straws. I got up reached across the desk and shook her hand. "I really appreciate your help."

I received a startled look as if my gesture conflicted with her judgment of the boy who had aced her out skipping a grade. She asked, "Do you remember when recess was over and we gathered on the back stoop of the school waiting to get in from the cold?" The scene came back to me dimly. I nodded. "And the time you fell off the railing and damaged your mouth?"

I remembered. That was the time Sis and W.D. and Red and me, came home with a busted arm, busted teeth, or, in my case, a fat upper lip. It was one of the few times I ever saw my mother cry. I laughed, said, "I looked like a monkey."

"I pushed you."

Had Mary Lou carried this bit of contrite baggage for all these years? Surely, this wasn't the reason she had consented to speak to me. I walked to the door, signed off sincerely with, "Thanks."

"Nick." I stopped, turned, knew damn well what was coming. "Jessie is my only child, and she has had a difficult life. She was the high school valedictorian and had an academic scholarship to college. But after that terrible auto accident she lost her . . desire."

Desire to do what? I waited, attentive to her remorse. "She had everything, beauty, intelligence, drive, every key to success." Mist formed in the corners of Mary Lou's eyes, but she held herself erect, pride surmounting her grief. "That earlier remark I made about Jessie playing games. She is very headstrong, but I don't want you to think I love her the less for it."

Only an idiot would have missed Mary Lou's resentment. It all seemed so trivial to me, skipping grades and all that nonsense, but bringing Jessie into the equation as a postscript presented her bitterness as a clear and present danger. Something had passed between mother and daughter that had aroused Mom's suspicions.   "I called Jessie last night and again this morning. She wasn't home."

"I'm sure there must be some explanation, but what it is I have no idea. I saw Jessica at the hospital, but afterwards I helped my niece clear out my sister's house." Lying is not so difficult once one gets in the groove, and I was in the groove.

Mary Lou's demeanor suggested she wanted to believe me if only to protect her vision of the daughter she loved. Why the hell was she checking up on Jessie anyway? Jessie was an adult. At the moment I didn't feel like the wise man that saw the date fall. When I left I felt those icy blue eyes on my back. The word skeptic came to mind.

Mamie

Mamie Esterhaus had been my homeroom teacher through grade school. She was a severe taskmaster who ran her classroom with an authoritarian bearing, ruler at the ready. At the time I failed to appreciate her moral lessons, poetic though they may have been in *SUNBEAMS,* but she influenced my untrained mind for something beyond a steady diet of comic books and pulp magazines. In high school Mamie confronted my reading habits once again. Unbelievably, she made English literature a treat not a chore. I wasn't much at parsing a sentence, nor did I miss many days at the Uptown pool hall, but my nights were devoted to *Chaucer* and *Green Mansions* and the tales of *King Arthur*. If it were not for her I'd never have gotten any farther than *Doc Savage* and the pulps.

I hadn't seen her since I entered the Marine Corps, but as I parked in The Manor lot I felt a surge of nostalgia. Sis, I was sure, in her regular visits had mentioned me, but to make certain I carried *SUNBEAMS* and the unknown photo along. I hoped she was alert because my intent was to search through an old lady's recall.

I paused in the common room of The Manor. It, like the main dining room, was spotless, an airy room bright with the morning sun. Exercise bikes, silent sentinels to a jogger's past, stood at rest in the far corner. The room was deserted. I peeked into the library. A gray haired codger with furrowed brow was intent on the stock market pages in the daily newspaper. The worth of his portfolio, I assumed, was a major concern of his day. I wondered what seniors without blue chip stocks did to ease their financial burdens. Their senior problems were closer to me that I cared to admit.

I strolled down a hallway to the assisted care section. Through closed doors television sets blared forth the morning soaps. It didn't really make a bit of difference because none of the "guests" could hear anyway. Occasionally, through an open door I got a wave and a faint, "Good Morning." More often than not I found myself returning a loud, "What?" My constant use of what used to infuriate Ellen. Now, no cared.

On the door her name, MAMIE ESTERHAUS, was etched on a brass plaque. I opened the door.

There wasn't anything special about the room. Bed against the far wall, a comfortable but aged chair, lamp, bookcase, TV set, a small desk holding reading lamp and a large numbered telephone. The ring would probably raise the dead. Needlepoint prints hung on the walls. Mamie Esterhaus sat in a wheel chair absorbed in a PBS travel show. She turned as I entered.

"Miss Esterhaus, I'm Nick James."

Her white hair floated a web-like sheen. Watery eyes loomed through thick wire rimmed lenses. Veins, blue and extended, ran across her hands, up her thin arms. She wore a shawl over her shoulders. Her body had gone to shit.

"Nicholas?" A smile of recognition brightened her face. She clicked off the TV, said, "Well for land's sake, sit down."

I sat in the only chair, asked, "How are you?"

Laughter canned from the past erupted weakly. "Look at me."

She wasn't the teacher I remembered, but neither was I the kid called Junior. Ann had told me she owned an apartment in The Manor, but now finding her in an assisted care room meant her health was failing badly. I didn't want to think of her next stop.

"I came home for my sister's funeral."

"Yes, I know. She visited me regularly. I'll certainly miss her. As I missed your mother when she passed."

Was Sis her only visitor? Her words were strangely, not of remorse lament maybe. I asked, "Do you have any family?"

"All dead and buried. As your mother would say, 'Not a chick nor child to care for her.'"

Her fingers fascinated me, in constant motion as if applying themselves to a needlepoint canvas. I said, "I noticed the needlepoint's, did you do them?"

"In my lonely days they were my salvation."

"Wonderful farmland scenes. Who designed them?"

"I did. They represent my youth. Even the horse and buggy."

Her lips turned up in a ghost of a satisfied smile. I said, "It's good to remember."

She chuckled. "When you get to be my age the past is the here and now. Can't say the same for the present."

I had to ask. "How old are you."

"That would be telling, but I'll never see eighty again."

"Amazing, you have lived so much of our history, through two world wars and the great depression, women's right to vote and presidents from Woodrow Wilson to Bill Clinton. That's something to be proud of."

"No, that's terrible." Mamie rolled her chair closer. "Never be the last one, Nicholas. When I go I'll go alone." And, as if she still had a ruler poised in her hand she reprimanded me. "Never end a sentence with of."

Which means what? Die young and have a crowd at your funeral?

I showed her *SUNBEAMS,* asked, "Do you remember when you gave this to me?"

She took hold of the book and read the inscription. Smiling, she said, "Yes, I remember. You were in some sort of trouble. I can't recall what it was but your mother came to me complaining that you obviously did not understand the meaning of fair."

"I let the air out of Mr. Benson's back tire."

Oh yes. He and your mother were of different parties and you decided to stop him from hauling voters to the polls. That was some more of your devilment."

"Devilment."

"Like the times you and Mathias Jackson sneaked up on the school's roof during recess and threw water bags at the girls."

"You must be mistaken. As I recall you caught Matt tossing water bags, not me."

"Oh, you were up on the roof, too. Maybe not at the same time, but you were up there."

It was true the past came alive for oldies. "He was expelled."

"How he became Chief of Police and Sheriff is beyond me. He wasn't much for books."

Her opinion, I surmised, was not the only voice of censure in Matt's past. I asked, "If you knew I was up on the roof why did you not report me?"

Her fingers stopped moving as marking a point in the past. "Because it would have embarrassed your mother."

This didn't quite jell with the Mamie Esterhaus I remembered. She was a tough article, never mollycoddled students, and believed in the dictum spare the rod and spoil the child. How she learned I was up on the roof was a mystery to me, but half the homeroom knew what Matt and I were up to. We were too smart by half.

I said, "I noticed a blank space on the inside back cover of *SUNBEAMS*. Ann found a photograph that fits exactly the space." I gave her the photo, said, "I wondered if you recognized the girls?"

"SUNBEAMS?"

Had she forgotten so quickly that I had given it to her? I pointed to the book in her lap. "My mother must have stored it away and Sis forgot to toss it out."

She opened it to the inside back cover tracing the missing photo with her spidery fingers, looking at the photograph of the four young girls all the time. A thin smile tinged her lips. She said, "It looks as if they were standing in front of a church, but the girls are unknown to me. Are you certain they are not your relatives?"

I knew she was telling me a fib. Not a lie, a fib. If she wasn't somebody I honored from my past I would have pursued the photo, but to become accusatory with her was unthinkable. Watching her fingers etch the blank space I knew it contained her past not mine.

Mamie handed back the book. It was an effort. Her frame was down to nothing, all skin and bones, no filling to it. She said, "I remember. When I gave you that book you were frightened. At the time I thought it was because you were in trouble with your mother, but afterwards I concluded that I frightened you."

Remembering that dank, dark house she called home I returned to the day she had given me *SUNBEAMS.* I said, "Until I saw Gene peeking at me from behind a curtain I was ready to bolt."

"Gene?"

"Gene Petersen. I saw him the other evening at Sis's wake."

"You were a good friend to Gene."

"He told me that he saw a man wearing a big hat and a long coat on the tracks with my father the night he died."

"Gene Petersen?"

"That's right. Charlie Cole wore a cowboy's hat and a long coat." I thought she had nodded off, but she expelled a faint grunt indicating life still existed in her wasted body. "Gene said he told his mother, Sarah, but she never reported it to Oscar Swensen. Frank Dowling told me that Oscar never knew that Gene saw a man with my dad but even so Oscar suspected Charlie Cole. I wonder why?"

"Interesting." She stared far off as if the something interesting belonged to her past. "Your sister kept me abreast of your career in law enforcement. I imagine you are a relentless detective. She was mighty proud of you."

Like Frank Dowling she was in and out of it. This was a one-dimensional conversation, nothing time consuming was in the cards. "You scared me, Miss Esterhaus, but not like Clara Reece. I repeated the story of Clara, from behind state hospital bars, screaming at Gene and me. Mamie produced a faint smile, but said nothing.

"Did you know Clara committed suicide?"

"Clara?" Mamie frowned, creating an image of the neighborhood lush. "Suicide? I recall she died in the state hospital, but I never knew she committed suicide."

"Apparently she died from rat poisoning that may or may not have been self induced." Mamie simply stared at me no words forthcoming. I was as bad as Oscar Swensen. Making assumptions based on a smattering of evidence.

"I must have heard wrong. Got it mixed up with Charlie Cole's suicide. You remember that don't you?"

Mamie hunkered down in her shawl as if a cold wind had passed through. "Terrible man. Certainly I recall his suicide. It was the talk of the neighborhood. The consensus was that he deserved to die."

From Mamie's tone it wasn't difficult to understand why she detested the bootlegger, everybody in the East End detested him. I wasn't here to put her under the lamp, but Mamie was one of the few left who knew the goings on in the East End a half century ago. Edge into it, Nick, bob and weave.

"I saw Duster Grimes yesterday."

"Terrible man. He gives the neighborhood a bad name."

"You know Duster was Charlie Cole's number two man?"

"I've heard."

"I'm convinced Charlie was murdered and Duster knows who killed him."

"I wouldn't know anything about that."

The old lady is telling me nicely that enough is enough. "I'm sorry if I in any way distressed you bringing up these terrible incidents, but there are not many people left from the old neighborhood."

"No, I'm among the few. You mentioned Frank Dowling. We are of an age."

"He is a wonderful man. He and my dad and Oscar Swensen were close friends. Which reminds me, Oscar told him that Sarah Petersen and Clara Reece were sisters."

Her eyes, cloudy with age, sought mine. "Sarah and Clara?" She paused spoke as if thinking aloud. "No, I did not know that."

I pressed the point, couldn't help myself. "After my dad was killed the Petersens moved into a home owned by Charlie Cole. I think that is interesting."

She grimaced and showed her teeth. "Charlie Cole! Why do you keep bringing up that detestable man?"

I had upset her and felt badly about it. I had no valid reason to believe that she knew Sarah and Clara were sisters or that she knew the Petersens had moved into a home owned by Charlie Cole.

Mamie was slumped over, her head resting on her frail breast, eyes closed. As my mother would say just plumb tuckered out.

I got up but to leave without saying goodbye wasn't right. I sat down at her desk, and taking up pen and paper, wrote a few words. It saddened me to think of her dying alone, without anybody caring. I told her I would write.

"I just want to die."

I turned. The old lady's eyes were cast in a far away mode, staring into a black hole known only to her. I didn't know what to say.

"It's terrible to get so old. I pray to God that He will take me."

Tears misted the corners of Mamie's eyes. Her hands were clasped across her meager chest as if entreating the Lord to remove her anguish. Her pain, I knew, was cerebral. She wanted to die and didn't have the physical strength to accomplish the deed. It came to me that she was pleading for someone, maybe me, to . . . A pillow over her mouth and nose for a few minutes and Mamie Esterhaus would be at peace. I shook my head savagely, choking back the terrible thought that engulfed me. I was spellbound by her poignant yearning. Then she closed her eyes and once more drifted off, her breathing back to a normal cadence.

I took in a gasp of air myself, dropping my shoulders in relief. My hand touched the telephone on her desk and wondered why someone near ninety and without family required a phone. I remembered Aunt Ida. She wasn't really my aunt rather a good friend with an indomitable spirit. Bed bound with both legs amputeed she kept her old Buick in the garage for, as she said, emergencies. She had a local mechanic take her car in twice a year to change the oil and check the engine. Like Aunt Ida's Buick Mamie's telephone represented a connection to life. There was no question in my mind that if Aunt Ida had sold her Buick she wouldn't have survived a month. But if Mamie pleaded to die why keep the damn telephone?

On the desk lay the frayed cover of a photograph album. I leafed through the pages, black and white photos only. Mamie was with her lady classmates posing in graduation robes before an Oberlin College sign, alone in cap and gown, no parents, no siblings, no photos of her growing up days. The album was really ancient, the pages cracked, a few photos once glued in now missing. I ran the photograph of the four girls against the missing slots but didn't get a match. I decided the dead and buried rightly belonged to Mamie's past, not to my meddling.

I closed the door softly.

I called the Sheriff's Office and left a message for Matt. "I'm going to see Duster. How about lunch at Hagens?" I thought about phoning Red, but to my brothers Hagens was their home away from home. As it would have been mine had I still lived in the East End.

I got in my rental and sat quietly for a few moments thinking about Mamie. Poor old soul just wanted to die. What was it Sis had said about Mamie - she called her a tortured soul. Well, Sis would have known.

Duster

I decided to dress down inasmuch as I was visiting Duster and thereafter having lunch with Matt and my brothers. I stopped at the hotel, hung up my navy sports coat and slacks, whipped off my tie and put on levis, a London Fog jacket and Texas boots. I felt better immediately. Casual was my middle name.

I suspected the old neighborhood was somewhat a retired community, my boarded up grade school halfway up the bluff was a give away that signified the little people were few and far between. I parked in front of Duster's house. I slipped the bottle of rye into my jacket pocket and walked to the porch. Duster wasn't sitting in his lawn chair taking in the world so I knocked on the front door. Getting no response I knocked a bit harder, still no response. I tried the door and it opened. I got a whiff as I moved into the living room.

I looked at my watch. Eleven fifteen.

The room was, surprisingly, clean and neat. A dark tan or beige wall-to-wall carpet showed little wear, drapes drawn across two windows fronting the street dimmed the room but not excessively. Copies of Utrillo were grouped on the wall fronting a sofa and sizeable TV set. Shelves containing an extensive collection of murder mysteries filled the wall behind two recliners separated by a small table and table lamp. A nearly empty fifth of rye and a half filled glass lay on the table along with a TV guide. The TV was off. The smell of death crept up the walls.

My eyes automatically memorized the scene.

Duster Grimes lay spread eagled in one of recliners. He had on a print, dressing robe of quality. A caked line of blood drifted down from his mouth to his chin. I took hold of his wrist. *Rigor mortis* had set in. I wondered if Duster was a diabetic because *rigor* would take only minutes in those cases. But the idea of Duster being a diabetic was nonsensical. He was, I knew, a drinker. I inspected but kept my mitts off the rifle lying on the floor.

It was a 06 Winchester, twenty inch barrel that could fire either .22 shorts or longs. It was magazine loaded, had open sights and a shotgun butt plate. In the old days the 06 Winchester was a common rifle used to shoot small game. It could easily be used to shoot oneself. The scene suggested Duster had committed suicide.

I checked the corner of the wall next to the front door and found markings caused by the rifle's sights. I smiled. Ellen's father had a similar rifle standing behind the front door. It gave me a start when we were back home dating. The only time he smiled was when we informed him that we had eloped. He said something about finally getting rid of her. Great guy. I missed him.

I walked down the hallway to a bedroom. The queen-sized bed had not been slept in and, except for a missing pillow, was made. I gave the room a quick toss, didn't know what I was looking for but covered my fingers with my handkerchief. A second bedroom was obviously not used, a single bed and a chest of drawers. I gave it quick look, nothing more.

It was eleven twenty-two.

The kitchen was large, a microwave and toaster rested on the counter, along with the phone. The usual appliances lined the wall next to the counter and a pine table with one setting and two chairs. The drawers underneath the counter were filled with the usual kitchen supplies. One drawer held a current telephone book, but no memo book listing Duster's personal telephone numbers. Nor were there any tacked on a sheet behind a cupboard door even though tacks remained suggesting that the numbers had existed.

Eleven twenty-seven.

I opened the back door, left it ajar as I reconned the garage. A two-year old Cadillac butted up against a tiny bench. Familiar tools hung from the far wall. I looked through the Caddy's windows.

I wanted to search the glove compartment but decided that hands-off was the wise course.

I returned to the house, closed the back door and went back to Duster. I kinda liked the old warrior even if he was full of it up to his eyebrows. He was a bit of a fooler old Duster, Cadillac, well appointed home gave me a hint that Duster lived far better that he projected. Would anyone believe Duster had Utrillo's oils hanging on the living room wall? They were only copies, but Utrillos?

I was stalling. The neighborhood was quiet. Had I seen anybody say raking the lawn? No. What about behind the curtain peepers? This was my third visit. Do you think nobody noticed? Really, Nick. I checked the telephone book and dialed the PD. The phone had no dial tone. I didn't have time to figure out why.

It was eleven thirty-five.

I went to my rental, tossed the pint of rye back in the glove compartment. I had been in the house twenty-five minutes. If no one had seen me I could fudge the time or declare I had been so shocked I just stood there unable to move. That would go over big when the locals discovered I had been a homicide dick. The truth would arrive. The only question was when.

I drove to the main drag and made the PD call from a gas station. I told the desk sergeant what had happened and that I would wait in front of Duster's house. He didn't seem too thrilled.

Two bluecoats squealed to a halt behind my rental. I got out, identified myself as the person that had found Duster and accompanied them to the house. One look at his body and they ordered me to wait on the porch. I was in Duster's lawn chair pulling on a cigarette when Lieutenant Dawson arrived with the forensic team. Dawson was maybe forty, graying, had a workout build and was very serious. He asked me to wait. Actually he said don't go anywhere. I had invented that line.

Matt

It was after one when Matt showed up with a deputy driving a sheriff's vehicle. He said, "What the hell ya doing sitting on the porch?"

"Waiting for Lt. Dawson."

"How long?"

"Half hour or so."

"Bullshit." He went in the house and quickly came out with Dawson. He introduced me to Dawson as a longtime friend who had called him stating I had intended to see Duster before I met him for lunch and he hardly thought I had knocked off Duster particularly before lunch, so we were going to Hagens and Dawson could see me at the station when we finished.

Which was a long speech for the sheriff. Dawson listened, gave me the once over, shook his head and went back to the house.

Matt dismissed his driver and directed me to my rental. "Drive," he ordered.

I laughed. "Dawson isn't exactly pleased."

"Screw him. He'd have had you sitting on the porch all afternoon."

"Did you tell him I was a homicide detective?"

"Hell no. But when he finds out he'll be pissed. Outsiders, if you know what I mean. By the way how long were you in there."

"You want to know?"

Matt said, "Not really, but I figure you tossed the house."

"Old habits die hard. My instincts tell me Duster didn't kill himself, but that's not for publication."

"When was he shot?"

"I'd say sometime around midnight."

"I saw the body. It looks like a suicide."

"I know it does. The 06 Winchester is fully capable of being used for that purpose. Duster could have shoved the short barrel into his mouth and pulled the trigger all at the same time. But my gut tells me he was murdered."

"Speaking of guts, let's eat."

We joined my brothers at Hagens and spent a lengthy hour chasing down V.O. with beer and tying into hamburgers and French fries. W.D. ever alert for the absent female form asked Matt about the missing Stella. He got a grunt in return, a sure sign that the on again off again was off again. I told

W.D. and Red enough about Duster's death to get the idea across that I hadn't just shut the door on his dead body without satisfying my curiosity.

Red said, "I don't get it. You talk to Duster about dad's death one day and the next day he puts a rifle to his mouth. If I remember he said Charlie Cole didn't have anything to do with dad. So why did Duster commit suicide?"

I said, "Beats me. I've told you what appeared to be a suicide. I can't say more than that."

W.D. said, "Or you won't." W.D. paused, grinned slyly as if telling me that all was well between us. He said, "Do you have this effect every place you go?" I stared at him, saying nothing. "What I mean is the bodies are piling up, Nick. Think about it."

I nodded. The thought had entered my mind, too.

On the way to the PD Matt pulled a file from a folder. "These are the only sheriff's reports I was able to find concerning the death of Clara Reece - an incident report signed by Parker Gould and a statement by Fraser Jamison, Director of the State Hospital. Fact is I'm surprised there was anything at all. In essence Gould concluded that she died of unknown causes, that he interviewed the guard that was posted in the building housing the violent ward, one Gary Blasingame. Blasingame clocked his rounds every two hours but on the night in question Gould found out he had missed half of his rounds. Blasingame claimed he had been drugged, but Gould reports the guard apparently was asleep. Gould recommended that he be fired.

"That's it?"

"That's it, partner. If Parker Gould prepared a summary report it's long gone."

"Conveniently disappeared."

"Got that right."

I said, "Jessica Landes showed me a hospital card dated May 13, 1953 that noted Clara's death was self inflicted. And her mother, Mary Lou Johnson told me this morning that office gossip held that she had ingested rat poison, which, if true, means cyanide. She also said that Pop Blasingame was fired as he was gone from the hospital within the month."

Matt gave me a sideways gander, said, "Jessica? You know Jessica?"

"Of course, she's Icky's secretary."

"She's had a tough life. I was on night duty inspecting the troops when her boy friend wrapped the car around a tree out on Route 6. Five killed, she was the only survivor. She was in therapy for over a year and I visited her often." Matt paused as if slowing down through a caution zone. "Her dad, Brainard Johnson, died shortly after the accident and Mary Lou took over the insurance business and Jessica's life."

"I noticed she walked with a limp."

"She was with child."

I had a sinking feeling. "Jessica?"

"We're not talking about Mary Lou, of course, Jessie. After the accident the doctor informed me she was five months pregnant. The baby died. I told Mary Lou but I kept it out of my report."

I sensed Matt knew nothing about my late night romp with Jessica, at least not yet. I said, "Poor kid."

"Poor kid is right. You have to understand Mary Lou is just like her mother. Her mother damn near went ape when you and not her precious daughter skipped a grade. Mary Lou is the same with Jessie. She cared for Jessie for years after the accident and through a messy marriage and divorce and, unfortunately, doesn't let Jessie forget it."

"And Jessie rebels."

"You got it."

"This is very interesting, but why are you telling me all this?" I hoped my sweat didn't show.

Matt said, "I don't think you ought to get caught in the middle between Mary Lou and Jessie. Jessie has a defiant nature."

He eyed me with meaning. "If you have any designs on Jessie I'd be careful, Nick. Mary Lou doesn't let the leash out too far."

Finally, I got it. Jessie had talked to Matt, and he knew her well enough to conclude she was the one that had designs. A jump in the hay for Jessica, I decided, wasn't a one-time ride. Jesus, life was complicated.

I said, "So what did Dr. Jamison have to say?"

Matt read from his statement. "Jamison authorized an autopsy and as Clara died on hospital grounds he, not the coroner, performed it."

I said, "In other words he authorized himself to do the autopsy. That's highly irregular if not illegal."

"Well, he did have an assistant."

"As if that makes it legal."

"Right. He signed a statement that Clara died from a self inflicted substance, origin unknown."

"I wonder how much that report cost the hospital."

Matt put the papers back in his folder, said, "For sure Parker Gould, the sheriff, and the coroner made out."

"But Oscar Swensen wasn't fooled."

"If you can remember that far back," Matt laughed, "The whole state was awash in gambling during the 50s that couldn't exist without crooked politicians and law enforcement officers."

I said, "We had bent cops long before the 50s. Which reminds me of the look you gave me when I was discussing Parker Gould being the sheriff's bag man with W.D. and Red."

Matt laughed. "We really were a couple of rascals. We'd hide behind the bushes down at the park spying on high school kids necking."

"Yeah," I joined him laughing, "and some more than just necking."

"When they moved to the back seat we knew they meant business."

I said, "That's when we spotted Icky's dad's Chevy and Charlie Cole's Ford with their lights out among the tombstones in the cemetery."

"Yeah, Charlie got out and handed Icky's dad a package. We thought it was some sort of a secret mission and Charlie was reporting to the deputy sheriff."

"My brothers thought that Charlie was giving him a bottle of booze and we thought it was a secret mission."

"And all the time Charlie was paying off the sheriff's bag man."

"We made a pact to keep or mouths shut."

"We didn't have a choice. One peep about what we had been doing and our parents would have locked us up."

I said, "And if we knew Oscar sure as hell knew. Speaking of Oscar it occurred to me that to believe, as Oscar asserted, that Charlie was murdered there had to be a second shot."

"How do you figure that?"

"If the rifle was standing by the front door as Oscar states it would have had to been fired before being placed by the body. The key is to whether Larry Hughes, the neighbor below the bluff that had originally called Oscar, reported a second shot. That's why I need the PD investigative reports."

Matt said, "Asking for reports covering Charlie Cole's suicide would be like waving a red flag in front of Dawson. Once he does a background on Duster he'll find out he was Charlie Cole's number 2.

You figure it out, Nick. Questions about Charlie Cole now are not healthy for you."

"You're right."

City Hall had the presence of an old man wearing a well-worn gray suit, high starched collar, standing erect in his mayoral splendor. I didn't know its age, but it held the city's secrets, one of mine included. We walked up the steps and entered. The lobby, hardly more than a wide hallway, was as I remembered it. The marble floor showed the imprints of age, and the same dark oak benches lined the walls. Above the benches, pictures of past mayors and early scenes of the downtown called to mind the city's history. A staircase ran up to the second floor where the magistrate once held court.

It was Halloween and my not so bright ideas of fun got Matt and me arrested. When I spoke with Pete Benson the other day he thanked me for making sure his son Zach got home safely. I hid Zach and Gene Petersen under a tarp in Wedman's garage before I made a break for it. As I hotfooted it this bluecoat eight feet tall put the arm on me. We were maybe fourteen years old. Jesus, was I scared.

I grinned, said, "I was just thinking about a little kid in court."

He laughed, said, "You mean the night we sat on these City Hall steps waiting for my dad to pick us up?"

"Yeah, that too."

"Something else?" Matt humped down next to me on a bench.

I said, "I had just made detective. I caught this kid, ten, eleven years old that had placed a concrete block on the main line railroad tracks. Skinny little guy couldn't have weighed seventy pounds. The DA decided to make an example out of him."

"And you didn't?"

"Yes and no. A passenger train had been derailed out east the week before this kid placed the concrete block on the tracks. It was a front page story and an editorial demanded action."

"How did you put the arm on him?"

"Simple really. I checked the nearby grade school for any students absent when the incident occurred. The principal delivered this little squirt to me, nice looking kid, very polite. The kid said he did it, but I couldn't believe it. I took him back to the scene and asked him to show me how he had done it. He hefted the block onto the tracks, didn't even work up a sweat. I almost broke my back getting the damn concrete block into the trunk of my car."

Matt got the picture, laughed. "So what was the problem?"

"At the hearing the court room was filled with law enforcement officers and this little kid. The kid was scared as hell so I put my arm around him, told him not to worry."

"I know the feeling," Matt lamented.

"So," I shrugged, "do I. Anyway, the DA makes a case out of how dangerous this kid is. You know the type. Heading for the governor's mansion on the back of a ten year old criminal."

"Sure do."

"What happened?"

"The judge sentenced him to a year at the boy's farm."

"Tough."

"I interrupted and asked the judge if probation might be in order since he had no previous history of trouble."

"I thought that was the DA's job."

"It was, and he was pissed at me. He informed the judge that not withstanding my unsolicited opinion it was a matter of grave public safety and the kid deserved the year. The judge stared at him for the longest time then amended his order. The kid got probation.

"I never forgot that little kid. When I told his parents they thanked me. Can you believe it? They thanked me."

"Maybe you were just thinking about the time we were caught."

"Maybe. I shook my head remembering. "My mother said I'd never get a job with a criminal record."

"We never had a criminal record."

"No record? I didn't know that."

"I was chief of detectives in Springfield when I applied for the chief's job here. My old man almost fell off the couch when I got the job. Anyway, when I took over the first thing I checked was our names, no record, not even a court file."

"But we washed squad cars."

"And polished brass."

"No record? I'll be damned."

"It was all a show."

"But it made the papers?"

"Yeah, and you know where we were the next Halloween."

"Ma locked me up with one of Mamie Estherhaus's books of knowledge."

"Oh yes, before I forget it, Dr. Fraser Jamison reported Clara's body was turned over to Stern's Mortuary."

I almost mentioned that Jessie had already told me but discretion, as they say, keeps a suspicious sheriff at bay. I said,

"That it?"

"That's it."

I said, "You get an A plus, sheriff. The way I see it if we can figure out why Clara was murdered we'll know who."

"Murdered? Where the hell did that come from?"

"No matter how you cut it, Matt, somebody had to have given her the rat poison. She was locked up remember? She sure as hell didn't get it by herself."

Matt got up, said, "My driver is about due. Lots of luck with Lt. Dawson."

I groaned as I got up. I had to admit I was too old for fooling around. That half-your-age stuff that Matt peddled spelled trouble.

"You look a little the worse for wear partner." This from a man that should know.

I stopped at the water fountain in the lobby, took two aspirin from a tin I always carried in my coat pocket. I washed down two tablets, sighed.

"You should watch your drinking."

Thank god he didn't say what else I should be watching.

Lt. Dawson

I walked down the staircase and a hallway through the only open door. A sergeant was busy on a computer, the obligatory cup of coffee chilling out within easy reach. Gray desk, gray chair, gray walls, he looked up, said, "In a minute."

The room was depressing. A drop ceiling with incandescent lights gave it the panache of a morgue. The smells of the dear departed were absent, but a certain mustiness lingered as if the walls dripped with tales of past interrogations. Or maybe it was just an old building.

I looked around for a chair, peeked into an office, saw a Lt. R. C. Dawson nameplate on an institutional steel gray desk. A steel gray chair with padding sat behind the desk, its brother waiting for the next victim faced the desk.

The sergeant said, "You Nicholas James?"

I nodded.

"Lt. Dawson said he was still tied up at the crime scene and for you to wait."

"In his office okay?"

There was a momentary pause while the sergeant wrestled with a momentous decision. "Not if you smoke."

"Is it okay outside?" A tad shy of smartass.

"Suit yourself." He didn't remark smartass.

I walked back to the lobby and saw the red circular sign with a lit cigarette bisected with a cross line. I got the hint. Walked outside and put my Zippo to use. Whether it was good use or not only addicts could answer.

I sat down on the steps and for the first time noticed that it was a great fall day, the sun cheered the sky, chilly enough for a light jacket or sweater. The trees were doing their magic. It was a time for nostalgia, and do you remember when we . . . fill in the line.

For someone who was not accustomed to waiting I took more than a few deep breaths, continuing to give my Zippo a workout. I was anxious to know what Dawson made of the suicide scene. Otherwise I would have left. That said it was a leap of faith to think he'd tell me anything. I hadn't the faintest what the problem was between Matt and Dawson but bad blood oozed from their attitudes.

The telephone still puzzled me. Had it been pulled out of the jack or had Duster simply not paid the bill? Everybody had a list of personal telephone numbers. Where was Duster's? That, to me, was more interesting than the absent dial tone. And then there was the missing pillow. The missing pillow was the key to whether Duster was murdered or committed suicide. Think, Nick, think.

Lt. Dawson said, "You look deep in thought. I apologize for taking so long. The coroner took forever. Follow me."

I followed. I sat facing him. He looked like I felt. Tired.

"Your name is Nicholas James." I nodded. "Tell me what were you doing at Duster Grimes's house this morning."

"First off, I came home for my sister's funeral, and have stayed on to help my niece clear out the family home." I gave him my sister's name and the address of our family home. "I was born and raised in the East End and grew up with Matt Jackson."

"Pardon me for interrupting but I asked why were you at Duster's?" Not surly, but not happy, either.

Obviously my friendship with Matt didn't cut it with Dawson. I said, "I saw Duster sitting on the front porch the other day and struck up a conversation with him. He was older and a bit of a fraud but we were both injured in the service, him in WWII and me in Korea. That's our only connection."

"How many times did you see him?"

His men had talked to the neighbors. I couldn't slip around this one. "As I said I saw him on the porch."

"Just once?" Attitude was everything and he had one.

I had sat where Dawson sat a zillion times and hated witnesses who made you pull out every scrap of information. "No twice." Pull you shit, pull.

Dawson sat back lost in thought. I waited. "He said, "Listen, James, I got off on the wrong foot. Your association with the sheriff colored my reasoning. It's no secret I don't like him, but tarring you with the same brush doesn't wash. So, let's start over."

Maybe he wasn't such a bad guy after-all. I told him about my law enforcement background and my first impressions of the suicide scene.

Dawson said, "Your background as Chief of Detectives is impressive. With your experience as a homicide detective what did you conclude when you first saw Duster?"

I was well aware of the proper use of a butter knife and Dawson was adept at spreading it on. I smiled. "Suicide was my first thought, but I would have to know the results of the ballistics test. That is, if the bullet hasn't been too damaged entering the brain."

He said, "It's true that the .22 long may have hit raw bone in which case it probably is damaged. The autopsy will be done today. I'll let you know."

"That's mighty handsome of you. I am well aware the mischief outsiders can do if they are of a mind to. I was in the house twenty minutes, from eleven fifteen until eleven thirty-five." My times didn't get a rise out of him so I concluded that he had a pretty solid idea how long I had been in there.

He said, "Anything else come to your attention?"

"He had a phone and a current phone book but no personal notebook listing private telephone numbers. There are tacks inside a cabinet door but no piece of paper listing often called numbers, doctors, neighbors, friends, you name it. And the dial tone was blank. I figure somebody disabled the phone. If it happened at the time of Duster's death it's important."

"You tried to call from Duster's?"

"How do you think I knew there was no dial tone? I didn't inspect to find out why."

"So you called from the gas station."

If this was a question I'd be damned if I'd answer it. I said,"I was visiting my old schoolteacher today. She's past ninety, her body has gone to shit and she still has a telephone. Who does she expect to call her? A game show? The lotto? Miss Esterhaus you have won sixty million dollars? The telephone is her lifeline.

"So, why is Duster's phone disabled and where are his personal numbers? His lifeline?"

Dawson laughed. He was much better when he laughed. "I can't answer, but I have a man at the telephone company. Is it your impression that Duster was a drinker? Reason I asked was that we located two cases of rye whiskey in the basement."

"Did he drink?" It was my turn to laugh. "There is no need to embalm Duster, he has taken care of that job already."

"The coroner estimates that Duster died sometime around midnight. He may be more accurate after the autopsy but I'd say midnight give or take a half hour."

I asked, "The neighbors didn't hear a shot around that time?"

He grinned. "The neighborhood is locked up tight by nine. And on both sides they wear hearing aids. I expect you could fire off a canon and they wouldn't hear it."

I said, "One other thing impressed me, Duster's life style. When I first saw his house on the outside I would have expected the inside to be a shambles, too. And the way he was dressed when I saw him on the porch I gathered he was on the near side of poverty. But inside he wore a classy dressing robe and if I'm not mistaken his whiskey was poured into a cut glass tumbler. Reproduction Utrillos for gods sake. Why was the outside falling down and the inside a study of Sir Malcolm enjoying an evening at his estate?"

"I'm sure I don't know"

"Were the neighbors ever in his house and did he ever have visitors?"

Dawson made a note, said, "I'll find out."

Bringing up the missing pillow was off the mark at this point. Dawson would rightly conclude he had a nut facing him not a homicide detective. If ballistics proved the 06 Winchester did not kill Duster I might mention the missing pillow, but not before.

I added. "I'm staying at the hotel downtown room eight-twenty. Tomorrow I'll be with my niece. You have the number. If I can be of any further service call me."

"I'll be in touch. By the way are you Red James's brother?"

"Sure am. What has the rascal done now?"

Dawson said, "Nothing unless you count haunting taverns a crime. I've known him for a long time. Great guy, full of bullshit, but a great guy."

I swept my eyes around his office. "By the way, when are you vacating this dumpster?"

"If you are still in town next week I'll give you a tour of the new police department."

Ellen

I nodded goodbye and drove back to the hotel. Evening was dropping a dark curtain on the East End. I was truly really beat. I required a drink and solitude. Last night framed my memory but I wasn't in the mood to see if there were any dates falling my way.

The bar hadn't received its quota of light bulbs yet, but the gloom was satisfying. I was about to grab a stool when I spotted Ellen sitting next to the same table she had occupied two nights ago. I signaled to Ralph. If I got his smile right it was one of knowing. He probably surmised I was running them in and out on schedule. Great for the ego but the reality was something else.

"Ellen."

"Nick."

She wore a navy blue pea coat over a gray turtleneck, hardly any makeup, and something was bothering her. She toyed with her wine glass. I lit her cigarette. I was afraid to ask her what she was doing here.

Ralph dropped my bourbon and a dish of mixed nuts on the table. He said, "I'll run your tab, Mr. James."

I think I said thanks.

Ellen said, "Ralph, I changed my mind. I'll have what Nick is having." She waited until Ralph returned with her drink. I lit a smoke for her and used my Zippo on my own.

"I've got some bad news. Frank died this morning. He was sitting in his chair looking at the river. His regular day nurse was on duty and I had stopped in to see if he wanted anything special at the grocers. He didn't answer. Oh, Nick, I'm so sad."

She took out a Kleenex and dabbed at her eyes. I wanted to embrace her but that wasn't in the cards, so I held her hand. I said, "I'm truly sorry. Frank was a grand old man. Although I kept at him about Oscar's cases I cared a lot for him. Is there anything I can do?"

"No, I wanted you to know and I brought you this."

She handed me a large folder. "Frank recalled that Oscar had given him these reports when he went into the nursing home. He died and Frank was left with this folder that I found in a file cabinet in the basement. He said to make certain he remembered to give them to you."

"Thanks, Ellen. I'll look at them tonight."

"Forget the reports. You look tired, Nick. You ought to go to bed."

I said, "I found Duster Grimes in his house this morning apparently a suicide."

"Gracious, no wonder you look tired. Was it awful?"

"It was my job." I could have kicked myself. The damn job was what led to Ellen giving me a permanent goodbye. "Matt Jackson rescued me from the locals, but my afternoon was spent with Lt. Dawson. He wanted to know what I was doing in Duster's house. I didn't lie but I didn't tell him the facts either. What I mean is I didn't say anything about Oscar's old cases. You understand."

"I think so." She sipped her drink, strong stuff for a wine drinker. "Maybe I shouldn't say this."

I interrupted, "But you will."

She smiled. "Smartass. Did I miss something? I thought you had retired."

"You are right. You are always right."

"I used to believe that line, too."

I said, "The day must be exhausting for you. We could stop somewhere for a quick bite."

Ellen said, "I can't, Nick. I'm picking up Frank's daughter, Virginia, at the airport. She's flying in from Kansas City. I made arrangements at the funeral home for the wake to be held day after tomorrow. You know you were right."

"Right? About what?"

Ellen said, "I made a fuss about you tiring out Frank when actually your questions gave him something important to think about. The last couple of days, I don't know, lifted his spirits. He looked forward to your visits. He told me he was certain you would solve Oscar's big cases. He really liked you, and thought you were a smart guy."

I said, "That's a mighty heavy load to carry around. Whatever you may think about me chasing these old cases I believe I owe Oscar and, in a way, Frank, too." I raised my glass, touched hers, "To Frank."

She responded, "To Frank." She got up. "I've got to get to the airport."

"Want me to drive you?"

"No. I have my car. Get some rest."

I said, "Remember I'm free. I'll be at Ann's tomorrow."

"Thanks, Nick."

I watched her stride out. If she had listened more to Frank I'd be out of the batter's box by now. I finished my cigarette and got up to leave. Ralph appeared as if on cue. "The chef has an excellent filet."

"Room service tonight. Make me a double to go."

Ralph prepared a package of mixed nuts along with my drink. I signed the tab. My tip could have bought several cans of mixed nuts. Ralph was happy.

Jessie

I set my drink and Frank's folder on the table along with my smokes and Zippo. I slung my jacket on the bed and removed my boots. I massaged my neck, stretched my back, sighed and groaned and otherwise acted my age. I plopped in the chair and looked at the folder but hadn't the inclination to open it. I opened the room service menu and was inspecting its contents when a knock on the door and a female, "Housekeeping," sounded. Eyes fixed on the menu I answered, "Come."

Jessie slinked in, wide smile on a wide mouth. "Pretty sneaky hey," she said and planted one on my mouth. To say I was astonished was an understatement. "Well you could say something like, 'Jessie how wonderful to see you,' or 'I've been hoping you would come.'

Your mouth is open, Nick."

I recovered, I think. "Jessie, how wonderful to see you."

She wore a western suede jacket with fringe and a tan suede man's cap. Blue jeans and tasseled loafers completed the outside upholstery. She draped her jacket on a chair showing off a white button down shirt. Kicking off her loafers she tucked one leg under her rear and sat down facing me. She kept her cap on.

"Don't worry, Nick, I didn't come to do anything."

Thank god I muttered to myself. I said, "I wasn't worried."

"Liar. You men are all alike." She took a sip of my drink said, "Fire water. Anyway, I came to find out how you're doing. I understand you found Duster Grimes today with a bullet though his mouth. Who is he anyway?"

So I went through the Duster Grimes story one more time. For all I knew she knew the reason why I had been seeing him, but I didn't walk through that door.

"You look beat, Nick." She grinned, "Maybe I ought to tuck you in bed."

"I don't think so."

"Well, you can feed a girl."

Safer ground by far. Enough about tucking in bed. I ordered a hamburger and fries for her and a filet and salad for me. We argued the merits of lite beer which, to me, there are none. We finally settled on Coronas.

I asked, "You know Sheriff Jackson well?"

"Absolutely. He's like my father. What I mean is that my real father died soon after I almost bought it in the automobile accident. Matt really helped me – and mother. You can't say anything against Matt to me."

"That makes two of us. What bothered me was Lt. Dawson made it clear he had no use for Matt."

"And you want to know why?"

"Yes. After an antagonistic bit of interrogation Dawson became friendly. In his place I don't think I would have been as forthcoming. But I have no way to judge why he hates Matt."

"Simple. His father expected to be named Chief when Matt got the job. For a couple of years he made Matt's life miserable. Matt got a bellyful and told him unless he retired he would fire him. Old Man Dawson opposed Matt the first time he ran for sheriff and is running against Matt again. Some of his charges are outrageous and untrue. Like father like son."

Our food arrived, just in time because Jessie was getting up a head of steam. She ate with passion, no fooling around, no asking me if I'd like some of her French fries or how's your steak and can I have a bite? We ate in silence, didn't have to put on a show for each other. She even drank beer like a man, none of that sipping and dabbing at her mouth. Girl after my own heart, and, I smiled, maybe my body.

She cleaned the table and put the tray outside the door. She pulled her chair over beside me. We smoked. She said, "What I really came to see you about was Clara Reece. I did some more digging in the old employee's files."

"Does Icky know?"

She laughed. "Dr. Gould knows what I want him to know. Anyway, we have male night nurses to handle emergencies in the violent ward. It struck me that the hospital had to have them when Clara did herself in. It took a bit of vamping with Hank, you remember 'nothing to nobody' Hank, but I found the names of the male night nurses back in 1953, Calvin Moore and Scott Mansfield. The night guard was Gary Blasingame who retired shortly after Clara died. He was an old man then so it is doubtful he is alive today."

I lit another cigarette for her but didn't interrupt. She continued. "I checked the current telephone listings for the area. There is no Calvin Moore listed but there is a Scott Mansfield at an address that is part of a development off Route 6. Here," she handed me card, "is his address. I didn't call him. He might not be the same guy but it's worth a shot."

"The wrong person sitting here is the detective. You done good, Jessie."

"I know that." She tossed her cap on the bed got up and sat on my lap. Nuzzling down she whispered, "You know, Nick James, you could grow on a gal."

"I think I already am."

THURSDAY

I came awake slowly, one eye at a time. Jessie's perfume lingered but she had made her get away without waking me. I glanced at the radio-clock. It was long past my wakening time no doubt due to a tough day at the office and an athletic night. I hadn't the slightest what I was doing with Jessie. Or what she was doing with me. She was a bit outrageous but under her cap lurked wheels within wheels. She wasn't the kind of dame you would kick out in the cold and it crossed my mind that she might be interested in more than fun and games. The reality, as I saw it, was that my December didn't belong in a picture with her May. I was thinking too much. Get up, Nick, shower and shave, Nick, take care of your laundry, Nick. I dressed and carried Oscar's reports to the coffee shop where I ate the continental breakfast.

Scott

The Scott Mansfield that lived at the address off Route 6 as Jessie described it turned out to be the son of the man I was seeking. His daughter-in-law directed me to his summer place on Campbell's Island up the Mississippi. I found Scott Mansfield sitting on the dock watching the river go by.

He waved to a lawn chair and poured me a cup of coffee from a thermos mug. "Got a call from my daughter. What's all this about?"

He still looked to be the powerful man. A mane of shaggy gray hair surrounded craggy features, a knife sharp nose bisected a pair of sunglasses. But his hands were afflicted with tremors and for the most part he held them clasped in his lap. I revised my first impression. He wasn't the man he once was.

I said, "I'm looking into the circumstances surrounding the death of Clara Reece. I know it's a long time ago, but I wondered if you remembered the night she died."

He stared at me as if to say not all the loonies are on the inside. "It must be 35, 40 years ago and yes, I was on duty. But before I say anything you'll have to explain yourself."

I told him who I was and that I had been homicide detective, that Oscar Swensen a local police officer had left me his files asking me to investigate Clara's death. My nose was growing longer but Mansfield seemed to buy my line.

"I knew Oscar. The East End lost a fine police officer when he died. If he asked you to do something for him I'm happy to oblige."

"It would be helpful if you could, so to speak, set the scene."

He gave me a skeptical gaze, said, "This is confidential isn't it?"

"Absolutely." As one of my Texas pals would say, "Don't get hung up on details. Let 'em talk."

"Well sir, Clara was housed in A building. Most all the inmates was peaceful, you know we had the Queen of Italy and King Arthur among our honored guests. And old Pat who passed the papers thought he was a pig." Mansfield laughed until tears misted the corners of his eyes.

I too remembered Pat and his, "oink, oink," when I gave him the newspapers. I interrupted and told him about the night the paper truck stalled and Clara scared the hell out of Gene Petersen and me.

"That mighta been before my time."

I nodded.

"Well sir, Clara was a handful when she went off talking crazy about her children, but she had her quiet times, too. Me and Calvin Moore had the night duty. We'd both been medics in the war and Dr. Jamison hired us at the same time. Anyway, that night we had run our checks of the wards and Clara was still alive."

"What time was that?"

"We started at ten and finished usually around eleven. Pops Blasingame was the night guard on duty. He sat up front in A Building with all the doors locked, except the front door and Pops locked that one when he did his rounds.

"It was his duty to clock in at all the stations every two hours. The reason I mention it is because the recorder showed Pops missed his last rounds that night which meant he was out of it for at least four hours. He swore that he musta been drugged, but that didn't go over at all with the investigation. Pops'd never lie about something that important, but he was an old geezer. Even so I believed him because he had never missed his rounds before, and that night he musta fell asleep or was drugged just after he had eaten his sandwich and had his coffee."

I asked, "Same time every night?"

"Yeah. Pops ran a regular schedule. He ate about two-thirty every night. He remembered drinking his coffee, but when Cal and me were there in the morning he checked his thermos in front of us and it was absolutely empty. Of course the sheriff's investigator took it to mean that Pops had emptied his thermos so that it couldn't be checked, but that was nonsense and Pops said so."

"Why was his thermos important?"

207

"Because he was asleep when Clara died of cyanide poisoning. Not that we knew anything official but after Pops woke up he checked all the inmates and found Clara dead. He called Cal and me and when we inspected Clara her lips were drawn up like a wolf's. I checked her breath to see if she was alive and it smelled off so I asked Cal to do the same and he said it smelled of bitter almonds. Cal had been a nurse before the war and he had run into poisoning cases. Anyway, he said she died of cyanide poisoning. We locked the room and reported directly to Dr. Jamison when he arrived for work. Cal told him we believed she had been poisoned."

"And what did he do?"

"Went to Clara's room first and then questioned Pops. That's when we learned that Pops claimed to have been drugged. I admit we found it hard to believe. Dr. Jamison inspected Pops' thermos and showed it to us. It was like I said empty. That was before the recorder was checked and showed Pops had missed clocking in."

I offered him my cigarettes and Scott took one. I lit them up with my Zippo and placed the pack and lighter on a wood table. He palmed my lighter, said, "You in the war?"

"Korea."

We smoked and watched the river. I suspected he needed time to reflect and I was in no hurry. Pushing always led to mistakes and in a business

208

where people's lives often hung in the balance judgment was everything.

"Cleaning crew gone?"

"Sure. All the employees were gone home, day nurses, admin staff, and maintenance people. Dr. Jamison took us back to his office and called the sheriff and the coroner's office. He swore us to secrecy, said the good name of the hospital was at stake. Of course we agreed. Then Pops and Cal and me went home."

"Was there an autopsy?"

"Of course. There was gossip that Dr. Jamison conducted the autopsy but that wasn't true. He, as I understand, was present but the coroner conducted the autopsy. I didn't know until the whole thing was over that the coroner ruled Clara died by her own hand therefore she was a suicide."

"No mention of cyanide?"

"No sir."

"But Calvin was certain that she was poisoned?"

"He's long dead but I'd swear by whatever Cal said. He wasn't a liar or the kind that'd make up stories. No sir, if Cal said she died of cyanide she died of cyanide."

"How could she get a hold of the cyanide?"

"We puzzled about that. Cal said that it could have come from rat poison and for sure rat poison was available, but it was locked up in the maintenance room in the basement."

I said, "It didn't necessarily come from the maintenance supplies. Anybody could have purchased rat poison."

"I guess so."

"And the sheriff never questioned you or Calvin?"

"The chief deputy did the investigation, man by the name of Parker Gould. Fact was Dr. Jamison controlled who was talked to. Unless he gave permission you were out of bounds. The son of bitch of a deputy reported if there was any fault it was Pops for sleeping on the job, and he recommended that Pops be fired. He concluded that Clara's death was self-inflicted."

"How did you know this?"

Scott Mansfield took in the river, avoided my eyes. Then he smiled as if remembering a covert mission only he and Cal were privy to. He said, "Still confidential?"

"Of course," I lied.

"Me and Cal stole his report for a look see. He recommended they fire Pops."

"And did they?"

"They gave him early retirement."

"And you and Calvin?"

"We were surprised that the coroner never called us. I presumed he had had a hearing, but I learned much later that he had not done so. In other words he ruled out of hand."

I asked, "So what do you think really happened?"

He glanced my way again, took a cigarette and my Zippo. "Nice lighter. This still confidential?"

"Just between Oscar, you and me."

He smiled. "I guess I can swallow that. The way Cal and I figured it, by the way Cal is dead, is that the coroner and the sheriff were paid off. That's just our speculation."

"Did you ever think that Clara had been murdered?"

"Maybe, maybe not. This was way too heavy for me and Cal. Nobody had seen Clara but us and Pops, and Dr. Jamison. I mean nobody else at the hospital. She was carted out of there early that morning before the staff came on duty."

"But you and Cal talked it over. How did she get hold of the cyanide? Who gave it to her?

"I ain't going any further down this road, Mister."

"I understand, but I was wondering if she had any visitors?"

"You don't give up do ya." Scott Mansfield wasn't exactly pissed but he wasn't smiling either.

I had passed by my welcome. Another rule best remembered. When it's time to let go it's time to let go. I smiled, said, "Forget I asked. Here's my telephone numbers in case you think of anything I should know."

He put my numbers in his wallet, a good sign that he wasn't too upset, but he shook his gray mane as if trying to figure out what to say. "Remember I told you Cal and me worked nights? How many visitors do you think she got at nights?"

"Sorry." I wasn't really but it was the thing to say.

"Fact is I wanted to ask you something."

"Go ahead."

"Me and Cal found out that Clara's sister, Sarah Petersen, signed the release papers when the coroner was finished with her body. That's interesting because nobody at the hospital seemed to know Sarah Petersen, and after you telling me that Clara scared you and Gene Petersen out of your wits I just wondered if Gene Petersen was related to Sarah Petersen?"

Scott Mansfield and Calvin Moore had done more than nursing at the hospital. I said, "He was her son."

"When you was running from Clara didn't he tell you she was his aunt?"

"Not a word, but then again knowing Gene maybe he didn't know."

Mansfield grimaced as if a sharp pain had knifed his gut. He shook gray mane again and said with feeling, "I shoulda told Oscar whats I shoulda done."

"You're not the only one who should have told Oscar what he knew."

Ann

I found Ann at the dining room table busy signing thank you notes for those who had remembered Sis. She looked up and smiled, motioned to an address book. "Mom must have known everybody in the East End. If not for her book I wouldn't have had half the addresses of people that contributed to the church. Like Mamie Esterhaus's address. Somebody at The Manor sent a card and twenty-five dollars in her name, with no return address, but Mom had it in her book."

She dropped her pen and gave me the once over. "The brothers called and told me about you finding Duster Grimes. I told you to stay away from him, didn't I?"

I reached across the table and kissed her. "Smarty girls shouldn't be ordering their betters around."

She snickered. "I inherited the rights from Mom."

"No fair bringing in the heavy hitters."

"So how was it?"

I went into my Duster story for the zillionth time and the grilling at the PD with Lieutenant Dawson. I added, "And Frank Dowling died yesterday. I miss the old man."

Ann said, "I bet Ellen was upset."

I said, "She came to the hotel last evening and," I showed Ann Oscar's reports, "gave me this folder that Frank had left for me."

"I just made out a thank you note for Ellen. She's using her maiden name. Did you know that?"

"No." What was her second husband's name? Herb something or other? At least she wasn't stuck with his handle. Of course James with a Nicholas attached had been long consigned to her dustbin.

"You want her address?"

"Sure."

"Came to the hotel, hey?"

She was fishing, but that water was frigid. I was saved answering her by the telephone. Ann went to the kitchen, listened and said, "For you Unk." She whispered, "It's the bulls."

Lt. Dawson

"Nick James here."

"Nick, this is Lt. Dawson. I left the crime scene photos at your hotel. I got the idea yesterday that you questioned whether Duster was a suicide. Is that right?"

"My hesitancy was instinctive."

"It had to based on something?"

I was being drawn in which, as a professional, pleased me and made me wary at the same time. "It's more smoke than fact."

"Do I have to dig it out of you?"

"Don't get in an uproar Lieutenant. It didn't make sense to me. For one thing, why was there a missing pillow? I didn't find it in the house. I might as well tell you I looked for it in the garage but it wasn't there. I believe that Duster's killer took it with him. Before I go on, let me ask, did you find it?"

"Why the hell should I tell you?"

"Two can play at this game, Lieutenant. I don't have to tell you a god damned thing, either."

Nothing came across for 12, 20 seconds. "Okay, we didn't find the pillow. In fact, nobody spotted it as missing."

I said, "The whole scene looked too pat. The mostly empty bottle of whiskey, the shot through the mouth, the 06 lying next to the body, made me uneasy. Only cops eat their guns, civilian's aim at their temples and half the time, miss or end up goofy for life.

"The old 06 Winchester fires a .22 long and if Duster had a thick cranium the bullet would like as not bounce off. So the shot through the mouth with a .22 made sense, but it didn't explain the missing pillow."

"Jesus, are you going to get to it?"

"I think the pillow was used to mask the sound of a second bullet being fired, but if so why was a second shot necessary? Only if Duster's Winchester wasn't used to kill him. In other words, Duster was wasted by a handgun that fired a .22, and the killer had to take that weapon with him when he left the death scene.

"To make the scene look as if Duster took his own life, he had to leave a weapon that fired a .22 long, and what better than Duster's 06 Winchester. The killer either just noticed the Winchester standing up beside the front door as was once the custom or he had been in the house before and knew it was there. I don't believe in coincidences. I believe the killer knew the Winchester 06 was there. Which is something for you to think about.

"Getting back to the Winchester it couldn't have been fired inside the house, hence the reason I went to the garage. Not to find the pillow, which, if I was correct, was long gone, but to smell the interior. There was no lingering odor of a firearm having been discharged in the garage, but at that time my argument hadn't time to take shape. I realized later that the garage wouldn't have been used. The pillow wasn't going to stop the bullet in the garage any more than in the house. A search would have located the second bullet somewhere in the garage, and the killer couldn't have that. So the Winchester had to have been fired outside. The pillow would have masked the sound so it had to leave the murder scene, too.

"But how much of a sound does a 06 Winchester firing a .22 make? It's more like a crack than a larger gauge rifle or sidearm. If X took the 06 and the pillow in the backyard, say between the

216

garages, its unlikely the neighbors would hear the sound of the shot. You might get lucky and find the second bullet."

"Dawson said, "You get all this from a missing pillow? No evidence of a second .22 caliber gun even exists, no evidence of a second shot exists. If you hadn't been a homicide dick I would have had your upstairs checked."

I said, "I told you it was smoke and mirrors."

Dawson admitted, "There were no fingerprints on the Winchester other than Duster's, but you'll be pleased to know ballistics reported the Winchester was not the weapon used to kill Duster Grimes."

He could have told me this at the outset, but he couldn't help himself from being an asshole. I said, "I thought a .22 hitting solid bone would collapse the bullet thus making the tests inconclusive. Now instead of a suicide you have a murder on your hands." I paused, expecting a question but none arrived. I said, "You were going to check on visitors?"

"Is that what I said?"

I didn't want to lord it over the man but I was sick of his shitty attitude. "I recall you saying yesterday that you had gotten off on the wrong foot. That foot is somewhere between the ground and your mouth, Lieutenant."

Silence. It was a struggle but his problem came out. "The foot you correctly surmise belongs to the

Chief who shoved it up my ass this morning for not tossing you in a cell overnight."

"You're kidding."

"Not so's you'd notice."

"I guess there is no use me asking why he took this attitude?"

Dawson laughed. His laughter sounded genuine, but I didn't have him line of sight, and lying over the phone is a national pastime. "Duster had no visitors, at least not from the neighborhood. The closest neighbors to his house are seniors. Not only did they not hear a shot what they know about Duster you could put in a half page memo. Duster's father was a loner, too, and a boozer. From all accounts Duster never worked unless you call running bootleg booze and working in a gambling roadhouse, work. He spent a long time in Army and VA hospitals, in and out of the hospital most of his life. I gather he was a most unpleasant fellow."

I said, "That hardly explains the Cadillac and the furnishings in the house. I got the impression there were two Dusters, one for outside consumption and one secret. Did you find any personal telephone numbers?"

"Just the telephone book. No personal book."

I said, "I think the personal numbers were listed on a paper behind the cupboard door over the telephone."

"I agree. There is still some paper under the tacks. You didn't mention the fact that the telephone line was pulled out of the jack."

Mark up one for the Lieutenant. I said, "I didn't see that."

He said, sarcasm etching his words, "You mean there was something you missed?" Then he recovered his attitude. "To be honest we almost missed it, too. The telephone connection ran down inside the cupboard wall where the jack was located. It doesn't make sense. We connected the phone and it worked fine. Why disconnected at the jack? Possibly there is a simple answer, but that I do not understand."

"Me either."

"The telephone company is still on hold. They are checking with their lawyers, need I say more."

I nodded as if I understood, but Dawson's problems with the telephone company were his problems. I had more than a sneaking hunch that my problems with Dawson and his chief related to professional jealousy and who gets the credit. Handing Dawson my thoughts on a platter was in my best interests. I said, "Let me, as they say, make this perfectly clear. Whatever I said relating to the crime scene would be better all around if my name wasn't mentioned. You understand?"

"I'm way ahead of you."

"When and where is Duster being interred?"

"He left a notarized paper in a tin box ordering that he be cremated and buried next to his parents. There is no memorial service. He'll be buried Saturday. The First East End Bank is executor."

"Kind of a bleak end."

"That's what I thought."

"Now all you have to do is find the murder weapon and you'll solve the murder."

"That had occurred to me."

I said, "Chief pressing you for an early solution?"

"He said something about hammering a wiseass Texan to confess."

"I'm neither a Texan nor in the mood to confess."

"Too bad."

I said, "I presume there has been no public disclosure relative to the ballistic tests."

Dawson cleared his throat, said, "I hope I don't have to ask?"

"Absolutely not. I'll not tell anyone."

"It'd be my ass if it got out."

"I thought there was a shoe already reserved for that space."

He hung up. He wasn't laughing.

Ann was putting on her coat as I dropped the phone in its cradle. She said, "I'm meeting some of Mom's friends for lunch. Not that you're a fifth wheel, Unk, but Hagens isn't exactly our style."

"Maybe do the ladies some good, temperance and all."

Ann said, "Seems to me you're the one who needs temperance."

"Sis had that line down pat."

"Speaking of Hagens I don't think you need to see W.D. and Red and the sheriff today. Give it a rest, Unk."

I said, "I'll do exactly what you say."

"Yeah, sure. No need to lock up," followed her out the door.

Oscar

I sat in a comfortable chair in the living room and opened the packet Ellen had given me. Oscar Swensen's reports were in three folders one each Michael James, Clara Reece and Charles Cole.

I opened my dad's file first. Frank Dowling had told me what Oscar had said about his death, but now I was reading a summary of the coroner's findings along with Oscar's notations in his labored hand writing. I was stepping into his shoes, and it gave me an eerie sensation as if I could look up and ask Oscar if this or that were true.

In some ways I was disappointed. There was almost nothing of substance that I didn't already know. My mother, via Oscar's testimony, said it was common for my dad to take a walk in the evening, so that on the night of September 10, 1940 he had simply taken his usual walk. He had not confided where he was headed. She had no explanation why he had been on the railroad tracks. Both Richard and Sarah Petersen, those living closest to the scene, had stated they were awakened from a sound sleep by the screech of the freight train stopping, hence, could add nothing to the incident. Oscar never spoke to Gene. Oscar stated there was no whiskey bottle near the sight of the accident, and the rumor going around that my dad was an alcoholic was decidedly untrue. Various neighbors backed up Oscar's statement.

Oscar testified that Michael James was a good friend who had shown no signs of despondency or otherwise was of a mind to commit suicide. The underlining was Oscars.

I finished Oscar's account little the wiser. If, as an eight-year old kid, Gene Petersen had spoken up and told the local police officer that he had seen a man wearing a long coat and a big hat on the railroad tracks with my father Oscar would have connected the dots. He knew Charlie Cole, knew his usual dress.

Whether Oscar would have been able to prove Charlie pushed my dad in front of Frank Dowling's freight train was the rub. But he would have had Charlie by the short hairs.

Why did Sarah and Richard Petersen move into a house owned by Charlie Cole? It seems obvious that they used Gene's information to blackmail Charlie. Something like, "we need an upgrade from our shack so unless you give us the Reimer's house we tell the coppers what Gene saw." But I knew there was something more to it. Just as I knew there was something more to Clara Reece's so called suicide. Call it what you will, I just knew.

I put the file down, no further along, feeling empty. My dad. Why was he there? Even my mom didn't know. I thought of the years she scrimped and saved for us kids and it damn near made me cry. She shouldn't have had to have these hardships. Me, a homicide cop had seen all the underside of humanity, and I couldn't tumble to why. I had to know.

I got up and searched the refrigerator for something to drink. Nary a beer or even a soft drink. Milk for heavens sake, and not the proper four percent that comes out of a cow with a smile, but that ought percent pale, chalky stuff reserved for underweight sissies. I half filled a glass, drank and gagged. It was awful. No self-respecting cow would be a party to skim milk. I thought about going to Hagens, but Oscar's writings held me captive.

I turned my attention to Clara Reece's folder. As with the Richard Petersen file I knew more about Clara's "suicide" than Oscar. The death certificate confirmed her birth as June 8, 1908, Armstadt, Illinois. Her death occurred on May 13, 1953, East End State Hospital. The date reminded me that the fighting in Korea ended in July 1953, but by that time I had been released from the hospital and returned to the States. My choices were either to reup or go to college. I was a Marine. I mean to tell you I was a Marine, but the thought of another, "police action," wasn't too high on my list.

I went back to Clara Reece.

Through not having the authority to stick his nose into county business Oscar slipped a fiver to a source and obtained the coroner's records. Sarah Petersen listed as a sister, claimed Clara's body that was picked up by Stern's Mortuary, in Andover, Illinois. If I could believe Frank Dowling's memory this was the first time Oscar knew Sarah and Clara were sisters.

Then he ran down Gary "Pops" Blasingame, the security guard, who had retired to a small acreage in Ames, Iowa. Oscar's crab like writing noted Blasingame was afraid because he had been warned that to talk would jeopardize his retirement. In my mind's eye I could see that huge police officer sweet talking Blasingame and somehow getting away with it. Blasingame claimed hospital gossip held that Clara had died of cyanide poisoning, but he protested that he had no personal knowledge of the incident. Nor knew how she had gotten hold of the poison if, in fact, she was poisoned. He named no names nor did he reveal that he had been drugged the night Clara died.

Given that Oscar knew Parker Gould was the sheriff's bagman his access to Gould's investigation was completely out of bounds. I got the idea from Oscar's account that Pops knew if the going got sticky there was more than his retirement checks at stake if he talked. The fall guy came to mind.

Scott Mansfield, the night nurse, was right. He and Calvin Moore should have given Oscar the whole sorry cyanide story. And jeopardize their jobs? Be real, Nick. Telling me forty years after the fact Mansfield felt reasonably free to talk. I say reasonably free because he wouldn't identify the person he and Calvin suspected.

It was clear to me that the hospital, in collusion with the coroner and the sheriff covered up the true cause of Clara's death.

Who had given Clara the poison and why? It was too late in the game to gather up the likely suspects, but it had to be one of the employees, someone who knew the internal workings of the hospital - doctor, nurse, staff, maintenance, cleaning, etc. Clara posed a threat possibly to an outsider, and if that was the case why was she a threat? Knowing who visited her may have answered the question but that answer was lost in time.

I was going down mine shafts that were long boarded up. I had run out of oldies to interview. Accept it, Nick, Clara was not a suicide and you are rowing upstream without a paddle.

Charlie Cole's folder was a thick one. He had been born August 12, 1890 in Wayne County, Illinois, died on March 9th, 1951. The death certificate recorded that he was an, "apparent suicide." At least for Oscar's sake there was some question about his suicide. I started to leaf through Oscar's reports and the coroner's hearing, but at the back of the folder in an envelope I found the "suicide" scene photographs. I was stunned. Astounded. I had been present at hundreds of homicides and had labored over their bloody photographs prospecting for a clue that would lead to the murderer. All splashed in deadly hues scarlet red and more red on a blanket of rainbows.

But this was the black and white of 1951. As I sifted through Charlie Cole's death scene I sensed the time line more than forty years ago shot by the reliable Speed Graphic camera. The room was larger than I thought but my youthful escapades spying on the bootlegger was never closer than the huge oak tree. It was dark. A lamp was on shadowing the scene. Multiple images clearly recorded the night Charlie Cole died. Charlie was spread out in a chair as if he had slipped half way down. One arm hung down as if he had tried to stop his slide but that was just a trick of lighting. Close up the dried blood wandered down his chin. No other mark of violence was apparent. He had been shot through the mouth.

A table next to his chair held a whiskey bottle and a partially filled glass. A 1906 .22 gauge Winchester rifle lay on the floor. An accompanying photo showed the space next to the front door where, I judged, the Winchester had stood. His boots were on the floor off to the side of his chair. He had black hair and hawkish features, a sharp nose and high cheekbones. His description written on the back of a photograph was that of a small man, five foot five, hundred thirty-six pounds. He'd never see sixty-two.

The telephone cord had been pulled out of the far wall. It dangled underneath the table upon which the telephone sat. I was transfixed. Oscar wrote that with the telephone out of commission he went home to call for backup.

At the hearing Larry Hughes, the neighbor who had reported hearing the first shot, claimed that he had heard a second shot. It occurred when Oscar had gone back home. The case detectives didn't believe him, but Larry Hughes refused give in. The coroner was undecided. This second shot was hugely important.

Oscar believed Larry Hughes and so did I.

I was living the sight of Duster Grimes living room all over again. The details of Charlie Cole's death even down to the disconnected telephone had been repeated – the same type weapon on the floor, the whiskey bottle and glass, the trail of dried blood drifting down the chin. Even a second shot.

I sat and smoked. An old murder repeated right down to the disabled telephone. I had reasoned out a second shot in Duster's death, but that it actually had happened in Charlie's murder stopped me cold. There was no question now Charlie Cole had been murdered. And so had Duster Grimes. Why?

I made a call, left a note telling Ann where I was headed, tossed Oscar's packet in the trunk and drove off. For the first time in this crazy affair I knew where I was going. I first stopped at the cemetery to speak with Sis, bring her up to date on my thoughts. It helped. Sis always helped.

Turn of the century farmhouses, white the color of choice, followed me down Route 67, they were protected by tall pines bent over from dueling the westerly winds. Silos, akin to the ancient guardians of the keep, shot skywards as if warning that ravaging hordes were approaching.Snow fences bordering the road were in place, the first line of defense set to trap the winter blizzards threatening man and beast.

Here and there low-slung modern brick homes, set respectfully apart from their ancestor's clapboards, signaled that a new generation had taken over the heavy lifting. The barns were newer and larger. Modern green coated machines, tucked away for winter repair, planted and reaped thousands of acres. The small farmer and his horse drawn team captured in sepia photos were just a memory.

Cable dishes brought in the concrete jungle where crime and drugs ruled in a way no ancient defenses could withstand. Sneaking through the atmosphere a modern day horde of cultural activists ravaged the values of life long ago and far away.

This was corn and soybean country, and despite the smug platitudes of the Denver crowd the landscape had a beauty all its own. No Rockies, but then again, no smog either. During the dog days of August corn tassels and blue skies dominated, but now the land was naked as a babe, waiting another planting season. This land fed the world.

The highway was eerily silent. Infrequent semis, a few Ford 150's driven by Ma and Pa at ought miles per. The death of Frank Dowling hit me in a way I didn't think possible. In truth, growing up I hardly knew him but in the last few days his presence gave my past meaning. I know I pressed him for information about my father's death, but I would have been happy just to sit and jaw with him over a cup of tea and a scone watching the Mississippi roll by. He hadn't disguised his feelings about Ellen and me, either. He understood us maybe better than we did. I wasn't the Marine Ellen vamped on the university campus, but seeing her again pleasured me. Unfortunately she didn't feel the same. I should have called her and asked if I could be of help in Frank's funeral arrangements, but my life with Ellen contained a lot of ifs. I would see her at Frank's wake tomorrow evening. Make a move for heaven's sake is what Frank implied. Frank was right.

I judged the turnoff to Mercerville to be two sights and a go-bye down the highway. When I had been a rookie cop "Two sights and a go-bye," had been the directions given to me by an old codger sitting on a fence line in rural Texas. I was way out of my territory but was hot after a fugitive from Tennessee that had sliced up his wife and tossed her into the pigsty. The pigs had a good feast.

Anyway, a relative of the wife slicer told me he was holed up with another relative down this country road. Where was the question? The old codger spat tobacco and explained to the citified dunce: "Take a sight as fer as ye can see and go by. Take another sight as fer as ye can see and the shack is on the left. Got it, two sights and a go-by."

He was right but the fugitive was long gone. Later I caught the slicer as his arms were wrapped around a gal watching Loony Tunes in a movie house. Slapped the cuffs on his right, her left. Locals were pissed at the commotion, but not as pissed as the gal when I told her what the slicer had done.

It took me three sights and two go-bys to reach the turnoff. I turned right and a few miles down the road right again. Business had departed Mercerville, pop. 693, without so much as a wave good bye. The Bijou theatre and Marks Department

Store were boarded up. Foggy windows and empty stores marked the death rattle of Main Street. I didn't have to ask why. Directions to a modern discount bonanza in nearby Andover had raped Mercerville's business district. So much for progress.

Mae Belle

I took a right on Grand, Mae Belle Foster's one-story tan brick sat well back from the street. I wended past inspiring oaks with fall foliage clinging desperately to their outstretched braches. As I got out the front door opened. Mae Bell, short and round, smiled me into her home

"Gracious, it didn't take you long." She peered up at me through granny bifocals. "You're a ruddy one aren't you? Come on to the kitchen, I have a fresh baked apple pie waiting."

Lots of energy in the old gal. She charged ahead through a long living room and down a hall as if leading the troops to midday mess. "Here, I'll take your jacket." It went on a hallstand.

"Take a seat. Coffee?" I nodded, watched her slide a slab of pie onto a plate. By the size of it I suspected Mae Belle had spent her life feeding starving farm hands. "Cheddar?" Again I nodded. She cut a thick piece and I dug in. It brought back the times I played baseball against farm-town teams. Sunday double-headers were a treat. Between the games the local wives and sweethearts fed us until our eyes popped. We never did win the second game.

Mae Belle talked as I ate. "Swede, you know, had a by-pass last year." I recalled Swede as a running mate of Red in the old days, but of the current Swede I knew nothing. "He is my second or third cousin. Never could figure out which. His grandparents and my parents owned farms side by side. The boys used to come down to swim in the lake north of town." She laughed, "Those were the days of real sport, let me tell you. W.D. and Red chased me all around." My questioning stare slowed her down. She smiled, said, "The only boy who caught me was the one I wanted catching."

I finished my pie, said my first words, "Delicious, absolutely delicious."

"There's plenty more." Mae Belle got up, but I held up my hand. "Couldn't down another bite, but thanks."

"You don't favor your brothers. W.D. is tall and dark, Red, well you know," titter, "was shorter and had red hair. Lots of devil in Red." She tittered again, paused at some recollection of the past. "They were a handsome pair, let me tell you." She considered her remark, said a bit flustered, "Forgive me, I don't mean you aren't handsome."

I grinned, got a word in. "No apology required. I am quite aware I don't have my brother's looks. W.D. is still tall, Red is still red."

"Well, Nicholas James what can I do for you?"

"Clara Reece. She was an apparent suicide when committed to the state hospital. Her body went to Stern's Mortuary in Andover. I'm trying to find out what happened."

"When was that?"

"May 13th, 1953."

She said, "I joined the WACS during WWII and served in General Eisenhower's headquarters in London, then in Brussels after the war. I received my captaincy before I mustered out." Mae Belle got up and rushed out of the room, quickly returning with a photograph of the general containing the inscription, "To Captain Foster, With Regards." Mae Belle held the picture with obvious pride. She continued, "The war was the highlight of my life. Isn't that a terrible thing to say, with all our boys being killed or injured? But the truth is, I enjoyed it." She placed Ike's picture on the counter. "Sorry, Nick. I can call you Nick?" She accepted my nod. "I'm being longwinded. The fact is I wasn't here and I have no idea when or how Clara died."

I said, "I understand Clara Reece and Sarah Petersen were sisters."

"They were twins." News indeed. I remembered Clara grabbing Gene when W.D., wearing that stupid diving bell, almost drown in the Mississippi. Mae Belle had stopped talking. She said, "You had a far away look, Nick."

233

I embellished the story about the time Swede and Red in a rowboat pumped air down to W.D. as he inspected the bottom of the Mississippi. If W.D. had had the strength he would have strangled them both."

Mae Bell laughed, filled my cup. "Sure about that pie?"

"Sure."

"They didn't look alike at all. Clara was a feisty one, had a lot of bounce. Sarah was shy, withdrawn, but pretty if you like faded. Clara ran off and married Joe Reece, a traveling man. He was always hanging around Marks Department Store pushing goods. My father said Joe abandoned Clara. Sarah married Richard Petersen, and, she too, moved away."

"When did Sarah and Gene move back?"

"The first time was a long time ago. Long before I enlisted in the Army, I know that."

"I mean permanently."

"I can't say for sure, but it must have been after Sarah's father died. I had signed over and was stationed in Brussels like I said. They were here when I got home. That was 1956."

"Do you know where they are interred?"

"Ummh. Let me make a call." Mae Bell was a hurrier. She trotted out of the kitchen as if she was running for a blue ribbon. I sipped my coffee, spotted an ashtray, but contained my desire. I was fingering the ashtray when she returned in a rush.

"You want to smoke, smoke for heaven's sake. My friend told me Sarah and Clara were buried in a small cemetery behind the church out along the Edwards River. I'll guide you there if you wish." I wished.

On the way she talked. It was a goodly drive, and she was a talker. Also a patter. She liked my knee. "They were odd ones, Clara and Sarah. My father said there was something wrong with the whole family. In the head you know. Richard Petersens folks farmed, but whatever could go wrong went wrong with the Petersens. They were not successful farmers, but grand people. Here," she patted my knee, "turn left just past the church."

The church had a steeple and a brass bell. It was just like the school I attended as a child; gray clapboard, steps with railing up to the front door, small stoop in back where I parked. I said, "Is it still in use?"

"Oh no, but the church and grounds are well tended, aren't they? We're mostly Lutheran and Methodist around here. I'm Methodist. What this tribe believed in is a mystery."

"What denomination were they?"

"They called themselves The Children of God. Something far out. Back in the old days everybody for miles around gathered in town on Saturday. In the summer our church groups took turns laying on an ice cream social in the park. But," Mae Belle gave a disgusted shrug, "not The Children.

There was lots of dancing. Gay old time I'll tell you. Anyway, these holier than thous," Mae Belle pointed to the church, "stood off to the side with their noses up in the air. One time Jimmy Nordstrom took hold of Clara and off they danced. Polka, I think. Her father about had a fit. He grabbed Clara and informed Jimmy he'd horsewhip him next time he laid his hands on her. Wasn't long after that Clara ran off with Joe Reece."

The cemetery rested on a rise a fifty yards from the church. Wrought iron fencing, belly high, enclosed the sacred ground. I followed Mae Belle to a tall gray marble stele standing precisely in the middle of the grounds. She said, "Here they lay, Herman Esterhaus and his wife, Rebecca."

If I was astounded with the photographs of Charlie Cole's death scene I was more so now. I stood wordlessly staring at the gray marble stele that dominated the cemetery.

"Are you all right?"

I mumbled, "You didn't tell me their maiden names."

"I thought you knew."

I shook my head no. The family name in high-etched letters held my eyes: ESTERHAUS. I sat down on a nearby marker, stunned.

Herman Eugene 1885-1949
Rebecca Cole 1890-1932
Mamie Louise 1907-
Sarah Rachel 1908-1963

Clara Ann   1908-1953
Fanny Naomi   1909-

Mamie Esterhaus had led me down the proverbial garden path. How had she kept her sibling relationship with Sarah and Clara secret all these years? And where was Fanny? Unless she was buried someplace else she was still part of the Esterhaus mystery.

Mae Belle interrupted my musing. "I was a child when Mrs. Rebecca died but I remember it well. It caused a stir let me tell you. She drowned in the lake. They said her row boat capsized, but there was a lot of speculation about that story."

"Speculation?"

"My father said Herman Esterhaus never allowed any of The Children out on the lake. He ruled them with an iron fist. Jimmy Nordstrom told me that he and his buddies used to creep up to the church on Sunday nights and listen to Herman preach the word of God. Hell, fire and brimstone according to Jimmy."

"What reason did they give for Rebecca's death?"

"The paper said it was an accident, but most folks believed she committed suicide. Local gossip held it that Clara was prostrate when they dropped her mother's casket in the grave."

Their headstones were lined up fronting the **ESTERHAUS** stele. Herman and Rebecca lay in the middle of the plot. Richard and Sarah Petersen and Clara rested to the left of Rebecca. On the right next to Herman were four blank stones.

I asked, "Where is Fanny buried?" Mae Belle shrugged, said, I have no idea." Three of the blank markers must be for Mamie and Fanny and her husband. The last marker must be for Gene. What a plot line for Agatha Christie. I asked, "How did Herman die?"

"As I said, I was in Europe, but if you don't mind a ride over to Andover I have a friend who would know."

We walked to the car. I wrote down the names and dates etched on the stele on a memo pad I found in a door-side pocket. Then I remembered the photograph of the four young girls I had left in Mamie's book of poems laying on the back seat. I took it out and held it up with the church showing in the background.

I said to Mae Belle, "What do you think? Could this have been where this picture was taken?"

She held the photo at arms length, finally gave up and put on her bifocals. "No, I don't think so, but the girls are Mamie, Sarah, Clara, and Fanny. It was taken before I was born, but I recognize them. They always wore white dresses on Sunday."

Another lie from the mouth of Mamie Esterhaus. Where was the picture taken? - Obviously another church, and another place, nineteen twenties probably. I was like a terrier worrying the hell out of a steak bone. Not a young dog but not old dog either.

Dolph

I didn't mind the ride. For once, Mae Belle remained silent as my mind worked furiously. Each of the daughters had fled the autocratic rule of Herman Esterhaus. And if my intuition was working, Fanny, too, had settled in the East End. But why hadn't they acknowledged each other? Even Oscar Swensen had not been aware Mamie was one of the sisters. What the hell was the reason?

The home Mae Belle directed me to dominated the center of Andover. Greek revival, more like a mausoleum. Doric columns held up the facade. Double hung windows monitored the downtown. High, black wrought iron fencing marched around the grounds. I parked at the curb, followed Mae Belle up the brick walk. She opened the door, yelled, "Dolph, Dolph, you here?" She motioned come on. Her steps echoed on the marble floor through to a room in the back.

An oldie resting in a recliner said querulously, "Damn you Mae Belle, no need to shout. Where the hell do you think I'd be?"

He spied me, cackled, "This one of your pickups, Mae Belle?"

I reached down, shook his hand, said, "Nick James, sir."

"Don't know any Nick James, do I Mae Belle?"

"He's W.D. and Red's young brother."

"Oh yes, I remember those rascals." Thin smile rimmed a set of false teeth. "Well, don't just stand there, Mae Belle, sit."

"This," she nodded to him, "is the last of the Sterns. Adolph Stern the Third. His family ran the mortuary until Dolph here sold out."

"Jesus Christ, Mae Belle, I got tired burying Mendon County."

Dolph peered at her through thick glasses, again with the false teeth, this time with a snort. Strands of brown hair streaked over his nearly bald pate. His skin had a papery thin creamy hue. When he smiled it was like etching being scrolled down a piece of parchment. Dolph Stern was an old geezer. Irritable, too.

"So what brings you here, Nick?"

"I've been running down the death of Clara Reece, formerly Esterhaus."

"You the law?"

Mae Belle interrupted, said, "Mr. James is a retired police officer and a decorated Marine." How she knew that I didn't know. Red's big mouth, I suspected.

"Marine huh. What war?"

"Korean."

Again Mae Belle chimed in. "He was almost carted off in a body bag but a buddy saw his finger move and saved his life."

"Saved your ass, that it." A sly glimpse hovered over Andover's one time undertaker. I nearly called him Digger but that was too easy. Besides, his surly manner was unpleasant.

"Absolutely." I was serious. There was nothing off hand about the body bag story.

"Pulling your leg, Nick James. I got a lot of respect for the Marines and the law."

If that was an apology I'd accept it as offered. I said, "We were out to The Children of God cemetery. The Esterhaus family seemed to have had a lot of tragedy."

"We buried a lot of them. Strange people. Yes, strange."

"How so strange?"

"I don't usually pass along rumors, but my dad told me Herman and Rebecca were first cousins. Herman Esterhaus brought The Children here from down south, Armstadt sounds right, but in Wayne County for sure. Seems they were run out of town for their religious beliefs."

Dolph adopted that sly look again as if he was about to impart a secret of great importance. "You know what you can get when first cousins marry, don't you?"

I nodded.

Dolph smacked his lips, sighed. "That wasn't the half of it. Rebecca did herself in because she caught Herman fooling around with one of the flock. Flock, get it, flock." He slapped his knee and cackled as if he'd ripped off a good one at the local men's club. When I didn't respond, he continued, "That's what my dad said. Rebecca was a suicide. Can't remember when that was."

I checked my notes, said, "She died in 1932."

Dolph shrugged, said, "That long ago. I wasn't in the business yet, but if my dad said it was so it was so." His frail fingers circled my wrist. Grip had the touch of a feather duster. "Lots of incest in rural areas back then." He nodded wisely as if insuring his slander was truth.

I had heard enough of Dolph's scurrilous gossip. I said, "Clara was an inmate in the state hospital. The press reported her death as a suicide, but a local police officer believed she died of cyanide poisoning. She died in 1953"

"Loony just like her mother."

"I understand Sarah claimed her body."

"That's right. Sarah brought her here."

"Did Mamie and Fanny come for the burial?"

He said, "No. I never saw Mamie at the burial, Fanny neither. The fact is this was a dwindling church group that kept to them-selves. No outsiders wanted. Mamie and Fanny could have come home plenty of times without anyone the wiser.

"I think Sarah came home to birth Gene but I could be wrong about that. She and Richard came back after Herman died. But I don't ever recall mention of Clara, Mamie or Fanny coming back to live. As I said, those church people were mighty closed-mouthed."

"Are any of them left?"

"No. They just disappeared into the woodwork you might say after Herman died. It was rumored they all went to California. Of course no one knew them so no one cared whether they stayed or went."

"But the church and graveyard are well cared for."

"Gene Petersen tends the grounds and church. Out of respect for his parents and grandparents."

"That's odd, Mamie not coming home for Clara's burial."

"I didn't say she didn't attend the burial, I said I didn't see her." Jesus, Dolph was a cranky old fart. He said, "My dad said that after Herman died the family marched to Mamie's tune. She inherited the whole shebang, and there was a lot of shebang to inherit. Fact is Mamie is a rich landholder. I got that on the Q-tee from a lawyer friend. Mamie is brilliant, too, college graduate as I recall."

"What was Fanny like?"

"Bit standoffish. She got the hell out as soon as she could. I heard she married some guy from down where they came from. Never knew his name."

Then I remembered the photograph of the four girls. I asked Mae Belle, "Would you get the black and white photo out of my glove compartment?" She jumped up and hurried out, didn't even put on her coat. Dolph whispered, "She needs a man, Nick. You interested?"

I laughed, said, "No sir."

"She's loaded."

"I think not."

Mae Belle returned in a rush, waving the photo, heading for the finish line. I said, "Give it to Dolph." She picked up a magnifying glass from a side table and handed it and the photo to the old man.

"Smart ass. I don't need that damn magnifying glass."

Mae Belle bristled, bent over and yelled into his ear, "You can't see without it you old fart."

Mark one up for Mae Belle. Dolph huffed, but he meekly put the photograph under the glass, asked me, "Who the hell are these girls supposed to be?"

"I thought they might be the Esterhaus sisters."

He shook his head like a horse shaking off flies. "Could be. The girls look as if somebody used a mixing bowl to cut their hair. Herman never allowed any display of fashion, man or woman, adults or children. But they were always neat as a pin. When they came into town the women

244

and girls dressed in white. Yes, they could be the Esterhaus children. Hard to tell."

I took the photograph, suspected the value of Dolph's memory was selective. Could be, maybe, hard to tell wasn't much to rely on for identification. I asked, "Do you remember a man by the name Charlie Cole?"

"Hell yes." Dolph turned to Mae Belle, ordered, "Get out the single malt girl and hurry up about it." He sat back with a sigh his eyes following Mae Belle's rear to a drinks cabinet. He muttered, "Sure you're not interested?"

The old geezer was pitiful. I laughed said nothing.

Mae Belle returned with a bottle of Scappa, 12-year-old single malt distilled on Scotland's Orkney Islands. She poured an inch into two tumblers, asked, "Water?" I nodded said, "Just a wee bit."

"You Scots, Nick?"

"My mother was born in Scotland."

Dolph tipped his glass to me, said, "Slainte!"

"Slainte!" I was a bourbon man but I savored the smoky whiskey, eyes closed. Slipped down without a whimper.

Dolph sipped, returned to Charlie. "Charlie Cole. Sure. We buried the bastard down south in a two-bit town, dammit I can't remember the name of that town, but it wasn't much. For years he had a still out on a stream leading into the Edwards River. Charlie ran his booze from there. Why?"

"An Unsub shot him in 1951. Made it look like suicide but it was murder."

"What the hell's an Unsub?"

I had to stop using copper lingo. I said, "Unknown subject."

He downed the whiskey. His lips actually smacked in pleasure. "We carted Charlie's body out to the Children of God cemetery, then had to turn around and bury him down south."

"How come?"

"Some lawyer, don't recall his name, shipped his body down from the East End. My Dad assumed Charlie was going to the Children's cemetery, but the lawyer called and ordered the burial in Burnt Prairie. By God I remembered." Dolph cackled, said, "'Put Charlie in a pine box and bill the lawyer for a silver casket,' is what my Dad said."

"Who paid the bill?"

"Never did know. With a lawyer talking who knows? Rebecca and Charlie Cole were twins, yep twins." Dolph peered at me to make sure I was listening to him. Satisfied, he continued, That'd make Charlie the uncle to all the Esterhaus girls."

Dolph poured for him and me, sipped, and took the reins again. "Rebecca was a very nice woman. Very quiet, religious and all that. She went out to the lake one evening and rowed out to the middle and jumped in. One of the Jones's kids saw it.

Anyway, when she was buried Herman wouldn't allow any of the Cole's from down south to come to the funeral. Which wasn't any loss as local gossip had it that they were bootleggers, too."

I said, "Let me get this straight. Rebecca drowns in the lake, Charlie took a bullet in the mouth, and Clara died of cyanide poisoning. They were all judged to be suicides, but with Charlie and Clara somebody got away with murder." I didn't mention Duster Grimes. I already had enough bodies to fill a cemetery.

Dolph said, "Don't forget Sarah. She tumbled down the stairs and died in the hospital from head injuries."

"Jesus, didn't any of them die peacefully?"

"The old man. He had a heart attack right there at the pulpit. Kneeled over praying the flock out of hell and damnation."

I said, "That was 1949."

"If you say so. Sarah, Richard and Gene arrived for Herman's funeral and never left."

"And Gene still lives in his grandfather's farm house."

Dolph drained his glass. Color up a bit. "Poor Gene. He tried his hand at farming, but he must have a lot of Petersen in him because he never made it work. John Dowling, our bank president, talked Mamie into leasing the land, I told you Mamie inherited the whole shebang didn't I." I nodded. "I expect Gene lives off the proceeds."

I said, "So he has been living alone ever since."

"Oh, he comes in to town for groceries. He drives a beat up truck, but he is well fixed."

"I saw him at my sister's wake."

"Gene? That must have taken a lot for him to do that. Gene sticks pretty close to home. Real strange fellow. Hardly speaks to anyone. Just like his Mama. Here, Mae Belle, top us off." To me he said, "Damn girl sits there daydreaming." I watched her pour, took the first sip straight. Nice aroma. Then I added a whiff of water.

"You look puzzled, Nick."

"I am. How could all these deaths occur without questions being asked in Mercerville, or even in the East End?"

Dolph gave me his false teeth grin again. "You were too young to remember travel back then. It took half a day to get down here from the East End." Dolph choked on the malt, began pounding his frail fist on the arm of his recliner. Mae Belle jumped up and patted his back. Finally, with a sigh, the old man pushed Mae Belle aside, said, "Get your damn hands off me you hussy." Mae Belle raised her eyes to the ceiling, shrugging her shoulders. It came through to me that in spite of the Dolph's irritable behavior Mae Belle was fond of the old man.

"Another thing. The Children of God lived apart from everybody. Whatever happened in their little world stayed right there. Outsiders, even the people they traded with, were never allowed into their circle. My dad told me they were armed to the teeth. They knew how to fire hand guns and rifles. Even the women hunted. It was different world back then."

"But Charlie?"

"Charlie paid off the sheriff, but his problem was shipping the rotgut back up to the East End. Sheriff here didn't give a hoot but the feds chased him down every time they spotted his auto. One time," Dolph cackled, "he got the notion he'd fly it up. This crazy bastard, can't remember his name, stole Lem Ranken's biplane intending to fly in Charlie's booze, but he was arrested when he ran out of gas." Again, the cackle.

I said, "I heard that Charlie was in debt when he was killed."

"Figures. He was about to lose his roadhouse because he was into the Shelton gang from southern Illinois. Tough guys those Shelton's, Charlie didn't pay up, Charlie was wasted."

It was a thought.

Dolph continued. "Charlie didn't give a damn about anybody. He even tried to blackmail the banker I mentioned. John got out his shotgun and told Charlie if he breathed a word of it he'd kill him. Course, I can't tell you what it was about, but it just goes to show you how far Charlie'd go when he needed cash. Hell, John gave Charlie a loan one time on just his say so, but that didn't mean squat to Charlie. He found out some smut about John's wife . . Oops, I'm talking out of turn."

I finished the single malt, said, "You have been more than helpful, Mr. Stern."

"Here, take my card. The single malt is always here."

I got up and helped Mae Belle on with her coat. As we left the room Dolph yelled, "If he starts chasing you, Mae Bell, for Christ's sake let him catch you."

I closed the door listening to his cackle.

She asked, "Want to stay for supper?"

We idled in Mae Belle's driveway, me thanking her every ten seconds or so, she stuck in the seat telling me stories about how Dolph had chased her when she returned from the WACS. I was in a hurry but I owed Mae Belle large. I asked, "What time?"

"Say seven. Got the directions okay?"

"Yes." Mae Belle fished for an invitation to accompany me, but I had to see Gene by myself. I waited until she opened the front door, waved when she waved. I hoped she didn't have the idea I was in the mood for chasing her.

Gene

I passed the church and cemetery, almost stopped to make certain I had not imagined the names on the Esterhaus stele. Possibly there was a simple explanation why the Esterhaus girls had fled the old homestead and autocratic father, lots of hell and damnation, no relief from the devil that contaminated mankind. No wonder they left. Dolph Stern's assertion that Herman and Rebecca were first cousins gave me pause. On hindsight it seemed probable Clara's mental illness stemmed from this alliance.

And what of Sarah? Even as a kid I decided she was spooky. Not Mamie though. If any of that tragic pedigree was sane it was Mamie. About Fanny I knew nothing.

I was still caught up in Clara's suicide. Clara was the key. Wrong, Nick, whoever slipped her cyanide was the key. The state hospital's old administrative files might contain the answer to who did the dirty deed, but without a warrant Icky would guard his preserve with the resolve only a paper pusher possesses. Jessica sneaking around the hospital records was an idea whose time had ended. I wasn't about to ask her to risk her job - again.

The sky was closing in and I wanted to get to Gene's before nightfall. I passed over the river and two miles further turned right on a gravel road. Another two miles and I turned into a dirt lane. Past a running stand of trees the Esterhaus farmhouse came into view. Through the open doors of a barn I spotted Gene's Red Boy. I smiled as I parked by the front door.

The house wasn't much, two story wood, twenty by thirty, dinky front porch, small windows. But it had a fresh coat of white paint. I knocked, waited. The door opened an inch. I caught an eye then it opened wide. "What ya doing here, Nick?"

Not exactly what I was looking for but about what I expected. "I was passing through and I decided to stop." Gene brushed the strand of straw hair from his eyes slowly as if making up his mind whether to smile or slam the door. Finally, "Come on in." As an afterthought, "Clean your shoes."

I brushed my shoes on the mat as directed, entered, skirted the stairs leading to the second floor. Was this where his mother had taken a tumble and died of a head injury? Our steps clattered on highly polished wood flooring. The living room ran the full width of the house. It was filled with furniture, all dark, hand made. Straight-backed chairs rested against the walls. A schoolmaster's desk, opened up showing a bible and crucifix, sat in the corner. I gathered Herman Esterhaus had conducted religious classes here, making certain his girls understood the wages of sin and perdition. I sat in a chair across from Gene. The room was clean, but a fusty smell permeated the air. Overhead, one of Edison's original light bulbs hung in a dime store shade. It was not lit. I got the impression the room was a shrine to the past.

Gene still wore his faded blue shirt and levis, waiting for me to speak. That is what it always was like with Gene. I said, "So this was your grandfather's home." He nodded. Is that his desk?" He nodded. "The furniture looks hand made." No response. Then he said, "I got something I want to show you."

I followed him through a door into the kitchen. He flipped on the lights. It was spotless. A metal-legged table with an unctuous green top sat before a large window, nineteen-thirties chrome chairs on each end. A dog of multifaceted parentage lay under the table. It got up and sniffed my shoes. I reached down and patted it. It retreated under the table, passive, like his master.

"That's my pal, Dodger." Gene spoke with feeling. Mangy cur was probably his only friend.

The sun disappeared over the horizon. Suddenly I felt the loneliness of Gene's existence. I asked, "Wasn't that the name of Charlie Cole's dog? The one Duster Grimes shot?"

Gene turned away, said, "Don't remember."

I said, "We were up in my spying tree watching Charlie and Duster and the McNally boys whoop it up. Old Dodger was yelping up a storm and Duster shot him. Then Charlie started firing at Duster and the gang. You remember."

Gene's words came out haltingly. "That was my dog Duster shot. After my Pa and Ma and me moved back here with my Grandpa, only he wouldn't take Dodger. He said he had too many mouths to feed as it was. My Ma gave him to Charlie. She said Charlie'd take care of old Dodger."

"But," I interrupted, "How come you didn't get Dodger back after you returned to the East End?"

Gene brushed back the yellow strands, but not his scowl. "Charlie wouldn't give him up. And my Ma wouldn't make him."

Did Gene know he and his mother had moved back to a house Charlie owned? Charlie had a streak of son of a bitch in him, but to keep a kid's dog was the worst kind of cruel.

"Remember it?" Gene pointed with pride to a half-moon oak end table standing beside a wood counter holding a red handled pump. A TV sat atop the oak end table.

I was set to ask Gene about my father's death, but I couldn't ignore Gene's obvious pride in my end table. I passed my hand across the finish. "Where did you get it?"

"Your sister had a garage sale, and I bought it. Do ya know how much I paid for it?"

Anything would have been too much. A wedge under the left leg corrected its slight leeward list. "I couldn't give a guess."

"I told her we were in shop together and she gave it to me for free."

I had worked on that damn table all one semester. My mother hugged me when I gave it to her for Christmas. I figured Sis gave it the old heave ho after Ma passed on. It sounded just like Sis.

I said, "I'm glad you have it." Gene smiled uncertainly as if the gesture was a rarity. "You like TV?"

"I like Opie. He's like you was."

I took that as a compliment. "What do you mean like I was?"

"Always in mischief."

I laughed, said, "Like the time I burned down the hillside and Charlie Cole and his rascals were arrested." Gene laughed. It was good to see. I continued, "The cops arrested the whole bunch, even Duster Grimes."

His laugh went down the drain with a gurgle. He said, "Duster Grimes was a bad man."

"I agree with you there. I understand somebody shot him dead."

Gene repeated himself, "Duster was a bad man." Then his eyes went far away. "I remember when you got arrested. We was hiding in Mr. Wedman's garage, you and me and Zach. You hid me and Zach under some gunny sacks and then you went flying out the door."

I interrupted. "And ran into a copper."

Gene repeated me. "And ran into a copper. I was scared."

"So was I."

Silence.

I said, "My mother was sure mad at me, but Miss Esterhaus saved my hide. She told her what I had done. It saved me from a whipping. I stopped to see Miss Esterhaus yesterday."

Uncertainty showed in Gene's face as if he should say something, but hadn't a clue. I said, "She's getting up there." His fingers worked on his levis with the same intensity as Mamie's. "I stopped by the cemetery." Knit one pearl two, something like that. Damn it, Gene, say something. "Remember the time we watched W.D. jump in the river with his diving helmet?" Smile back again, fingers out of yarn. "He sure cussed Red and Swede."

Gene nodded furiously enjoying the scene. I said, "How come Clara Reece grabbed you? I thought she was going to throttle my brothers."

Fingers back tracing his levis. I pushed on. "Remember when she scared the hell out of us?" Beyond the window leaves were flying in a swirl and branches were swaying to an upbeat tune. "It was just like tonight. Clara was at the bars screaming and hollering at us." Gene remained mute. "You were with me when I drove the paper truck up to the state hospital. Brother, did we hightail it. Why in hell you didn't tell me she was your aunt?"

He was breathing hard, small beads of sweat erupted from his forehead. "You oughta not swear. Swearing's a sin."

"They said she was poisoned."

Gene peered me though his straw strands, said, "That ain't true. She died right there in the hospital. Heart gave out." It was the way he responded, forcefully, determined, unlike the passive Gene I knew. He was not lying. Probably it was the story of Clara's death his mother told him.

"Sorry, Gene. I was mistaken about Clara." I backed off. "Matt and me were talking about that Halloween the coppers arrested us. You got home that night okay didn't you?" Gene got up and went to the stove. He lit a burner with a match, set a coffee pot on it. He passed a towel over his face, his shoulders drooping. He poured coffee into two mugs and returned to the table, breathing back to normal.

He said, "I got home okay. Thanks to you."

"No thanks necessary. I knew you were okay, but I was worried about Zach." The truth played out differently. Gene would have been a mess had the coppers grabbed him, not Zach. I sipped, asked, "Matt said you hid out that night in Miss Esterhaus's house. That so?"

No response.

I said, "Remember the time I was in trouble and Miss Esterhaus gave me a book of poems?" No response. "I wondered why you were in her house, but she is your aunt, too, isn't she?"

Gene muttered. "You shouldn't ask me these questions. You're my friend."

"Why? Did your Aunt Fanny live in the neighborhood?"

"It ain't right."

What was so mysterious about Mamie and Fanny Esterhaus? Whatever it was I wasn't going to get it out of Gene. To hell with the Esterhaus menagerie, and Charlie Cole, and Duster Grimes, and the rest of this crazy quilt nobody gives a rat's ass about. I got back to my purpose.

"Why did you tell me that a man wearing a big hat and a long coat was waving his arms at my dad on the railroad tracks the night he died. Why tell me now? Help me to understand, Gene. Why now?"

Nothing.

It was cruel what I was doing to Gene, but this was my dad I was talking about. "It was Charlie Cole wasn't it? Maybe you didn't recognize him at the time, but later you remembered. Charlie had on that long coat and a cowboy hat when Duster shot Dodger. Why didn't you tell me then?"

He gripped the table, knuckles white, the sweat beads had grown enormously. Like silver baubles hanging from a chandelier trembling in a sudden breeze. "Did Charlie push my Pa in front of the freight?" Now his fists were pushing back and forth on his thighs. I repeated, "Why didn't you tell me then? You said I was your friend. Why didn't you tell me then?"

Gene was in another world, spacing out. I had to get to him before he lost it completely. "You told me you told your mother. Did you know Charlie was your mother's uncle? Is that why she didn't tell Oscar?"

Low moans now coming from Gene. He was close to panic, his head shaking back and forth, slurring his words. "Don't know," is what I believe he was saying.

"I grew up without a dad, Gene, not having a clue as to why he died. If I had known Charlie Cole was there with him the whispering bastards wouldn't have whispered he had committed suicide. Hell, if Oscar Swensen knew Charlie was on the tracks that night he would have resolved my dad's death. And I would have grown up without a hole in my heart."

I was playing a dangerous game. Gene wasn't the first psycho I had had to deal with. One time I was trapped in an elevator with a crazy Arab who believed an Israeli hit squad was waiting outside to kill him. Like Gene, enormous droplets of sweat popped out on his forehead. Guy damn near killed me.

"I discovered Duster Grime's body. He was killed exactly like Charlie Cole. Shot through the mouth with a 06 Winchester rifle. Who would know how do that, Gene?"

Gene's fists suddenly stopped kneading his levis, his words came out choked. "Charlie was a bad man."

Even as I pressed I couldn't bring myself to believe Gene had shot Charlie, or Duster for that matter. Gene hadn't a mean bone in his body but I had been fooled before by timid types who had committed heinous crimes.

"Did you shoot Duster? Shoot him when he was drunk? Good for you. Charlie and Duster, two no good blackmailing bastards would never threaten you and your mother again."

Gene screamed, laid his head back and screamed, "MY MOTHER, MY MOTHER." I damn near fell off my chair. Jesus, he was scary. Just like crazy Clara clinging to the bars screaming.

"MY MOTHER, MY MOTHER."

He jumped up and ran down then hall. I tackled him at the front door and we struggled, damn beads of sweat slapping in my face, Gene still screaming. "MY MOTHER, MY MOTHER." I tried pinning his arms, but he easily threw me aside. Crazy man strength. Overpowering. I didn't stand a chance. He ran back to the kitchen. I cornered him by the back door, panting, chest heaving. My police defensive tactics weren't worth a shit. His eyes were revolving around the room like the strobes on a trooper's squad car. I made my move. The last thing I remembered was the club in his hand, and his screams: "MY MOTHER, MY MOTHER."

I forced one eye open, saw a pair of shoes, heard through a tunnel, "He's coming out of it." I moved my head, moaning. "He's moving his head." Another voice: "With that lump on your head you'd moan, too." Both eyes open now: "He must have a thick skull." That wasn't the only thing thick about me. First voice, a woman's: "He's a former homicide detective." Second voice: "He took a real blow." Woman again: "His brother said he was nearly killed in Korea." Second voice again: "It'd be a shame if he bought it in Mercerville."

I fluttered my fingers. Jesus, my head hurt. Arms pulled me erect and sat me in a chair. I had trouble focusing.

"I'm Deputy McCabe. You know Mae Belle. Can you talk?"

I pointed to the small refrigerator, mumbled, "Ice."

"Get some ice," this from Mae Belle.

The deputy asked, "What do I put it in?"

"A towel for Christ's sake." Tough broad.

I held the ice to the side of my head. My God it was tender, lump the size of Texas. I took in a breath, let it out slowly, "Where is Gene?"

Mae Belle peered into my eyes. Her face was gray and worry lines crossed her forehead like newly plowed ground. Her hands were steady as she inspected my eyes. "Amazing. They don't show concussion, but he has to go to the hospital." So what does she know? The room slowly developed shape. Deputy McCabe was a big bastard. He asked, "What happened, Mr. James?"

"Gene went nuts. I think he hit me with a club." I got out my aspirin box, motioned for water.

"It was a baseball bat."

I took down four aspirin, said, "First hit Gene ever made."

"Mae Belle called us. When you didn't show for dinner she came here and found you on the floor."

I grimaced. "I missed dinner, I guess."

Deputy McCabe said, "You missed more than dinner, partner. It's almost eleven."

"Is Gene's truck gone?"

"Yes."

"You'll have to pick him up. He's crazy."

The deputy said, "We already got him. He drove his truck into the lake. You think you can travel?"

"Sure. But I don't think I can drive."

Mae Belle said, "I'll drive him to the hospital. He really needs to see a doctor."

Deputy McCabe objected. "The sheriff will want to see him first." Mae Belle got her back up but the deputy insisted I see the sheriff. I didn't argue.I didn't say anything.

I lay back in the passenger seat, staring at the sky. Stars were out. Stars were in, too. Every bump in the road was shock. Mae Belle pulled off the road bordering the lake. Strobes flashed from a paramedic ambulance and several squad cars. A tow truck was backed up to the lake. It had hooked onto the rear axle of Gene's pick up. He'd never call it Red Boy again.

I got out and motioned Mae Belle to stay in the car. She ignored me and took hold of my arm as if I was too weak to navigate. She was right. Sheriff Hansen introduced himself and said, "We found him inside the cab filled up with water. The windows were cranked up." I spotted a bundle laid on out on a carrier. "Gene?" I asked, knew the answer.

"Yeah. The way I figure he ran his truck into the lake on purpose. His hands were together as if he was praying. Did you have any idea he'd do this?"

Did I? I said, "No."

"Something pushed him over the edge."

I nodded. Something for sure.

"You know anything about the family?"

More than I wanted to. I answered, "His grandmother committed suicide in, I gather, this lake. One of his aunt's committed suicide in a mental hospital, and his mother, I understand, fell down the staircase and died."

"You knew him a long time?"

"We grew up together, Matt Jackson, Gene and me."

"Sheriff Jackson?"

I nodded. Lord, my head hurt.

He walked us to Mae Belle's car and said to her, "I'll want to talk to him tomorrow, but he needs to get to the hospital."

We followed the ambulance back to Andover General. My head would not stop throbbing, lights seen only by me flashed on and off as we covered the miles. Mae Belle walked me into the emergency room and talked me through the paper work. This Indian from Bombay prodded and swabbed, signed me up for X-Rays and an MRI.

Spending the next day in a flimsy gown and booties wasn't in the scheme of things I had to do. Besides, I had no intention of facing an interrogation by Sheriff Hansen. Whatever explanation I made concerning Gene's suicide would only lead to further questioning. I grabbed a protesting Mae Belle and headed for her car. Two nurses in white nearly caught us in the parking lot but I ordered Mae Belle to rev her up. For the first time I noticed she drove a Jaguar. One-armed it. She had a heavy foot, too.

We slowed down passing the lake. Gene's red truck and the law had disappeared. God, my head ached. I swallowed three more aspirin from my tin, shivering as they went down sans water. The clock on the dashboard registered three am.

She cut the lights and coasted into Gene's driveway. I had the idea that Mae Belle got a charge out of playing copper. My car was still there. The house was dark. No coppers were standing guard.

I knew what I was seeking. Where to find it was the question. I sat for a moment trying to think what Gene would have done with it. Damn, I never expected him to commit suicide.

"Listen, Mae Belle, I have to toss this place. I don't have a warrant so it's completely illegal. I'll be able to talk myself out of it should I get caught, but if you're here you'll be left hanging from the yardarm, so to speak. So what I want you to do is drive off and forget you ever saw me."

"Charmer." She got out and followed me.

One of the upstairs bedrooms still contained the effects of Herman Esterhaus. A black suit and wide brimmed black hat were hanging in a closet, and white shirts in a dresser drawer. Gene's bedroom held a bed and dresser with a lamp on top. Clean, neat, stark. In his closet were the identical black suit and black hat as worn by his grandfather, plus black oxfords. Nothing. I felt Mae Belle's breath on my neck.

I went downstairs, checked Herman's schoolmaster's desk in the living room. Bible, sermon notes in meticulous script. The kitchen went quickly, drawers, cupboards, pantry, and refrigerator. Zero. Where was the dog? Probably took to the hills, except there were no hills. Get your ass in gear, Nick. I found a switch along side kitchen door that lighted the door to the barn.

Mae Belle followed me to the barn.

I clicked on the interior light. It gave off a golden glow. Shadows drifted eerily from farm tools lining the walls. A bench sat in the back corner, small tools, pliers, hammers hung in a row on a pegboard above it. Drawers were filled with the oddments a worker would use for small jobs. Nothing.

A ladder rose to the hayloft. It was dark. I searched for a light switch, but found none. I went back to the bench, and from a drawer, took a flashlight. I climbed up, took in the sweet aroma of hay. It smelled like Matt's parent's barn. Only now instead of two kids eavesdropping covertly on the adult world from the hayloft door, I sought proof that might explain a murder. Nothing.

I went down to the barn floor, Mae Belle's eyes tracking me. I shrugged, kept searching. I found the gun wrapped in a paper sack tucked behind some tractor manuals in a drawer of an old pine table.

A Colt "Official Police" .22 long caliber six shot, six inch barrel revolver with checkered walnut grips, pre WWII. I put a pen in its barrel, and with a handkerchief protecting my fingers I cracked open the cylinder. It held five unused rounds, one empty shell casing. Surface oil and dust crusting the barrel told me that the revolver may have been used to kill Charlie Cole, but not Duster Grimes. It wouldn't even fire in its present condition.

I replaced the weapon. I could sense Mae Belle wanted to ask questions, but as a good soldier she knew the meaning of need to know. She kept her mouth shut.

I walked back to the kitchen. About to flick off the lights, I spied the TV atop my old oak end table. I removed the TV, picked up the labor of my youth, and said to Mae Belle, "I made this end table in shop class. Gene would have wanted me to have it."

Mae Belle grimaced. "I don't think so. Risking everything over a nothing piece of . . . furniture would hardly be worth it. You better leave it, Nick."

I gave her a proprietary look and I picked it up, and put it in the trunk of my car. She said, "It isn't even straight." I got the idea that spending a lifetime with Mae Belle meant never getting in the last word.

I followed the Jaguar to her house. The road blurred and every bump in the road was an adventure in pain. Jesus, my head hurt. I shut off the engine and bent over the steering wheel. Mae Belle opened the driver's door and led me inside. I argued but it wasn't much of a fight.

I said, "I can't let the sheriff get to me tomorrow."

Mae Belle said, "I know or at least I think I know, but you can't drive in this shape. I'll hide your car in the garage."

"Give me a couple of hours."

"At least."

She put me to bed.

FRIDAY

The strobe lights alerted me. I pulled over to the side of the road and keyed off the engine. I cursed my heavy foot, the last person I wanted to see was a county copper. I had passed the Mendon County line so I didn't have to worry about Sheriff Bob Hansen getting his mitts on me. But a ticket I didn't need. I rolled down the window.

"Your license, please." Courteous, but wary.

I produced my wallet, handed him my Texas license and a retired PD identity card. I must have looked like yesterday's hash.

His nameplate spelled out Wilson. He fingered the license and looked me over. Pointing to my head, he asked, "What happened?"

I touched a spot behind my left ear. It was sore as hell. I said, "I'm on my way to meet Sheriff Matt Jackson. He will identify me."

As if that was an explanation.

He turned and went to the squad car. Standing outside the car, holding the mike, eyes still intent on me, he radioed in. I couldn't hear what he said, but saw him nodding. He returned to me, said, "Sheriff wants to know if you will meet him."

I nodded, asked, "Where?"

More mike talk. "He said you would know where."

Officer Wilson returned my identity cards. "I'm not trying to be nosey, but you look like you need a doctor."

What I needed was more sleep.

The Boys and Matt

If there is a certainty in life it exists in Hagens Tavern. The neon lit clock on the wall showed twelve-thirty. The big balers had finished mopping up their plates and were making for the door. The old-timers were still at the bar fighting the battles of WWII. The way I felt I ought to be sitting with them.

"Mae Belle called me." Red pushed away his hamburger basket, felt his breast pocket for a fresh stogie. "She's a bit put out you left so early. Said you snored."

W.D.'s eyes lit up with an old flame's interest. "She said what?"

I said, "Don't listen to the red head. I spent last night in the emergency room." Lies were becoming a habit with me.

"You okay?" This from Matt. He was into Canadian rye with a beer chaser. Hagens' boilermakers were a generational habit that one could savor in a chancy life.

I said, "They took an MRI."

What I did after escaping from Andover General was better left unsaid. Nobody would know that Mae Belle was with me when I found the Colt .22 in Gene's barn. She had the guts of a stand-up guy.

Matt downed a shot, laughed. "MRI, huh. Empty like a light air balloon. Seriously, Nick, you don't look so hot. I never saw a guy with a black ear before."

I said, "I don't even recall Gene swinging the bat. The doc said I was lucky I hadn't received the blow straight on."

W.D. took a sip of beer. It was his second glass, a record for my eldest brother. "Gene?"

Slide past this one, Nick. I gave them a diluted account of my face to face with Gene Petersen and the suicide scene at the lake. I played up the hospital treatment as if I cared. I had amnesia about what Dolph Sterns told me about the Esterhaus family.`

"Did you think Gene killed Duster Grimes?" W.D., like the TV detective, just wanted the facts, Ma'am.

I smiled, ducked the question. "I don't know what drove him to commit suicide in the same lake as his grandmother in 1932. He just went crazy on me."

W.D. was relentless. "Somebody shot Duster."

Matt eyed W.D. "How do you know Duster wasn't a suicide?"

He motioned to Red.

Matt eyed brother number two "So?"

Red took the dead cigar out of his mouth and looked it over as if it was a long lost friend. It was disgusting. "I got it from a PD pal."

If Red knew Duster Grimes was murdered half the taverns in the East End knew it. Red took a leap back through time, said, "Maybe it was Duster who shot Charlie Cole. You said Oscar Swensen believed Charlie was murdered."

I said, "When Charlie bought it Oscar's immediate reaction pinned the dirty deed on Duster Grimes. Later he came to the conclusion that Duster didn't kill Charlie, but that he saw the person who did. I think Oscar was right on the money."

W.D. said, "You seem certain."

"I am."

"So who killed Charlie?"

"I don't know."

Matt said, "You must have an idea."

"Nothing that would make the ten o'clock news."

"Let's hear it."

"Back in the 50s Charlie was up to his ass in debt to the Shelton gang that operated out of southern Illinois. At the same time his gambling operations at the Antlers Inn went south. This was a time of political change when the administration cracked down on gambling operations. Rogue taverns were closed down. Likely as not Charlie's Antler's Inn met this fate. Faced with demands from the Shelton gang Charlie couldn't pay up and he was wasted."

W.D. said, "You're saying some gang from southern Illinois shot him?"

"It listens."

Matt said, "Listens my ass. You must have something better than that."

I shrugged, said, "Maybe Gene, but nothing better."

W.D. donned a serious face like a proctor admonishing his favorite student. "Why?"

Matt interrupted. "Gene? The Gene we knew killed Charlie? Puny Gene? Charlie would have chewed him up."

Red's eyes caught up with mine. He said, "Jesus, Junior, if Gene killed him what was his motive?"

Motive? Opening up the Esterhaus family can of worms would only lead to questions I was unable to answer. I considered telling them I had located the .22 handgun in Gene's barn probably used to kill Charlie, but I decided to lie instead. "Gene all but admitted he killed Charlie before he nailed me with a baseball bat."

Matt said, "Sheriff Hansen called me. He's not too happy you skipped." I shrugged. "He thinks Gene was into something heavy and you were on his trail. He's pissed off you didn't contact him before you confronted Gene. And he's really pissed you ran off before he could talk to you."

I laughed, quietly. "That's ridiculous. I'm not a homicide detective anymore."

"He doesn't know that."

"He's dreaming."

"He told me Gene's house had been searched. He figured it was you."

I said, not kindly, "He's blowing smoke."

"His deputy told him that an end table sitting in the kitchen is missing."

"You can tell the nosey bastard it's mine."

"Yours?"

"Now boys." I looked up and Stella stood at attention, hands on hips, laughing. "Another round? And I mean whiskey, not boxing gloves."

I said, "This man of yours can be a horse's patoot."

"Tell me something new." Stella bounced off to the bar.

I turned to W.D., said, "Remember the end table I made in shop? Sis gave it to Gene after Mom died."

W.D. snickered. "You mean somebody other than Ma would put it in their home?" That was about as sharp as W.D. ever spoke to me. Kinda mean I thought. "I got it in the trunk of my rental. Want to see it?"

Matt said, "The question Sheriff Hansen asked me is when the hell did you take it?" The deputy said the end table was in the kitchen when you went to the lake. He remembers because a TV was sitting on top of it and now it's sitting on the floor." Matt presented an attitude I didn't much care for. I shrugged.

This was the High Sheriff on his high horse, all because of a missing end table? Not likely. It dawned on me that he was upset because I hadn't taken him along to Mercerville. I intended to ask him a favor, but favors from the sheriff had suddenly dipped to the bottom of his list of things to do for Nick James.

W.D. said, "Forget who killed Charlie. Nobody cares about Charlie Cole. What I want to know is why Gene waited over fifty years to tell you that an unknown man was on the tracks with dad. Well?"

"I questioned him, sure. But I got beat up for my efforts. I don't know why he told me that story. And now we'll never know."

Red chimed in, "But you don't believe Gene killed Charlie or Duster?"

"No."

"Doesn't leave many candidates," Red added.

"This is where I came in." W.D. chased down a whiff of suds. "Red and me have an appointment."

He dropped a three tens on the table. "Ann asked about you."

I nodded, said, "I'm headed there now."

I watched my brother's escape through the rear door then turned to Matt. "I wondered if you could obtain some state hospital records for me."

"The state hospital!" Matt's eyes shot up as if I was asking him to make a surreptitious entry.

I said, "I'm not asking you to do anything illegal. Being the sheriff you have the authority to ask Icky for personnel records."

"Personnel records? When?" His tone wasn't friendly. I didn't think he knew about Jessie and me, but there was a caution sign waving.

"When Clara Reece died. May 13th, 1953."

"In your right mind do you think Icky would open up the hospital files on a case that his father covered up? If anybody is smoking dope it's you, Nick."

Matt fiddled with his beer glass, eyes seemingly interested in the neon beer sign on the far wall. "I can't help you, Nick."

I was so damn tired I hadn't the strength to argue. I said, "Fine." I got up and left the sheriff with his heartthrob. Stella smiled and waved as I departed through the rear escape hatch. My rental took me back to Sis's house.

Somebody who knew the inner workings of the state hospital had a huge reason to see Clara dead. It had to be an employee, but my list of suspects was composed of bodies long buried. Parker Gould simply didn't fit. He may have conducted the investigation surrounding Clara's, "suicide," but he had no prior access to the nut ward.

I had no workable reason to approach Icky to review the state hospital's old personnel records. Even if they existed it was an iffy proposition at best. One word from me about his father's cover up would seal Icky's mouth forever. I couldn't blame Icky. I would do the same thing. And bringing Jessie into the mix possessed a personal responsibility I refused to accept. Getting any further between mother and daughter could lead to an involvement I had no desire to pursue.

Matt puzzled me. His refusal to use his authority to check the records for me was absolute. I might have passed it off for plain stubbornness but for one reason.

He never asked me what I wanted from the records.

Ann

As I drove to Ann's I couldn't erase Fanny Naomi Esterhaus from my thoughts. The Esterhaus grave marker showed her being born in 1909, but her death had not etched in, nor was there an individual headstone. I knew she was still alive, more intuition at work than fact. She would be eighty-four. Where was the question.

I pulled in back of Sis's garage. The dumpster beside it was filled with her stuff. No other word for it. My sister's stuff, the meaningful items of her life being tossed away. I wondered who would toss my life in a dumpster. Forget it, Nick.

Ann was sitting by the kitchen table, coffee cup in hand, looking a bit tousled. Not like Ann at all.

"Taking a break?" I asked.

She jumped up, concern washing her face, screamed, "What happened to you, Unk?"

Damn, I should have shaved and showered. I sat down, accepted a cup, lit up and went through my night in Mercerville. I lied through the business of my hospital ordeal, joked again about the vacuum in my MRI images. I gave her bits and pieces, but said nothing about the Esterhaus family. Charlie Cole, I discovered, was an easy fall guy for everything bad that had happened to Gene. It wasn't hard to put the blame on the bastard.

I asked, "Did Sis ever mention anybody named Fanny?"

Ann frowned, said, "I don't think so."

"Or Naomi?"

"No. Why are you asking?"

"Gene Petersen had an aunt named Fanny, and, if she's alive, I thought I'd tell her about his death. The problem is nobody knows who she is. Or was."

"Afraid I can't help you."

"What about Sis's address book?"

Ann nodded, got up and picked it up from the dining room table. "Here it is."

The address book was filled with names of people Sis knew, cared for, sent birthday cards to, and entered the dates of their births and deaths. It was slow going. I paused at old familiar names, bringing back their faces to the time when I was a youngster delivering papers to the East End. Ann watched as I smoked and sipped coffee. There was no Fanny.

I dropped the book on the table, disgusted. I was certain Sis knew someone named Fanny, but it was not to be.

"Here, let me look," Ann said.

I peered through the kitchen window at the bluff. I was disgusted with myself for telling my brothers that Gene was responsible for Charlie's, and by inference, Duster's deaths. Fortunately, Matt was so damn mad at me for refusing to come clean with his law buddy, Sheriff Hansen, that me laying the blame on Gene fell through the cracks of his anger.

Like Oscar suspected, the reason Charlie met his death was because he blackmailed somebody, and that somebody murdered him.

Ann pointed to a name. "What about her? No way, Sun City."

Another name caught my eye. I rolled it across my tongue like savoring a tasty stew. Address The Manor. Possible? I was reaching.

Jessie

I almost fell asleep driving to the hotel. I needed a shower and a few hour's shuteye and clean clothes before I made an appearance at Frank Dowling's wake. I took Oscar's investigative packet with me. Why I didn't know. I was so damn tired I was about to drop. I trundled up to my room and opened the door.

"You bastard." Jessie stood hand on hips, fury in her eyes.

"Huh?"

"You told me you could be trusted. She was shooting darts at me and not missing. "You stood me up last night and now I find our you were down in Mercerville chasing some skirt."

I said, weakly, "To be sure I was in Mercerville, but I was not chasing a skirt." The truth was going nowhere.

Jessie sat down, picked up a cigarette and tried to light it.

Disgusted, she threw it down. "Well?"

Who did she think she was talking to? I almost told her to go to hell, but my cooler side prevailed. Holding onto the high ground

I turned my head and showed her my ear. "For your information I spent last night in the hospital."

"What hospital?" I suspected she had been lied to before.

Behind granny glasses her blue-blue eyes traced my head with concern. Without cheaters she had no depth perception, but she traced my hurts with the touch of a feather duster. It wasn't just my head that was pounding. My arms were splotched with ugly, discolored bruises.

Her perfume was something tony, the kind that drew you in even though you knew it was bait and you were the victim. It smelled wonderful. Tears came to her eyes. Bastard I could take, tears I couldn't. I laid the hospital story on thick, made more of the fake MRI test than was necessary. By this time I almost believed it.

She wore a solicitous manner in a way suggesting she possessed a proprietary interest in our future. It could be that I had said something foolish during our night's exercises. Our first night together had had the impact of a car wreck. The second time around the velvety ride of a Town Car, she drove I rode. But now I was too weak to defend my honor, assuming I had any honor left.

She whispered, "You poor baby. Your head looks terrible. And you smell, too. Let Jessie give you a shower and put you to bed."

I got the idea I wouldn't be showering alone.

Frank

The travel alarm awoke me at six. The other side of the mattress was uninhabited. I prayed my thanks and struggled out of bed, showered again, shaved and otherwise wakened to a goodbye sun. I put on my funeral parlor Navy blue suit, white on white shirt, and red striped tie. I was slow to admit it but burning the candle at both ends was a young man's sport. Jessie, having the competitive edge due to age, had nearly extinguished my candle.

Matt Jackson must have told Jessie about my trip to Mercerville. She said he was her father figure. Thankfully he left Mae Belle Foster out of equation otherwise my lie about an all-nighter in the hospital would have flown like a limp flag in a hurricane named Jessica.

I read the note she had perched upright on the table. She gave me her phone number and said she expected wine and dinner at eight. She knew I was going to Frank's wake. That was acceptable. My plans to leave on a flight to Texas tomorrow might be more difficult to explain. Might be?

I leafed through Oscar Swensen's investigative packet, and tucked my dad's file into my suitcase. I compared the death scene photos of Duster Grimes that Lt. Dawson had left for me and the forty-year old shots contained in Charlie Cole's file. Except for the time frame and dress they were almost interchangeable. I dropped Charlie Cole's file including the damning photos of his death scene on the front seat, except for one photo that I stashed in the glove compartment.

I drove to the funeral home and signed in. Although the sign-in log showed fifteen or twenty crabbed signatures the names that followed were in a more readable handwriting. I assumed these were the children, like me, of Frank's generation. There were not too many present.

Pete Benson cornered me on my arrival. He still amazed me, erect, black hair, sans glasses, a spring to his step. The aging process seemed to have passed him by. He recollected the night Charlie Cole had died when he had seen Duster Grimes at Vic & Sues Tavern.

"Do you suppose that had anything to do with Duster being wasted, Nick. I got it on the grapevine that you found him."

"You're right I did find him, but as to being connected to Charlie Cole's death, I don't know. As I recall from what you told me Charlie died in 1951. Long time ago."

Pete nodded, said, "I guess you want to see Frank."

I still called him, Mr. Benson. And he still smiled.

I stood in front of Frank's casket, praying. I detested it when somebody remarked that he or she, "looked natural." There was nothing natural looking about death. Frank didn't look like the Frank I knew, but who does lying in his casket. He was a grand old man and his death had a marked effect on me. I paid my respects to his daughter and shared a bit of my youth with her as it related to her father.

Ellen

I turned and saw Ellen. She smiled. I melted.

"How are you doing?" I asked.

"I should be asking that question, not you. I didn't realize you had found Duster Grimes when we spoke the other evening." She ran her fingers gingerly over the side of my head, said, "Lord, Nick, what happened?"

I said, "I need a cigarette, you interested?"

She smiled, gathered her coat and we went outside.

"Well?"

I once again used my Zippo on our cigarettes. I reconstructed my Mercerville story line once again. What was real and what I described was a script only the Hollywood crowd would appreciate.

"And Gene committed suicide?"

"Yes."

"But why did he attack you?"

"I was asking him about the night my dad died and the probability that Charlie Cole was responsible for his death." I added, "You know, of course, what I was talking to Frank about?"

She exhaled, said, "Yes, Frank told me about Charlie Cole being mixed up in his death. It was Gene who told you about seeing a man on the tracks with your father. That's true isn't it?"

"Yes."

"So why did he attack you?"

"If I knew that I'd know a lot of things."

Ellen stubbed out her cigarette in a standing urn. I followed. I said, "I'm flying back to Texas tomorrow."

"I thought Ann was having a sale tomorrow."

"She is. I'll leave in the afternoon."

Silence.

"Another smoke?" I asked.

She shook her head no.

"Listen, Ellen I may never get the chance again and if I don't say it now. Remember the vacation we took to New England? It was our first fall together. We saw this old farmhouse in New Hampshire, and you said what a great place it would be to settle down. I'll move wherever you like. Even back here."

The farmhouse in New Hampshire wasn't going anywhere. I wasn't worth a damn when it came to expressing my feelings. I loved her and couldn't even say it.

"Oh, Nick, but it wouldn't work. I'm sorry. I truly am."

I watched her walk inside. My gut was churning. It felt as if I had swallowed a cold brick. I lit another cigarette, cursed the day she had approached me on the university quad, cursed Frank Dowling for suggesting that she still had feelings for me. What a sucker, getting dumped again by the same broad. Nasty tone, Nick. No matter how I reasoned our relationship, it still came out with me losing. She may have forgiven my addiction to the Job now that I had retired, but my involvement in the Charlie Cole/Clara Reece/Duster Grimes deaths only proved that I hadn't changed a wit. To her, I was still the Nick James she said no thanks to.

Even so I knew she loved me.

Lt. Dawson

I was at my rental when Lieutenant Dawson grabbed my arm. He said, "I was looking for you inside."

"And I was just about to drop you a packet at the station."

"Packet of what?"

I opened the car door and gave him the file. "These are the investigative reports of Oscar Swensen, a PD officer long before my time and yours. His photographs of the death scene of an old neighborhood bootlegger by the name of Charlie Cole is, when you review them, remarkably like the Duster Grimes we saw dead in his living room."

Dawson took out the photos and walked over to one of the overhead parking lot lights. He went through them, mumbling. "Jesus Christ, where did you get these?"

I lit another smoke. "The man inside the casket."

"How long have you had them?" A touch surly from the Lieut.

"You're getting close again to being an asshole, Dawson. I hand you pure gold and I get a shitty response. You know where you can shove that attitude."

"I'm sorry, Nick."

He offered me a cigarette. I took no notice, but under similar circumstances I had adopted the same aggressive stance. My temperature dropped back to normal, and I knew then what I was going to do. I asked, "How do you handle anonymous sources?"

"What?"

"I mean how do you cover information given to you in confidence when you know damn well know who it is?"

Lt. Dawson said, "Keep the identity in my hip pocket. But in a trial all bets are off."

"I'm not concerned about a trial. I'm more concerned about brother officers." Sheriff Hansen came to mind.

"I can promise that."

"Charlie Cole's death was made to look like a suicide, the same as Duster Grimes. Neither man was shot by the 06 Winchester found lying by their bodies. But the weapon that did kill them had to be capable of firing a similar .22 caliber bullet." I cleaned up my Mercerville story not drifting far from the suicide of Gene Petersen and my finding the Colt .22.

"By this time Sheriff Hansen has searched Gene Petersen's barn and found an oil encrusted Colt "Official Police" .22 long caliber, six inch, six shot revolver with checkered walnut grips in a paper bag. What's important is that this is a pre-World War Two weapon. Plastic grips only came into being after the war.

"I believe this weapon killed Charlie Cole and you will too when you read Oscar's file."

Dawson said, "So when I ask him for the gun he may get shirty when I refuse to give him the name of my source."

"You got it. Of course you might as well know Sheriff Hansen is already pissed because I didn't stick around, so whatever you say about your anonymous source will be suspect. Just keep me out of it."

He nodded. "This Colt .22 you found in the Petersen barn sounds like the twin of the weapon that killed Duster Grimes. Did Gene kill Duster?"

I said, "He sure as hell is the primary suspect, but as he committed suicide there won't any proof. As to the Colt .22 I found in Gene's barn I'm just guessing that it was used to kill Charlie Cole. I'm good at solving old dog cases."

We exchanged cards. He seemed disappointed when I told him I was flying back to Texas tomorrow.

The Manor

It was dark when I parked near the assisted care entrance of The Manor. The door was locked with a numbered sequence dial, but an oldie smiled and let me in. So much for security. Mamie's room, I judged, was down the hallway and to the left. I had a sense of foreboding, but it was of my own making. This was going to be difficult.

I stopped at the nurse's station seeking the head nurse. I found her behind a desk overflowing with files and paper, a light heavy weight looking crisp in her starched whites. A bronze plaque announced, "Verlee Haines."

"Yes?"

I introduced myself, added, "My sister visited many of your patients."

She sat back, folding her arms across her bow, wedding ring the size of a basketball hoop. Damn formidable presence. "Your sister was a dear. If anybody was a saint, she was. I'll miss her." She paused, waiting for me to get it out.

"I wondered how Miss Esterhaus is doing."

"Oh, you must be the man that visited her the other day." Not much was missed in The Manor. "Have you known her long?"

"She was my grade school and high school teacher."

"That's nice of you to remember. Mamie isn't doing too well."

"Will she make it to a ninety?"

"Doubtful, very doubtful."

"I'm sorry to hear that."

"If not for your sister she wouldn't be here today."

"My sister?"

"It must have been eight, nine years ago. That was before Mamie moved from her apartment to assisted care. Your sister found her in the bathroom bleeding. She had slit her wrists. Of course your sister immediately called the nurses' station. I was on duty. We rushed her to the hospital."

I said, "My sister called her a tortured soul. I wondered why she said that." Thank heavens Sis never told Ann that Mamie had tried to kill herself. Good for her.

The starched uniform rustled, ice frosted her tone. "Well, I can't say what Mamie said, and her family doctor is dead."

Had I a best foot it was time to put it forward. I said, "Miss Haines, I understand the privilege between you and your patient, but did my sister tell you why she tried to commit suicide?"

Frost still there. "I don't believe I should."

"There is no privilege between you and my sister."

Grin as wide as the Mississippi. "You are the clever one, Nicholas James. Law enforcement man if I remember rightly."

I said, "My sister?"

She nodded and smiled. Her smile was worth the trip.

I said, "Miss Haines, what you tell me stays with me."

"That's Mrs. Haines." Prim and proper, no nonsense. "Your sister told me that Miss Esterhaus was incoherent when she found her. She moaned about having abandoned her children, that she had ruined the lives of everybody she touched."

"Did she ever try it again?"

"No. We were very careful, all the doctors and nurses. We monitored her moods, if you will, but no, I was not aware of any further attempts."

I got up to leave, then asked, "Does Miss Esterhaus have many visitors?"

"Besides your sister, only one, her nephew stopped by every month, sometimes twice a month. He lives near Mercerville. I have his address if you want it." Why, for heaven's sake hadn't I had the brains to see Mrs. Linebacker the first time I was here?

"Thanks, Mrs. Haines, but no." I was halfway down the hallway when I heard her call. "Mr. James." She crooked her finger and I walked back. "I forgot. Dr. Gould used to stop by."

"Dr. Parker Gould?"

"Yes. I believe he was her student also. Do you know him?"

"We were in the same classes."

"He counseled her for months after the incident. You could ask him, but I doubt he would tell you anything."

"Patient-doctor?" I chided.

Verlee Haines frowned, said, "You're head doesn't look so good."

I faked a grin, said, "I was in an accident yesterday."

"Maybe you should be in bed." Nurse Haines's considerable arm swept the geriatric set lined up against the wall in beds and wheel chairs. "You would be under my care."

Verlee was a bit of okay. "You'd be my first choice."

She grinned, said, "Just don't take too long. I'm retiring next year."

Nurse Haines turned and marched back to her office, an impressive sight. I made my way to a screened in lounge area set between the nurse's station and the assisted care rooms. I sat down, lighted up and thought about Mamie's attempted suicide. She abandoned her children. What had she meant by that? Clara raved about, "the children," too, before she was found dead. What had she meant? Were they both rambling about the same children? The Children of God, the religious sect run by their father?

I suspected Icky knew what she was "tortured" about. After all he had counseled Mamie after she slit her wrists. And, learning that Clara Reece was

Mamie's sister, he must have reviewed Clara's psychiatric file. Finding his father's investigative report must have been a blow. Icky was no dummy. It must have been apparent Parker Gould Senior had taken a bribe. No wonder he destroyed Clara's file.

But I was getting sidetracked. Mamie abandoned her children.   *Her children.*

I smoked, studied my notes filling up the ashtray. I had no idea of the time. I called Dolph Sterns. The old bugger was as querulous as ever. The only time he brightened was when he offered me Mae Belle Foster as a blushing bride. Dolph said if I wasn't so damned cheap I could buy a paper and find out for myself that Gene was born May 13th, 1932 in Mercerville. I wondered aloud if he knew the exact date when Gene's grandmother had committed suicide. Dolph wondered aloud if he was some damned information service. I hung on while he checked the burial records.

Rebecca had died in the lake May 23rd, 1932. Dolph's father's notes showed that Rebecca and Charlie Cole were not only brother and sister but verified that they were twins. I wondered aloud how his dad knew that. Dolph's reply was not fit to print.

I thanked him. He was still pushing Scotland's single malt whiskey and Mae Belle Foster's body when I hung up.

Fanny Naomi Esterhaus would not go away. She was like an itch that scratching at only made more irritating. I put in a call to Scott Mansfield. He was not happy that I remembered he was on duty the night Clara Reece died. He hemmed and hawed, but finally confirmed the identity of the person whom I suspected. She was a cleaning lady who worked in the security building the night that Clara Reece died of cyanide poisoning. I asked him what specifically Clara had been raving about. Silence. His breathing was audible over the phone, but at least he hadn't hung up on me. He was afraid he would have to testify. I assured him there would be no trial. "The children," he said reluctantly. He asked me when I was going back to Texas. Tomorrow, I said to a dead line.

Although the name I sought in Sis's address book was Fanny Esterhaus, I had tucked the name Frances Johnson, Apartment 272, The Manor in my memory bank for future reference. Don't ask my why, maybe because she lived in the Manor or had a name that somehow resembled Fanny. Until Scott Mansfield verified that Frances Johnson was working the night Clara Reece died her identity as Fanny Esterhaus was only speculation. Somewhere along the line Fanny had changed her name to Frances. I knew I would find out the reason why, but that could wait.

I walked up a level and through the halls to the apartment quarters. The nameplate on the door identified Frances Johnson as the occupant. I knocked and heard a come in.

Frances Johnson was standing erect, dressed in a blue pants suit. She appeared to be much younger than her eighty-four years, hardly a line in her face, absent crow's feet. She wore her brown hair in a sort of pageboy. I suspected it was dyed, but if so, only her hairdresser knew for sure. She bore a confident air, one I hadn't expected from the cleaning lady who was on duty in the state hospital the night Clara Reece was murdered.

I said, "Mrs. Johnson, I'm Nick James."

She smiled and asked me to sit. "Oh, I remember you, Nicholas. You passed our papers, and were a classmate of my daughter's. The neighborhood was so thrilled when you came home from Korea alive. I was so sorry to hear of your sister's death. She had many friends here. She was mighty proud of you."

Did she really not suspect that I knew? Sugar coating good old Nicholas had a false ring. I said, "Thanks. Everybody loved my sister."

"What can I do for you?"

More than one could sugarcoat. I said, "Ann and I were going over Sis's address book and we spilt up the names of some people to visit." I prayed my lie would hold water.

"That's so nice. May I offer you a cup of tea and shortbread cookies? Your mother was Scottish wasn't she?"

"I'd be most obliged. Yes, she was born in Scotland."

Frances Johnson smiled as if giving away a secret. "She still had a brogue."

As I drank my tea I wondered if that was how she gave Clara the cyanide. "Have a cuppa, dearie?" My God.

We talked of Frank Dowling and my dad's death, of the old neighborhood, what ever happened to? It was all very pleasant, but I saw in her eyes the spider that centered me in her web. Having an opening I said, "You must excuse me, Mrs. Johnson, I'm going to see my old teacher, Miss Mamie Esterhaus."

"Oh, I'm sure she will enjoy your visit."

No matter how I cut it I had no proof, and proof, after all, is what a lawman is all about. It was a circumstantial case at best. Fanny Naomi Esterhaus, aka, Frances N. Johnson was Clara Reece's sister and she was a member of the char force working the night Clara died. And, yes, Judge, she gave Clara the rat poison. Scott Mansfield doesn't remember? Mr. Scott Mansfield you say you can't remember yesterday much less forty years back. Sorry, Mr. James. Case dismissed.

So what about Mary Lou? She told me gossip in the admin section held that Clara died from rat poison, but she didn't tell me that her mother was a part of the night char force. And why should she? I didn't ask her about her mother. Despite not being forthcoming with me I didn't believe Mary Lou knew anything about her mother being the sister of Clara Reece and Mamie Esterhaus.

Then again my objectivity was colored. I didn't give a rat's ass about Frances Johnson or her daughter Mary Lou Johnson, but her granddaughter was another matter. Jessica didn't deserve another tragedy to affect her life.

Not from me.

I was walking to Mamie's assisted care room when Verlee Haines grabbed my arm. Hell of a grip. "Where you been?"

I mumbled something inane, but Verlee was caught up in her own story. "I apologize, Nicholas, but it fell through the cracks. I just spoke with Sheriff Bob Hansen in Mendon County. He found Mamie's name and phone number in Gene Petersen's personal effects. The day nurse didn't inform me, but he called Mamie sometime this afternoon about her nephew's suicide last night. He drove himself into a lake. Suicide. You know that?"

I nodded.

That ticked her off. "Coulda told me." Her eyes mirrored the fire that was building under her starched whites. "In any event Sheriff Hansen got to thinking," she rolled her eyes, "and he was wondering how she was doing and wanted me to check on her. He said she didn't say much to him this afternoon. She began crying and hung up. I surmise he figured he fouled up. The news must have been awful for her."

A security guard was standing outside Mamie's door. Verlee spoke to him, but what was said, I didn't hear. Quite frankly, I wanted to talk to Mamie, but if she were too upset to talk now that would delay my return to Texas. I had the notion I was a carrier of death. Blame the messenger wasn't too far off.

"You can come in," Verlee said.

Mamie was sitting in her wheel chair, her hands resting under a comforter, eyes trained on a point far off. Nurse Haines spoke quietly and calmly to her. The hum of the desk phone off its hook caught my attention. I placed it in its cradle. I said more to myself than Verlee. "Who called her?" I took an address book from the top drawer. Frances Johnson's phone number was underlined. She undoubtedly told Mamie that I had visited her. And what had she imparted to her elder sister? I didn't know exactly, but whatever it was didn't spell good news for Nick James.

"You've got ten minutes."

I said, "Thanks."

Verlee's gazers swept my body. Not quite Jessica's lasers, but close. "Let me know someday, lawman, just what the hell is going on here." She stalked out, starched whites whispering crisply as she marched down the hall.

Mamie said, "I've been expecting you." Reedy voice, not much force to it. Tears misted her eyes.

I said, "I'm sorry about Gene. I don't understand why he committed suicide."

"I'm sorry, too, Nicholas. Gene never should have told you he had seen a man on the tracks with your father the night he died."

She drew the revolver from beneath her coverlet. I was momentarily frozen, it was as if time didn't exist. I heard the shot and the smack of the impact. I grabbed my chest, but didn't feel the hurt. The old lady shot me. Without a god damned change of expression she shot me. I remember sliding down, my back against the wall, sitting on the floor, hands holding my chest, her face blurring as I did so. No emotion, no nothing from her. Then I heard another shot, but I couldn't feel where it hit me. I was sliding into nothingness, like going down a steep hill into a black hole. Shot by an old lady who couldn't even get out of a wheelchair. Jesus Christ, not something a homicide detective would feature on his resume.

Why? Why? Why? I knew why her sister, Frances, called her. Kill the bastard. He knows. What the hell did I know? I should have listened more closely to Dolph Sterns when he said that The Children of God knew all about guns.

Jesus, what a hell of a way to die.

MARCH 1994

Southern Illinois

I flew from Houston International to St. Louis, hired a rental car and drove to southern Illinois intent on finding out exactly why Mamie Esterhaus had shot me. What had I known that made it necessary for me to die? Mamie's second shot, I found out during my recovery, wasn't meant for me. She had turned the Colt on herself – committed suicide with a .22 long through her mouth and into her brain - just like deaths of Charlie Cole and Duster Grimes. A Colt .22 long lodged in the brain seemed to be the Esterhaus murder weapon of choice.

I wasn't seeing too well when this happened, not breathing too well, either. Thank heavens Mamie thought I had cashed it in otherwise she would have made certain I was dead. During the long winter months I gnawed on the bare bones of the Esterhaus suicides/murders chewing over why

Mamie's last words to me were what Gene told me about my dad's death.

I wasn't a cheerful recuperator. I was the mean-spirited type that pulled up the blankets and treated all visitors the same, shabbily. All in all I was a horse's ass. My Texas detective pals were used to this side of my sick bay attitude and except for calls avoided personal visits. If not for Matt running interference I would have had Jessica and even Mae Belle as permanent guests. They called and my thready voice convinced them I was not faking my convalescence. I would have welcomed Ellen, but except for a call or two she expressed no interest in coming to see me. Of course, having lived with me, she knew my moods.

Did my nosing around these ancient piles of death force Mamie's hand? You bet your sweet ass. But why was my death necessary? Answering that question was what I was after.

From St. Louis to Fairfield, the Wayne County seat, was a nothing run. Even in southern Illinois early March weather could be nasty. Cloud cover shadowed me, not a hint of sun, but the fields were lined with tractors doing what they do to fill the world's bellies with corn and soybeans. My chest told me rain was in the forecast. Ever since I had taken Mamie's bullet I was now a weatherman of sorts, although I would have gladly gone through life without this gift.

Robert R Glendon

As I entered Fairfield I remembered Herb, a Marine buddy of mine, who was born and raised on a farm outside Fairfield. Every Sunday without fail, Sunday after Sunday, his family ate fried chicken. "I mean to tell ya I like fried chicken, but I'm no sum-bitch about it." He took a mortar round when we were advancing backwards – Marines never retreated - after the Chicoms crossed the Yalu River. Fried chicken and my pal were forever intertwined. I didn't dwell on his memory, I'm not one to brood, but entering Fairfield brought him back. I laughed aloud. I was no sum-bitch about fried chicken, either.

I introduced myself to the county clerk as an historian researching The Children of God religious sect. Mrs. Vera Raines, a charming lady who refused to let her age get in the way of heavy lifting, pulled birth, marriage and census volumes for me. Mamie Louise (1907), Sarah Rachel and Clara Ann (1908), and Fanny Naomi Esterhaus (1909) were all born in Armstadt, Illinois. Herman Esterhaus, a farmer, and Rebecca Cole Esterhaus, a housewife, was given as their parents. Francine Mays, a midwife from Burnt Prairie, signed a notarized letter verifying each birth.

Richard Petersen (1909) was also born in Armstadt. He married Sarah Rachael Esterhaus in The Children of God church in 1927. Herman Esterhaus, minister, officiated. There was no record of Gene's birth. Vera asked if Gene Petersen's birth

302

was important. Absolutely, I replied. She asked if I minded if she called the nearby county clerks which would save me a trip, and wasn't any problem for her. I gave her Gene's probable birth year as 1932. She phoned the county clerks in Albion and Carmi, adjoining counties. There was no birth listing for a Gene Petersen. I didn't think there would be, but didn't say that to Vera.

According to Vera, it was now Nick and Vera, the town of Armstadt had all but closed down along with the closing of the nearby coalmines in the 30s. A few tumbledown farmhouses and shacks remained, but no one lived in them now. There wasn't even a post office.

The 1920 census records of Wayne County were the last showing the Esterhaus family, the presumption being that they had moved to Mercerville sometime during the 20s decade. It came to me that if I wasn't on the proverbial wild goose chase it was all but impossible in the year 1994 to uncover that which I suspected to be true. Yet I was certain that even after 74 years some records or some person existed which would point to the truth.

Vera wondered if being an historian, I didn't want to research the Shelton brothers who were quite famous gangsters. "Born right here", she claimed. I said I would be delighted, but my time frame was restricted. She allowed as to how my frame didn't appear to be restricted. A tad sassy, I thought, so despite her wedding ring, and her gray hair, and her frumpy dress I invited her to dinner. Vera grinned, said she was too old for fooling around, but she needed an hour to close up shop. "Pick me up behind the building."

I asked her directions to the cemetery. I found Herb's gravesite and talked to him about Korea, and laughed about the time I was almost zipped up in a body bag, and how I always thought of him when I ate fried chicken. I looked around lest somebody would see me talking to myself. They put people away for less than that.

We drove to Mt. Vernon and ate in a B&B that once was some personage's mansion. The dining room glistened from a crystal chandelier, and chairs and tables were hand waxed to a high sheen. Lace tablecloths suggested the ease and comfort of fine dining from the days of hoop skirts and stovepipe hats. A no smoking note artfully settled in a cut glass ashtray brought me back to the current century.

It was far enough away from Fairfield not to tempt the locals with wagging tongues. Vera had changed her dress from frumpy to smart. She was a delightful companion. From a floor to ceiling mirror destiny glanced at me, but, like Dracula, I avoided destiny's beckon. Vera had said she was too old to fool around. I hoped she meant it.

Over a martini for me and wine for her Vera told me more than I wanted to know about the famous

Shelton gang of Fairfield. She ordered a breast of chicken dinner that triggered my recollection of my Marine pal's chicken story. Her laugh was inside out, not enough to shake the dishes, but a lot more than a titter. It died out when I told her he was killed in Korea.

She remembered that Aggie Blaine, the daughter of Francine Mays who had signed the Esterhaus birth certificates, resided on the far side of Burnt Prairie. She said that the town was once a bustling mining and mill town that sported three banks. Aggie Blaine, she said, was a character, but if anyone knew anything about the Esterhaus clan it was Aggie, via her mother, who also knew chapter and verse about the Cole's who were White County natives. When I asked what she meant by, "character," she just smiled.

Burnt Prairie, the smile again, was just down the road no more than 15 miles from Fairfield. As I parked behind the county building she said, "Your friend is buried in Fairfield, isn't he?"

I nodded.

"It was good of you to visit him." She reached across the seat and kissed me. "I'll bet you had misgivings about what I was up to?"

"It had crossed my mind."

She laughed, got out, and said, "Never on the first date. Come again." I said I'd do just that, knowing damn well that I wouldn't. She knew it, too.

The following day was a clone of its yesterday, cloudy, chilly, misting, typical March promising rain. I found what was left of Armstadt a few miles south of a burg named Golden Gate, a suburb of Fairfield. The only thing left of Armstadt was a whistling wind whipping through the shingles of barns and a few standing houses, like drunks desperately trying to remain upright. I found The Children of God church off to the side of a country lane, forlorn and abused by the weather. It was here that the Esterhaus girls stood long ago dressed in their Sunday white, all prim and proper waiting for their picture to be taken. I had the photo to prove it.

I continued south under an I64 overpass. Two miles further on a sign announced Burnt Prairie. The town would never make a *Country Living* magazine spread. Houses with caved in roofs, or caved in porches, leaners defying gravity. A bleak pile of lumber stood shakily on a street back from the main road. It must have been the mill, but was now but an echo of a time when it gave substance to a viable town. Enterprise had blown out of town a reminder of the Great Depression, mine closures, and the loss of the mill. The three banks Vera mentioned wouldn't be paying out any more interest. But standing proudly against this aging rot were white steepled churches giving hope where hope was desperately needed.

Aggie Blaine

Aggie Blaine was an eighty something living in a log house built around Abe Lincoln's time. A 38 Ford, still drivable, lurked under an overhang ready to make the run to Burnt Prairie. Between gales of laughter and firing up a pipe that smelled of cheap tobacco Aggie gripped my arm as if I'd try to escape. She reminded me of the Texan that hung over the fence by the side of the road all day long hoping that somebody would stop by.

Compared with the outside the combined living/ dining room was a fooler. Comfortable lounge chairs with a casual table between, several colorful hand woven rugs over a spotless hard wood floor, a round oak top wire table and chairs that once fueled the young crowd at the local malt shop stood in the corner. Opposite was a corner cabinet filled with a display of depression glassware.

Aggie handed me an ashtray. "Smoke 'em if you got 'em."

I offered her one of my ready-mades, and dropped the pack on the table within our easy reach.

"You a copper?

I figured there was no use in doing the history professor routine. The old dame knew coppers, an acquaintance probably learned first hand from the opposing side of the bars. If so, I was I trouble.

"Was once."

"Not too long ago?"

"You're right."

She took another cigarette. I lit for her. She inspected my Zippo lighter, said, "Marine huh. Which war?"

"Korean."

"My Jim was a Marine in World War II. Got shot up on Iwo" She motioned to a photograph on the wall behind me. "He used to drive for the Shelton's. That's his .38 Ford outside." Aggie had an eye cocked on me as if I was raw meat waiting for the grill.

"You know about the Shelton's?" I nodded, she continued. "They controlled the whiskey and gambling joints from Peoria to St. Louis, and all the rural towns, too." I'd about had my fill of the Shelton gang, but they were big stuff in southern Illinois and I dared not offend their exploits.

"I used to go with Jim down to Georgia to pick up a load of whiskey. It got too hot for us in Florida so we'd take a truck down to Jekyll Island, that's in Georgia, and make our contact on the Inland Waterway, then drive back." She got lost in a cloud of cigarette smoke and memories. I waited. Aggie was rough cut. She wore an old print dress and boots that smacked of fieldwork and hard times. Yet she possessed a certain pride about her that only tough people facing tough times had experienced. I admired her.

"Me and Jim were just youngsters. When the law got wise to the Inland Waterway we'd make contact off shore on the Atlantic side of the island. We didn't dare use the island because of the high mucky-mucks with their yachts had a fancy club on the island – you know, Rockefellers and such. So what you here for?"

I went into the Esterhaus tribe and The Children of God. Along the way I mentioned Charlie Cole.

She fired up, "That no good bastard. He worked for the Shelton's in a tavern up St. Louis way. When we delivered a load he always treated us like dirt. Charlie smart mouthed one of the Shelton boys, and he lit out upstate when they decided he should be pushing up daisies." Aggie laughed. It was a whole body laugh, lots of flesh shaking.

I waited while she wiped her eyes then brought us back on course. "I understand he and Rebecca Esterhaus were brother and sister. He is supposed to be buried here in Burnt Prairie."

"He is, sad piece of garbage that Charlie. He was born crooked. They were twins, he and Rebecca. She was a wonderful lady. Everybody admired Rebecca Cole. She never should have married Herman Esterhaus, my Ma'am said. They were first cousins, but the Cole's and Esterhaus's were thick as thieves so that explains it, I guess. Or maybe it was because he owned so much land here abouts. It was a shame she committed suicide. My Ma'am birthed all the Esterhaus's girls. She told me old Herman was a controller. You could see it with that religious tribe of his. They did exactly what Herman told them to do. Which reminds me Herman Esterhaus was a twin, too. Thomas, I think, was his name. He died young."

I said, "I'm interested in his grandson, Gene Petersen who was the son of Richard and Sarah Petersen. He was born in 1932, but the county records don't show his birth. I was wondering if your mother knew anything about him?"

Aggie got up, groaned and stiffened her back, muttered a blasphemy, and went into the kitchen. She returned with a mason jar filled with white liquid and two cut-glass lowboy whiskey glasses that I judged to have been lifted from some high mucky-mucks island club.

She poured generous slugs into the glasses, sat down and waved her glass to me saying, "Here's to Jim." I repeated, "Here's to Jim." Thank heavens it was not required that I speak immediately. I may have said before that I am no stranger to whiskey, but this stuff was potent.

Aggie smiled and poured again. "Damn good juice, I made it myself." She tossed it down in one swig. She didn't pose with a little finger extended, nothing lady like disguised her pleasure. She would have made a great drinking partner for Duster Grimes, but he was dead as I would soon be if I continued to sample Aggie's prime whiskey. I breathed deeply and likewise took a full gulp.

She capped the Mason jar that I took to be a good sign. "Well now, you're looking for a baby boy name Petersen born sometime in 1932. Can you be more specific?"

"No"

"Is it really important to you?"

"Yes."

"How important?"

"Worth a couple hundred?"

"That all?"

I pulled my wallet out and counted three fifties and a hundred in twenties. I captured her eyes and said, "That's it."

"But you could get more?"

"I could but I'm not going to."

She laughed, another flesh bouncer, struggled to her feet and said, "What I show you goes no further than this room. If it's what you want you can give me those fifties."

She went into the bedroom, closed the door. In a few minutes she shuffled back carrying a ledger. The cover appeared to be of some age. "My Ma'am always kept a record. She was midwife to many families hereabouts, and she was trusted to keep quiet when the questions of who did what to who came up. But she protected herself should compromising questions arise in the future. Understand?"

I nodded.

"When she died she willed me this house and this ledger. Even Jim didn't know about it. Oh, he knew I had it, but he didn't know what it contained, not that he couldn't a guessed."

She handed it over. A slip of paper marked a page. I opened it and read:

On May 13 and 14, 1932, twins, a boy born at 11:52 pm and a girl, born at 12:15 am, were born to Mamie Louise Esterhaus, age 25, father unknown. Place of birth was The Children of God church in Armstadt, Illinois.

Present were Herman Esterhaus, his wife Rebecca Esterhaus, and

Miss Mamie's sisters, Sarah and Fanny. Also present was Charles Cole.

Signed: Francine Mays, Burnt Prairie, Illinois

Dated: May 14, 1932

The document was notarized with a Wayne County seal and dated May 14, 1932.

I must have inspected the page for several minutes. I handed the ledger over to Aggie along with the fifties and twenties. Twins! Why hadn't I tumbled to that bit of information? I figured that Gene was Mamie's son but twins? I needed another drink. I asked she nodded. It hit me like a heavyweight. I gasped, recovered and said, "Do you have anything to add?"

Aggie said, "Their births were not registered in any of these nearby counties. They must have been entered in the county covering Mercerville.

That's what Ma'am said. Course their registration could have been delayed. That wasn't uncommon in those days."

"What do you mean?"

She said, "People just didn't get around to it. My Jim didn't have a registered birth certificate until he went into the service. I understand there were some school districts that required a birth certificate when the child entered school. But that wasn't a hard a fast rule. I'm not sure that it was a State rule, but it could have been."

"But this record by your mother is unusual. What did the Esterhaus clan do? Pack up and head for Mercerville?"

"I guess so. Ma'am said they had two cars. And there was no place for them to stay in Armstadt. Herman had sold all his property except for the church. So, I guess they went back home."

I said, "And they came back to Armstadt to have your mother midwife the birth because she had done all the birthing in the family. Herman knew he could trust her."

"That's right."

"I'm beholding to you, Aggie. I'll not compromise your mother's memory. Or you."

Aggie smiled. "If I didn't think I could trust you, you never would have got a smell of my Ma'am's ledger."

"I thought from what you said about helping the Shelton's run their whiskey that you didn't trust lawmen."

She turned serious. "You was a Marine, and I can tell you been hurt. And my Jim was a Marine and he got shot up. You was a lawman and my Jim was elected county sheriff." She stared at me as if that proved I was a stand-up guy.

Her reasoning kind of lost me, but if I passed muster I wasn't about to question her. Aggie was a bit of okay, but I resisted the impulse to kiss her. That kissing business can get a guy in trouble.

East End Cemetery

It was topcoat and scarf weather clouds obscuring the sun, chilly, misting almost rain kind of day. I needed more than my London Fog jacket as I shivered strolling through the cemetery that held the graves of my growing up family. It was mid-morning and the promise of spring was yet in my eye. I stopped at Sis's grave, told her that I had cadged a dinner and a bed from Mae Belle Foster last night. I could see her giving me a jaundiced eye but getting a kick out of my Mae Belle description just the same. At least I think so. I explained what I was about to do and I could almost see her nodding, good for you. It was important to me that she understood. I caught the figures of W.D. and Red standing before my parent's graves. I had thought of asking Matt but this session was for family only.

When I was a kid my brothers were twin rocks that gave me a dimension of what it meant to be a James. I grew up thinking that I was part W.D. and part Red, unknowingly taking from each what fit me, pieces of their personalities and substance, bookish like W.D. and outgoing like Red. Without a father to set the rules of conduct they were my male guides. Or, given my mood, the dank day and the lonely cemetery and all that, was I thinking too much? My personality was of my dad's making no doubt. Were W.D. and Red simply just throwins that happened to live in the same house I did? Too deep, Nick, don't go there. As I saw them standing in familiar poses I wondered if they ever saw something of themselves in me? I thought not.

Red, dressed for the North Pole and looking off-put without his usual half-smoked cigar prop, said, "What's up, Junior?"

W.D., wrapped in a raincoat, suspiciously London Fog, and a Scot's hat, waved an umbrella as if Red had said it all.

"You'll understand why I picked our parent's graves to play this." I took a mini cassette recorder from my pocket. "Don't ask questions until it's finished. This tape is a copy of an original reel-to-reel tape. There are some lengthy pauses in it, some are obviously emotional, but it is complete. Any questions?" The brothers shook their heads no. I started the tape.

*"My name is Thomas Edward McNally often
called Ace McNally. The date is August 12th, 1967.
I am speaking into a recorder in Oscar Swensen's
den in his home. Officer Swensen promised that
the tape would remain secret as long as I was
alive. I make this statement freely. It is something
I should have done long ago. I am responsible for
the death of Michael James. I have often prayed
for forgiveness, but I know that can't be.*

(The tape runs silently for twenty seconds)

*"I was the youngest of our family. My brothers,
John and Jeff worked for Charlie Cole, the
bootlegger who lived up on the bluff.*

*In the spring of 1940 I joined them. I didn't
relish Duster Grimes who lorded over me, but
I tried to act like Charlie. I even bought a long
canvas coat and floppy hat and strutted around
like Charlie.*

*Anyway, I had started taking flying lessons, and
thought of a plan to make myself more important
to Charlie. I found a farmer's plane for sale down
near Mercerville not too far from Charlie's still on
the Edwards River. I put my idea to Charlie. He
says okay. I'd fly up his booze to a landing field not
far from Charlie's Antlers Inn out on Route 6. My
brothers and me and Duster that drove the rural
roads dodging state and county coppers hauling
whiskey wouldn't do any more worrying. Flying up
was the answer to copper problems.*

(The tape runs silently for ten seconds)

"*Anyway I get a ride down to Mercerville and sweet talk this farmer into letting me take his plane for a spin. I figure I'll do a fly over Charlie's still on the Edwards River and then up to the Antlers Inn proving to Charlie that I can do it. Sort of a dry run. But I run out of fuel and had to make an emergency landing at the Moline Airport. I was arrested for stealing the plane. No matter what I said that damn farmer filed a complaint and I was sunk.*

"*So I'm transferred back to the Mendon County jail. Well sir, I expected Charlie to stand my bail but he wouldn't hear of it. I was really ticked off. Here I thought we had a deal and he wouldn't stand a few hundred dollars. Neither of my brothers or my dad had the money so I'm stuck in this crappy jail charged with grand theft.*

"*My dad borrows the bond from Mr. James. My dad tells me not to breath a word of it to anyone about Mr. James lending him the money as he does not want to be connected in any way with Charlie Cole especially in court records. He also says that Mr. James advises that I should tell the judge that if he'll void the charge so that I don't have a criminal record I will join the army. I wasn't to keen on this idea, but my dad says I should thank Mr. James for giving him the bail money.*

(Tape runs silently for ten seconds)

"*So I met Mr. James one night when he is out for his walk and tell him how thankful I am. He tells me that I ought to join the army and straighten out my life. I'm not too happy about the army business, but to get back at Charlie and to pay back Mr. James I tell him all about Charlie's whiskey business. Everything about his still on the Edwards River, who he pays off, passing off his illegal booze in regular whiskey bottles at the Antlers Inn, when deliveries were expected, and his deal with this guy Dr. Nathan who sells his elixir called Nathan's Jaundice Bitters that cures bad bowels and every other disease known to man from his converted bread truck in all the rural Mississippi River towns up to the East End. He even had the nerve to set up in that empty lot down on Main Street in the old neighborhood. The old doc's elixir is nothing but Charlie's booze mixed with rose water. I oughta know because I helped bottle it down at Charlie's still.*

{Tape runs silently for ten seconds)

"Meeting Mr. James secretly went on for a couple months. What Mr. James did with the information was up to him. Getting back at Charlie was all that was important to me. Then Charlie's booze at the Antlers Inn was being confiscated and he was arrested. The same thing happened every time we ran up loads from Charlie's still. Dr. Nathan was being run out of the rural towns. Even you confiscated his elixir when he set up in the neighborhood. Charlie finally got the idea that somebody close to him was ratting him out. He

didn't exactly accuse me but he said he'd kill the bastard who was informing on him. I was really scared. I remember the date. It was September 10th, 1940. I met Mr. James down by the tracks as usual and I guess I got riled. I told him Charlie was going to kill me and it was all Mr. James's fault because he was feeding you all the information I'd given him. He said he'd never given Oscar anything and to stop waving my arms like a crazy man. He laughed at me and turned to walk away. I was so mad I pushed him in the back and he fell and hit his head on the rails. He just laid there and I just stood there. I was stunned. Then I heard train coming so I panicked and pulled Mr. James off the tracks and ran like hell.

(Tape runs, thirty seconds. Sounds like McNally crying)

"I hid out at my uncle's farm. I didn't know till the next day that Mr. James had died but I have to admit that I sensed it that night. The papers said the police investigation hadn't identified anyone who had been with Mr. James nor had seen him that evening. So I took the easy way out. Since no one had seen me I was in the clear. I did what Mr. James told me to do. I went before the Mendon County Judge and told him I'd join the army if he dropped the charges. I even had the army recruiter with me. The judge agreed and I left the courtroom with the recruiter. I served in the Army Air Corps then the U.S. Air Force ever since September 27th,

1940. Nearly twenty-seven years without a blemish on my record. I served honorably in World War Two, the Korean War, and recently in Nam. I know this doesn't make up for the death of a fine man, but I was so scared of Charlie and the fact that I had caused Mr. James's death that I have remained silent till now. I had no intention to do what I did, but I guess that makes no difference. When I saw you at my dad's wake it came to me that I ought to confess. There's never been a September 10th in all these years that I haven't had to drink myself to sleep. I'm one sorry son of a bitch. May God forgive me.

"Thomas Edward McNally. August 12th, 1967."

(Again the sound of weeping. Tape completed)

I said, "That's it."

Red said, "So the ride Swede and me gave him down to Mercerville eventually led my dad's death."

I said, "Our dad."

"Sorry. This is a real shocker. It's just that I remembered telling you the story about Ace and the plane – when was it, last October?"

Red had just taken on a load that was too heavy even for a Marine vet of World War Two. I said, "Taking on the blame for dad's death is unacceptable. Ace made the deal with Charlie to fly up his booze long before you and Swede drove him down to pick up that plane. It was just a ride, don't make any more of it than that."

W.D. said, "I agree. McNally is the sorry son of a bitch that started it all. But how and when did you get the tape, Nick? And why didn't Oscar do anything about it when he got it? When was it 1967?"

"I got it from Virginia Grant, Frank Dowling's daughter a month ago. The reel-to-reel tape and Oscar's sealed envelope were among papers she found in Frank's lock box. Oscar's cover letter instructed the sealed envelope be sent to a member of the James family after Thomas Edward McNally died. She remembered me from Frank's wake and sent it to me. She wrote that it was up to me to open the sealed envelope or not as I saw fit. About Thomas Edward McNally she knew nothing. Oh yes, she apologized for not writing sooner, but didn't give a reason why."

Red said, "Why you? We were at Frank's wake, too"

"I don't know. Maybe Ellen told her to send it to me."

W.D. again. "Why didn't Oscar do anything about Ace's admitting to dad's death in 1967?"

My eldest brother was stuck on why, as I had been. I said, "If I read Oscar Swensen right he was straight copper. He gave Ace his word he wouldn't compromise his statement. There never was a question of him going to the DA. He had given his word."

W.D. said, "It must have been a real blow for him to hear Ace confess when all the time he thought Charlie was the main suspect who had something to do with dad's death."

Red added, "But when Gene Petersen told you about the man in the long coat and big hat you zeroed in on Charlie, too."

I said, "I invested my reputation in Charlie Cole having killed dad. When I heard Ace's statement saying that he wore a long coat and a floppy hat to impress that bastard Cole, I tell you it pulled me up short. I was wrong tagging Charlie for dad's death. I'm disgusted with myself."

Red said, "Get real, how were you supposed to know how Ace was dressed in 1940 for Christ's sake."

"Thanks, Red."

W.D. said, "I take it Ace McNally is dead."

"No."

"You mean you didn't follow Oscar's instructions?"

Red interrupted. "Nick doesn't owe Ace anything. Oscar made the promise to him, not Nick."

I nodded. "Ace currently lives in Austin, Texas with his wife, Alice. They have two married children and three grandkids. After thirty years in the Air Force and another ten as an auto mechanic Ace is fully retired. They are members of a country club and have a wide circle of friends. Ace was living the good life until the good life bit him. He has lung cancer. Doctors say he has three months to live. What do you want to do about the bastard that killed our father?"

W.D. looked at Red then at me. They turned their eyes downward toward our parent's graves as if expecting a miracle answer. I said, "There is no chance at all of prosecuting him. Even if the local DA agreed he would be tried here not in Austin. I have press and TV contacts in Austin who would jump at the chance to report it the way we would want him exposed."

Red shook his head no but said nothing.

"Or we could confront him privately and make him sweat not knowing whether we were going to prosecute him or go public."

This wasn't going the way I expected. My brothers were not helping me out of the pit I was digging.

I gave it another try. "No matter what we do Ace has to know that we know. There's no free pass just because Ace is terminal. I grew up without a dad, and I still see myself as a kid crying and asking God why. Now I know who and why and this self-described sorry son of a bitch is not going to die without knowing that we know. That's a promise."

Red mumbled, "I say let's go to Hagens."

W.D. bowed his head and said, "Let us pray."

Hagens

Hagens had a jilted look about it. Without the bar stools filled with the 30s crowd and the ambulance chasers yet to fill the round tables, it was lonesome sight and it smelled of stale beer. I caught a familiar figure in a far booth, hung up my jacket and dropped a manila folder on the seat across from the High Sheriff. We exchanged insults then a waitress named Madge appeared. I ordered coffee and a shot of VO. Matt was still working on a shot and a beer.

I lit a cigarette, asked as I exhaled, "Where's Selma?"

"Don't ask." Not exactly surly but close on.

The brothers filed in and sat down. Madge dropped the VO and coffee on the table for me. Red said immediately, "Short beer and VO for me and W.D. This is my brother Nick from Texas."

Madge eyed me as if an outlander from Texas might contaminate the joint. She said, "Brothers, huh," and marched off.

W.D. said, "It's been bothering me all the way back from the cemetery. Didn't Oscar know our dad had Ace's information on Charlie Cole's operation? After all, they were best of friends."

Matt interrupted. "What's this?"

I held up my hand to Matt. "Oscar wrote that our dad never told him about his secret meetings with Ace. What happened was that an anonymous caller rang the PD several times that summer exposing the bootlegger's operations. At that time Oscar thought the source was someone in Charlie's gang."

Red asked, "But the anonymous calls?"

"Were made by our dad."

Matt again. "Will somebody tell me what's going on?"

I reached into the manila folder and took out my mini recorder. "Listen to this, Matt. In fact listen to it in the head. Just don't let anyone overhear."

Matt shrugged and stepped down the hallway to the men's room. I said, "Don't worry about Matt. He knows how to keep his mouth shut. About what we do with Ace McNally, that's different. That is just between us."

Red lit up a new cigar and settled back, prime time satisfaction glowed from his face. I reached into the folder and handed W.D. Oscar's letter to Frank Dowling and his sealed comments covering Ace's taped statement, and a second mini cassette.

I said, "You and Red now have everything I got from Frank Dowling's daughter. If you don't have a mini recorder, buy one."

Matt returned and placed his bulk next to me. Handing me my recorder, he said, "Astounding. Who would ever have believed that that silly ass McNally was responsible for your dad's death? I'm not going to ask the obvious questions as they are none of my business, but how are you boys taking it?"

Red slowly twirled the fake Havana giving it an inspection worthy of a Marine Corps DI. "After all these years kinda numb."W.D. said, "That's about as good a word as any. Numb."

I wasn't numb I was mad as hell. I kept seeing that son of a bitch pushing my father on the railroad tracks and not doing a damn thing about it. I used my Zippo on another smoke, calming myself. I said, "I have a long drive ahead of me and I gotta fill the inner man." I signaled Madge. W.D. ordered a cheeseburger basket, I seconded. Red and Matt preferred to stay with the VO.

"Long drive where?" This from Red.

"Mercerville. I stayed with Mae Bell last night and I'm booked in at the same place tonight."

With the ketchup bottle perched over his French fries W.D. said weakly, "Mae Belle. You mean Mae Belle Foster?"

I mumbled through a mouthful, "The same. A true friend, and a person you'd want with you when the going got sticky."

"Sticky?"

Matt explained, "Like when you're in somebody else's premises without permission."

Red laughed, eyed W.D. "Like the time you and Mae Belle were in her father's barn without permission."

W.D. pushed away his empty basket, ignoring Red. "If Charlie Cole wasn't responsible for dad's death why did Mamie Esterhaus shoot you?"

"The same question I asked myself when I thought I was dying. During the winter months recovering from my wound the why never left my mind. I had a pretty good inkling why, but when I listened to Ace's statement I finally knew our dad's death hadn't any direct connection to Charlie's murder or that of Duster Grimes. It was my incessant poking around that waved the red flag. Mamie was afraid I was on the cusp of finding out her secret, the reason why she killed Charlie and had Duster wasted.

"I spent the last three days digging in southern Illinois, in a town no longer existing called Armstadt, and another town just hanging on called Burnt Prairie. The Esterhaus girls, Mamie, the twins, Sarah and Clara, and Fanny were all born in The Children of God church in Armstadt. You remember the photo of the four young girls standing in their Sunday best in front of a church? That was taken in Armsdadt.

"Until sometime in the 20's, their father Herman Esterhaus, and his religious sect owned substantial lands in the area. But they sold out and bought huge acreage roughly between Mercerville and the Edwards River. Again, they built a church exactly like the one in Armstadt.

Red asked, "Is this Armstadt near Fairfield?"

"Near enough."

I signaled Madge for a refill. When she left I said, "My inquiries with the local county clerks failed to locate the birth record of Gene Petersen."

Matt said, "Who is the key to this story, I take it?"

"Absolutely. I lucked out and found the daughter of the woman that acted as midwife for all the Esterhaus births. Fortunately, the mother kept a personal, but secret, record for all the births in which she served as midwife. It cost me a couple C notes to see that journal, but I will not name either mother or daughter.

"Census records list the number of individuals in a family, but births in a rural area may have gone unrecorded for years, or recorded not at all. That's where the midwife's journal came to be important, to substantiate a birth years after it happened."

Now for the lying, or as I preferred, not telling the complete truth. "At 11.52 pm on May 13, 1932, in The Children of God church in Armstadt, Illinois Mamie Louis Esterhaus gave birth to a male child, name unknown, father unknown. Present were her parents, Herman and Rebecca Cole Esterhaus, her sisters, Sarah and Clara, and her uncle, Charles Cole."

"My God," said W.D., "She had a bastard."

"Right. So I called Mae Belle and she personally checked the birth records of Mendon County. At 11:52pm on May 13, 1932, in The Children of God church in Mercerville, Sarah Rachel Esterhaus gave birth to a male child named Eugene. The father was Richard Petersen. The midwife who attended Mamie's birthing sent a notarized statement claiming she attended the birth of a male Esterhaus child in The Children of God church, *location not stated.*

She didn't exactly lie but neither did she admit the birthing occurred in The Children of God church in Armstadt not in Mercerville, nor did she give Mamie's name. Other notarized letters attesting to Eugene Petersen's birth were attached to the birth record: One from Rebecca Cole, Sarah's mother and one from Charles Cole, Sarah's uncle."

Red said, "So Charlie Cole knew Mamie's secret. No wonder she killed him."

"Look at these." I pulled the photos of the death scenes of Charlie Cole and Duster Grimes from my folder and handed them to Red. I waited until he passed them across to W.D. and Matt. "Charlie was killed in 1951 and Duster last year, forty-two years later for Christ's sake, yet the crime scenes, as you can see, were eerily alike. Both had a 06 Winchester lying by the body as if they were the suicide weapons, but the actual weapon that killed Duster and shot me was a Colt, Official Police, .22 long caliber with checkered walnut grips. I found an exact twin Colt, Official Police, .22 in Gene's barn that had been fired a long time ago. Not proof for Charlie's murder, but I'm not making a case for trial."

Matt held out Charlie's crime scene photo. "When the hell did you get this?"

Ignoring Matt, I said, "In both murders the telephone lines were disabled and both men were, if the levels of the whiskey bottles were accurate, drunk. How else could you shoot your victim through his open mouth unless he was in a drunken stupor?

"Sorry, Matt. Just before my trip down to Mercerville Ellen found Oscar's old investigative files in Frank Dowling's cabinet and gave them to me. One other thing, Lt. Dawson told me the PD finally obtained Duster's telephone records and the day prior to night of his murder he made numerous calls to Mamie Esterhaus. Her connection to Duster's murder wasn't hard to make."

"Why didn't you take me with you" Matt had a hard edge to his voice much as I would have had in similar circumstances.

"I only wish I had," I lied. "If you were there I wouldn't have gotten Gene's baseball bat across my head."

W.D. said, "I follow you. Mamie killed Charlie but it isn't clear to me why she did it."

I said, "Mamie had the two essential requirements of a blackmail victim, a secret she was desperate to keep and money. She had inherited all her father's land holdings and, of course, she was Gene's birth mother. Charlie was deeply in debt and had no compunction blackmailing his niece."

Red waved his stogy, chiding me. "Nice guy. I remember you telling us the Shelton mob did him in."

I laughed. "And here I thought you slept through that lecture. Mamie was simply an inviting target. He blackmailed her and she killed him."

Matt chimed in. "Reasonable, no proof but reasonable. And Duster Grimes saw her entering or leaving Charlie's house the night he was murdered?"

"Correct. Duster's story about being in an Army hospital in Chicago that night was a bunch of crap. Mamie traded one blackmailer for another. But Duster's saving grace was that he had no knowledge of Mamie's secret. I doubt he tapped into Mamie until after he retired from the Army. Mamie had to figure she could control Duster as long as his demands were not excessive. Just enough to keep him off the unemployment lines and a ready supply of booze."

Matt said, "Ever think you asked one too many questions? Mamie must have believed Duster was going to crack, but it's hard for me to believe that Gene killed him. What about the missing sister, Fanny? You haven't mentioned her."

"My thought exactly. I had an ex-copper pal of mine who is an expert tracer get on Fanny Naomi's trail. She and her husband, Glen Stanley, who farmed near Bolivar, Tennessee, were killed in a head on automobile accident on August 3rd, 1966. They had no children."

It was easier explaining the fictional death of Fanny Naomi Esterhaus than the reality of Mamie's living sister, Frances Johnson. Anybody interested in the truth might claim I had just lied to my best pal.

"So we are back to Gene having murdered Duster."

"The only thing I can say is that he was the only one who could have given the Colt .22 to Mamie after Duster was murdered."

Red said, "You did a hell of a job, Nick. I really mean it, a hell of a job. About that other matter, we talked it over and whatever you want to do has our support."

"I'll get the tab." I watched my brothers tug on their coats and depart by the back door. They had slowed down a tad, my future in another decade minus a year. It knew it was up to me to handle the Ace McNally matter when I got back to Texas. I could do that.

Matt

Matt eyed me, said, "You're looking better. Last time you looked like shit."

I said, "I prefer death warmed over instead of shit."

"You know, Nick, W.D. isn't much of a drinker."

I laughed, "Red makes up for him. By the way old pal whatever happened to Selma?"

Matt grunted, actually grunted. "She ran away with a mope half her age. Last I heard they're playing house in Punta Gorda, Florida."

"Got a replacement?"

Another grunt. "Jesus, you're really nosey."

"You're right." I applied the old Zippo to a smoke, inhaled and told myself not to worry, secondary emissions in Hagens were enough to cashier a guy. "I want to thank you again for all you did for me when I was laid up."

"No thanks necessary."

"It was nice of the director to offer me two weeks free care in The Manor."

Matt said, "He was scared out of his gourd you were going to sue. Plus you had the TLC of Verlee Haines."

"I asked her to marry me."

"You're joshing."

"Well yeah, but her husband wasn't laughing. He was the size of a NFL tackle and a security guard at The Manor."

Matt opined. "What the hell, Verlee could have played tackle."

I said, "Plenty of heft and the vocal cords of a Marine DI. She didn't let the press get to me. Or anyone else she didn't approve of, like the coroner who took my statement. She told him I had amnesia and if he didn't understand that he could pack up his briefcase and get out."

Matt said, "I was there too, Nick."

"Right, you helped."

"Thanks a lot."

"You're welcome."

Matt shook his head in disgust. "What about Clara Reece?"

It was difficult dissembling to Matt, but a soupcon of fiction might get me through this murderous brew. "Clara Reece was poisoned. It could have been self-inflicted, but if it was murder I haven't a clue who did it." I had a clue all right, but I hid the truth behind the fact that, as a lawman, I had no proof. "For example, Oscar Swensen's investigative file was of no help, and Icky's father, Parker Gould, obviously filed a fictional report that surprise, surprise is no longer extant. Icky's father was a thief wearing a badge."

Matt waved Marge over, ordered two VOs. "I've had enough of the Esterhaus family."

Not as much as I had.

He said, I thought in a hopeless way, as if his burden was too great to handle alone. "You know, don't you?"

"Know what?"

"About Jessica."

I did not want to walk this trail with Matt, but he was sadly in the mood. I gave him a lead. "What are you talking about?"

He bent over, hands together as if in prayer. "It was crazy, just crazy. I had applied for a detective's job in Springfield. Mary Lou was engaged to Brainard Johnson which is funny if you think about it because her maiden name is Johnson. Johnson marries Johnson and they form the Johnson and Johnson Insurance Company. Convenient if you think about it."

Matt laughed as if the mere thought of a liaison between two Johnson's was joke on someone I'm not quite sure who.

"Mary Lou sold me an insurance policy, and it just happened. Soon after I moved to Springfield she married Brainard. Hell, I didn't even know until after the auto accident that nearly cost Jessie her life."

Details I didn't need but Matt was intent on plowing old ground. "Jessie was just eighteen, a beautiful girl, bright, she had a scholarship." He choked, caught himself. It was painful watching him struggle. "If Jessie lying there near death wasn't enough Brainard died of a massive heart attack. I helped Mary Lou out, commiserated with both of them. When Mary Lou told me I was Jessie's father, I damn near fainted. Looking at Jessie, all broken bones and despair, it just broke me up. And I couldn't tell her I was her father."

"Mary Lou refused to let you tell Jessie?"

Matt nodded. "She said Jessie's life was complicated enough." I wanted to say something meaningful, but as usual mouthed some nonsense you could get from reading a sympathy card. The consolation was that he knew there was nothing I could say. Friends always know that. Then I remembered Jessie saying she confided in Matt as if he was her real father. Deep thinker that I am I decided that life was a screwed up mess.

"I'm sorry."

I could hardly hear him. He mumbled, "Mary Lou is really concerned."

This was becoming difficult. I said, "You mean she suspects my intentions?" I didn't add honorable.

"The question is age. You, me, Mary Lou are of an age. She could put up with a fling. It's the long term that disturbs her."

It was out of my mouth before I realized that I was talking to Matt Jackson, Jessie's father, not Matt Jackson my lifelong pal.

"What long term?"

"Jesus, Nick, sometimes you don't have a clue."

Matt hit the target that time. I said, "I apologize for sounding so unfeeling. Jessie means a great deal to me, but I'll be upfront with you. I never expected our being together was going any place. I'm old enough to be her . . . well I'm aware

of the differences in our ages. Tell me, what don't
I know?"

"Jessie says she loves you."

I swear I gulped. "And?"

"She intends to marry you."

"Does she know about Ellen?"

"They met while you were still sedated."

"And I wasn't told?"

"Jessie admires Ellen. She says Ellen is very
mature about the situation."

I bellowed, "You mean she told Ellen she was
intent on marrying me! Jessie's a child."

"She's determined."

I waffled, "I wish I had known about this
before."

Matt was back to mumbling. "I don't blame you,
Nick. I know Jessie acts impulsively sometimes."

Sometimes? Matt's old saw in Hagens came
to mind - half your age plus ten. I'd bedded his
daughter. How or why it happened meant nothing,
I had abused his friendship. It would never be the
same between us. Never. We sat in silence.

I left Madge a huge tip, obviously not thinking
straight. We walked slowly back our cars, talking
of escapades in sneakers, of better times when our
lives were simpler.

Matt asked, "You going to see Jessie?"

"Not after the bomb you threw me."

I waved to him as he churned up the rear tires. Dammit, why did he tell me Jessie was his daughter? My life was complicated enough.

Heading south toward Mercerville the weather turned ugly, the sky had a gray-black tinge that foretold rain, or worse. Wind gusts charged my rental car savagely as if they had it in for the snaky but puny midsize. Like the Shelton gang of southern Illinois lore who clanked down Main Street in a used a WWII tank for protection I should have given more thought to March in the Midwest. The lion had roared in and refused to depart.

I should have been expansive, but my spirit was shrouded in gloom. It wasn't taking a bullet that was so depressing. That was physical. But being caught up in the mysteries surrounding my father's death and the enigmatic Esterhaus clan suicides, seemingly without answers, that was depressing. I had spent months closeted in my Texas condo hampered by the march of time and deaths of those who might have been able to help me. But now I had answers. I knew why my dad was on the railroad tracks and who caused his death. But why Mamie felt compelled to shoot me that I'd face up to alone at the cemetery. It was time for the complete truth, not the varnished version I'd given my brothers and Matt.

The Children of God Cemetery

The church had suffered. The front gutter had broken away, paint peeled from the window frames, the back stoop steps listed to port as if acknowledging *The Children of God* ship was sinking fast.

I took my copy of *SUNBEAMS* from the front seat. I scanned Mamie's inscription to me signed in her precise hand ages ago. I smiled. I must have acted up because those dratted poems ruined my baseball season. I carried my manila folder and the book of poems as I walked up the rise to the cemetery. The ground was scruffy, leaves lay in sodden clumps. Several tree limbs lay hard against the wrought iron fence. I brushed the seat of a wrought iron bench and sat down.

The grounds, like the church, required a caretaker.

The **Esterhaus** granite monument was as I remembered it, the centerpiece of hallowed ground. The numerals, 1993, had been freshly etched in the stele acknowledging *Mamie's* death.

Herman Eugene	1885-1949
Rebecca Cole	1890-1932
Mamie Louise	1907-1993
Sarah Rachel	1908-1963
Clara Ann	1908-1953
Fanny Naomi	1909-

When Mamie had slit her wrists years ago in The Manor she was moaning about *her children* not her child. And Clara, before she was poisoned, raved about *the children*. I didn't know then what either sister meant but when I called Dolph Sterns he told me that his dad said there were two Esterhaus babies when they buried Rebecca in '32. Sarah had a new baby and either Clara or Fanny had one too. Hard to remember which one, said Dolph.

Mamie had two babies. Twins a girl and a boy. My God, I was dim. Herman had a twin brother, Rebecca Cole and Charlie were twins, Clara and Sarah, too. The whole Esterhaus shebang was awash with twins. And I didn't catch on until I saw Francine Mays' midwife journal.

She recorded that Mamie had birthed twins, a boy born at 11:52 pm on May 13, 1932 and a girl, born at 12:15 am on May 14, 1932. Gene's falsified birth certificate had been filed in Mendon County the day of his birth, but Mary Louise Johnson's birth record was not filed until August 12, 1937 – *five years later and just prior to her entering grade school.* And who was the teacher that accepted her birth certificate? Mamie Louise Esterhaus of course.

Clever. I had to admire the planning that went in to filing these false birth records: Gene's filed on May 13th, 1932, and Mary Lou's filed on August 12, 1937. Same midwife affirmed the births, backed up by good old Charlie's notarized statements. Even the dates of their births varied by a day, Gene born on May 13th and Mary Lou May 14[th.] Oh yes, Mary Lou's parents were listed as Joseph Johnson, father, and Frances N., mother.

When Ann pointed out a name in my sister's address book I caught the name Mrs. Frances N. Johnson, living at The Manor. At the time I wondered if Mamie's sister Fanny Naomi might be Frances Johnson, but it was just a passing thought. As Matt said, I was smoking dope. Her name hadn't surfaced during my inquiry and I had no factual reason to believe that Frances N. Johnson was Fanny Naomi Esterhaus.

Then I called Scott Mansfield, my state hospital source. I gathered that he was sorry he had ever heard of Nick James. He claimed he couldn't remember, but I was good at buttering and I buttered Scott Mansfield real good. Yes, Mrs. Frances Johnson was a member of the night cleaning crew when Clara Reece died and yes, her daughter, Mary Lou, clerked in the office. Scott Mansfield wouldn't lose any sleep if I left for Texas on the first stage. In fact that is precisely what he said.

So Fanny Naomi had married and had altered her given name to Frances N. sometime before agreeing to be the proxy mother for Mamie Louise's bastard girl child. Mary Lou Johnson, my classmate those many years ago, bore the middle name, Louise, just like her actual birth mother, Mamie Louise Esterhaus.

And when the time came it was Frances who slipped cyanide into Clara's nightly drink. "Here, dear sister, Mamie doesn't like for you to talk about the children. No more screaming about the children, hear!"

What could I have told Matt? What the hell could I have told him? By the way Jessica's grandmother was a killer. What if he asked me for proof? Well, Matt old pal I haven't got any, but my years as a homicide dick inspired me. Jesus.

How Frances Johnson concealed her family background I haven't a clue, but I am certain Mary Lou had no knowledge that her true mother was Mamie, nor that her proxy mother, Frances Johnson, a night cleaning woman at the state hospital conspired with Mamie to bring about their sister Clara's death.

What a controller, Mamie Esterhaus. She not only gave her children to Sarah and Fanny but demanded that their husband's keep her secret, too. Charlie Cole should have known better than try to blackmail her.

A few raindrops began to splatter on the ground. I felt the cold, zipped up my jacket, carried my manila folder and Mamie's book of poems directly in front of the Esterhaus monument, the headstones at my feet. I spoke to Mamie, to her alone:

Mamie

"You had to have them near you, your birth twins. You must have lived in fear lest the Esterhaus instability showed up in Gene or Mary Louise. Your father and mother were first cousins and you realized the problem early on. Clara showed signs of dementia so you couldn't allow her to become Gene's proxy mother. Sarah was never quite with it, but her husband, Richard was stable.

"Poor Gene. Forever lagging behind, the butt of schoolmate's cruel harassment, unable to protect himself, mentally or physically. Sarah wasn't much of a protector, either. You pressured Charlie Cole to give them the Reimer's house. Or did you secretly pay Charlie for the house? Regardless, it was *vital* that you saw to Gene's upbringing.

As to Gene's twin sister, Mary Louise was a gifted, outstanding student, loads of friends, a natural leader. And your sister Frances proved to be the perfect mother. There was nothing proxy about her care and her love for your child. Frances stood up for Mary Lou, doted on her, gave her a proper home.

"How did it go? Frances was working nights in the security ward at the state hospital. She must have been frantic that Clara, in her ravings about the children, would expose the truth. So she went to you. It was you who provided the cyanide and

Frances who carried out the deed. You and Frances murdered your sister. How diabolical.

Suddenly, cold rain came down in a fury cleansing the head stones. The pines guarding the western edge of the cemetery shielded me from the worst, but it was a losing proposition. I tucked Mamie's *SUNBEAMS* under my jacket, but it was already soaked.

"It must have been pure hell for you. It was bad enough when Charlie blackmailed you, but then you had to deal with Clara, too. I give you credit. Only a brilliant mind could have gotten away with their murders."

The gravesite told it all. I went on talking to Mamie's headstone, convinced of my logic. I looked down at the headstones, silent reminders of the dead.

Left: *Richard - Sarah Rachel- Clara Ann – Rebecca Cole*

Right: *Herman Eugene– **Eugene Herman** – **Mamie Louise*** - two blank stones.

"Gene was laid to rest between you and Herman." It was sleeting now, punishing me with icy droplets. My so-called rain jacket had soaked through. Water threaded down my neck onto my shirt. I shivered.

"And now for THE secret. If it had become known that your own father sired your twins the scandal would have ruined the religious group he inspired, The Children of God.

"Incest is such an abhorrent crime."

I was shouting through the downpour, I must have looked like a loony left out too long. "I can't believe you were a willing partner, but just the notion of doing it with your own father sickens me. What did your unfortunate mother think when she realized who made you pregnant? Not too hard to figure that one out. Ten days after your twins were born she committed suicide. The shame of bringing into the world babies who were the product of her husband and her eldest daughter was a humiliation she could not live with.

"They all died violent deaths: Your mother Rebecca, your sister Clara, your son Gene and you. Even your sister Sarah pitched down the staircase. And those that got in your way - Charlie Cole, Duster Grimes, almost me. All to prevent the world from knowing your bastards were sired by your father."

I wiped water from my face, but the effort was useless. I couldn't see more than ten yards, and my shoes were sinking in the muck.

Pointing my finger at the Esterhaus stele, I had the presence of a prosecutor charging the guilty with high crimes. Lightening hit a maple shearing off half the tree. I jumped as it hit the ground. The pines were bent over, water rushed between the headstones carrying along winter's debris. It occurred to me that Mamie was paying me back.

"Your secret lay in these graves until I started asking questions."

Shouting wasn't doing it. My words were lost in the storm's roar. What the hell was I shouting for anyway? I mouthed the words. "Mamie, damn it, listen:

"When Sheriff Hansen called you he mentioned I'd been with Gene just before he committed suicide. Right then you knew I'd been digging deeper into your contemptible secret. That night in The Manor when I saw your phone off the hook I knew you hadn't made a phone call, *you received one.* It was from Frances. What did she say? 'Kill him, he knows all.' Is that what she said? 'You have the gun, Mamie. I gave it to you after I killed Duster. Kill him.'

"It was only when I was sliding down the wall with a .22 in my chest that I understood Frances had killed Duster. The entire death scene at Duster's was clever, damn clever. You read my mind think perfectly. Make it look like Charlie's. Nick will make the connection, Duster's death scene exactly like Charlie's. And he will conclude Gene was responsible. He is a linear thinker, smart but linear. He knows I'm too frail to have killed Duster so he will blame Gene. Yes, dear sister, you kill Duster, and if it becomes necessary I'll kill Nick.

"You were as crazy as Clara, but a quiet crazy, the crazy that kills without remorse. But,"

I laughed, "so is your sister, Frances. The whole damn family's crazy."

The downpour began to ease, and, for the moment, it was not quite so dark. Then, filtering between the pines, I saw Gene's figure emerge, mouthing the words, "My Mother, My Mother." My end table sat on the ground beside him. I was hallucinating, I knew that, but his presence was overpowering. I understood he knew Mamie was his mother, but I hoped he hadn't heard all that I had said. I stood motionless as if my slightest move would break the spell. But I had to tell him. I owed him.

I yelled, "It's just between us, Gene. No one will ever know."

He brushed back his hair, seemed to smile, then picked up the end table, turned around, and faded away slowly. I cupped my hands over my eyes, shielding off the rain, but he was gone. God, who was the nut now?

I placed *SUNBEAMS* on top of Mamie's headstone. I yelled, "The photo of you Esterhaus girls is inside. I found the church down in Armstadt where it was taken." I waited as if expecting an answer, said quietly, "I don't want it any more. And I don't want these anymore." I pulled the notarized records and notes from my folder and tore them to bits. The wind did the rest.

I trudged back to my car, got a fresh pack of cigarettes out of the glove compartment. My hands shook as I used my Zippo. I was soaked from head to toe. I caught my face in the rear view mirror and wondered who it was. Madness.

The storm passed over, making its way northeast. The heavens slowly brightened. I sat for a long time pondering the Esterhaus tragedy. Let the dead stay buried. W.D. said that. I reckoned he wasn't the only one who would disapprove my digging into this sinkhole of evil. The way I looked at it the innocent ones who had died violent deaths might now rest in peace.

I drove to Mae Belle's feeling as if I had gone the distance in a fight that should have been called. God, I was beat. I needed a hot shower, a glass of Wild Turkey, and bed. And I didn't need any help, thank you very much.

APRIL 1994

San Antonio, Texas

He was laying on a hospital bed, partially propped up, eyes closed, breathing faint and labored. A sheet covered him up to his waist, a white gown thereafter. Not knowing him as a man I could not tell if, or how much, his body had deteriorated, but the lines ebbing across his face were those of a very sick, very old man. I sat along side his bed staring. The lung cancer had advanced to his brain. He was definitely terminal. I felt cheated finding him in such a state. It was like beating the crap out of a cripple, but I could care less. He killed my father. That's all I cared about.

I had taken a private flight from Houston, and pondered all the way just how to handle this bastard. What if I found him comatose or worse yet dying? But he was simply lying there with his eyes closed. His wife usually visited him at noon and stayed the rest of day. I had the better part of two hours alone with him but I temporized, not the same hotshot detective I knew so well.

His eyelids fluttered open and he focused on my face. "Who are you," he whispered.

I forced a smile. "I grew up in the same neighborhood as you. Remember the old East End on the banks of the Mississippi?"

He smiled, seemingly nodded. "But who are you?" It was a struggle for him to get out the words. I decided that there wouldn't be too many words left for Ace McNally.

"Oh, you wouldn't remember me. But you'd remember my father, Michael James. I have a tape I'd like you to listen to." I held my mini recorder next to his ear and pushed on the play button. As he recognized his words admitting to pushing my father onto the railroad tracks he closed his eyes tightly and shrunk up as if trying to disappear within his own body.

"How?"

"How did I get the tape?" He nodded. "Oscar Swensen kept his promise to you. He never exposed you, but unfortunately for you, I never promised. All I see in Ace McNally is a coward who killed my father and ran away. You owed my father. He bailed you out of jail, advised you to join the Army. And how did you repay him? with appreciation? with gratitude? No, you ranted and raved and waved your arms, and in a fit of frenzy you killed him, that's what you did."

"No, no, I didn't."

"Didn't what? Didn't kill him?" You miserable bastard. I grew up without a father, my mother without a husband, my sister and brothers without a dad all because of you. Here," I took a black and white photograph from my jacket, "this was taken of all of us in the back yard in the summer of 1940. I'm the little guy standing in front of my dad.

"What is it? Fifty-four years ago? Fifty-four years you have lived without paying a price, fifty-four years without being held responsible, fifty-four years going scot-free, no accounting legally and none morally. But no longer, I promise you no longer."

He lay there helpless, crying now, a mist drifting down his cheeks. Christ, he didn't even have the strength to cry. I forced the photo into his fingers. He mumbled, "What?"

"You mean what am I going to do? Oscar is dead. That ought to give a breather. The one witness to your taped admission is dead. But I have the original tape and a big surprise for you. You were seen that night on the tracks with my father. Remember the Petersen family who lived in that run down shack between the tracks and the river? Their son, Gene Petersen saw you. He was just a kid my age, one of my school friends. He told me he saw you waving your arms at my dad.

So I have a witness damn your soul and he is ready to testify."

So I lied.

"Please."

"Please what? Don't tell your wife? Don't tell your kids. Don't tell your grandkids? It bothered me that you made Oscar Swensen promise not to release your confession until after you were dead. It puzzled me. You made the tape in 1967. You were 47 years old and about to retire from the Air Force. But it all became clear when I found out you weren't married until 1969 to a much younger woman, and didn't have children until the 70s.

"Then it made sense. You were single in 1967. The only person you gave a shit about in 1967 was yourself so making Oscar promise not to make the tape public until after you were dead was a reasonable but shortsighted request. You may have figured that your confession after you were dead gave you absolution of sorts. But there is no absolution for you now. None.

"But now you have a family. Your wife and children are precious to you. What you are really concerned about is that I will expose your secret. What a story it will make, ten o'clock news, front-page stuff. The stuff newscasters live on. I can do it you know. Trust me, they'd go for the story of how I found the man who killed my father in 1940. They'd play your taped confession on TV, and my childhood buddy would tell them how you waved your arms and threatened my father.

"Or you can just die. You do know you are going to die?" He nodded. "I'll promise you no press, no exposure, if you do just one thing." I could tell his mind, what was left of it, was grasping my words. I dropped my head close to his. "You want to hear your option?" His nod was imperceptible, but it was there. "You must place my family's photo in your folded hands in your casket when you die. Oh yes, I know you do not intend to be cremated. I will be present at your wake and funeral so do not think you can destroy my photograph. If you do not agree I will expose you for the sorry son of a bitch you are. My father's death goes with you for eternity."

The photo had fallen from his fingers, but I tucked it firmly in his hands. "Remember, if the photo goes with you when you die there will be no exposure. Surely the peace and comfort to your wife and children is worth my small request. But if I fail to see the photograph in your hands your family and the world will know."

I last saw him holding onto the photograph gasping for air with a vacant stare in his eyes. I paused at the door hoping the son of a bitch would die then and there. He didn't. I left.

OCTOBER 2002

Ace McNally died ten days after my face-to-face with him in San Antonio. I didn't attend his wake to see if he still held the photograph of my father in his casket. I prayed that he had sweated out my threat of media exposure during the last ten days of his miserable life. He died knowing that my brothers and me knew that he had killed Michael James, but that wasn't enough for me. When I first heard his taped confession all I thought about, dreamed about was vengeance. Vengeance would be mine, I promised myself. Then I learned he was dying, and it was as if a candle had been snuffed out. I'd never be able to hurt the bastard the way he hurt my mother, and Sis and W.D. and Red, and me. I wanted him alive and well, not some piece of shit lying in a coma. I never heard him beg for mercy, please don't tell my wife, think of my kids, words I craved to hear. I had to satisfy my anger with the meaningless threat of exposure. Meaningless because I had no intention of inflicting his wife and children and grandkids with TV cameras shoved in their faces, caught up in a crime they knew nothing about. He didn't know that, but the sorry son of a bitch only lasted ten days. Ten days was a blink in the eye in the life my father would have had and shared with me.

In the tape Ace asked that God forgive him. It's a good thing he didn't ask me.

New Hampshire

After my talk with Ace McNally I decided a change of venue might adjust my outlook. It wasn't just about Mamie shooting me, but my life was in the dumper. Retirement sucked, Ellen rejected me again like a record stuck in the same old place, and as far as Jessica was concerned the thought of marriage chilled me. A head shrinker might have diagnosed me with depression, but depression wasn't Nick James. Let's just say dealing with the Esterhaus murders and suicides left me a little down.

So I sold my condo in Texas and moved to this nothing village or Notch as they are wont to call such places in New Hampshire. I took the job of constable that paid a salary commensurate with the crime level. The local real estate agent conned me into buying a run-down two hundred year old saltbox, with a straight face as he claimed, a history. The only person of note who had not slept in it was George Washington.

I still have trouble with the native's lingo, but when the old gaffers down at Ed's Cafe invited me to sit for a spell and have a cup I knew I had arrived. They were good, solid people. I just couldn't understand them.

Then Jessica moved in. "Here I am, your very own girl/child. Wanna fight it?" I didn't. Eyes alight and enthusiasm run wild she worked along side me as I rebuilt this clapboard mistake they called a house with a history into a livable home. She gave it personality and to me a lot more. The only serious argument we had was over the placement of my scrubby end table I had lifted from Gene Petersen's kitchen. Of course, she never knew anything about Gene and cared less to know about my youthful work of art. I was satisfied with the fiction that as soon as we completed work on this 200-year old disaster it would grace the living room. Jessie gave out with a satanic smile. I knew damn well it would stay in the barn.

Every four years presidential contenders listened to the locals vent their views making believe they were interested in New Hampshire politics and the state of the nation. The townies laughed about this local that told the leading contender that he hadn't made up his mind to vote for him as he had only met him twice. And, bless her, Jessie joined in. She was good at venting.

Jessie died of cancer on a fall day two years ago. She was optimistic to the end worrying more about me and our home and the townies that needed her help. She never complained even though the diagnosis was preordained, and she died in pain. I was devastated. I buried her in a glen shadowed by the White Mountains. Matt was there along with the locals she captivated. When the service and church luncheon was over Matt returned to the house with me. We sat with a glass in our hands watching the magnificent view. In the fall the colors are dazzling, but that day and for the longest time after the colors were, to me, subdued as if I was saying a long goodbye to Jessie.

I remember how Matt started out. "You never told Jessie did you?"

Considering it was the day I buried my sweetheart I wasn't thinking too swift. "Told her what?"

"That I was her father."

"No, I never did."

Matt was sort of talking to the distant mountains as if afraid I would hear him. "Gene never killed Duster Grimes. If there ever was a bunny rabbit it was Gene. I'm sorry Gene belted you with a baseball bat, but no, Nick, Gene never killed Duster."

I sat and smoked and feared what was coming.

"And you not knowing who poisoned Clara Reese was an obvious deception. Nick James would never have rested until he had solved Clara Reece's murder. I know Nick James."

Matt got up and walked outside watching the sun disappear over the mountains. I poured myself more bourbon, in fact, a lot more bourbon. I had lied and covered the sad Esterhaus tragedy so that Jessica would not learn the truth of her heritage, nor would Matt who was her father. But maybe now was the time for all the truth.

I said, "The murders were committed to preserve Mamie's secret. Charlie Cole, Clara Reece, Duster Grimes. And the suicides, Mamie shot herself, her mother Rebecca Cole and her son Gene drown in Mercerville's lake.

"In May, 1932, she gave birth to twins, an unnamed boy and a girl, father unknown in Armstadt, Illinois."

Matt sucked in his breath. "Twins? Bastards? Who was the father?"

"Her father."

"My God in heaven, incest." Matt paused trying to handle what I was telling him. "I take it Gene was the boy. But the girl?"

"Mamie saw to it that they were reared close to her. Her sister, Sarah and her husband Richard raised Gene, and Frances Johnson, the fourth Esterhaus sister and her husband, claimed Mary Louise for their own. You must realize by now that Mamie controlled all of them."

Matt said with a hint of reproach. "Frances Johnson never died in an automobile accident in Tennesse."

"That's right."

But then his face softened. "All lies to protect Jessica. It's about Jessica, isn't it?"

Not too much detail, I told myself. "Her grandmother Frances was a member of the state hospital's char force, and she conspired with Mamie to poison their crazy sister Clara Reece. And with Mamie's guidance Frances, not Gene, shot and killed Duster Grimes. Jessica never knew any of this."

"But did Mary Lou?"

"No." A positive no distanced Jessica from the entire Esterhaus legacy of violence. What her mother Mary Lou did or did not know was an unknown.

Matt said, "That day at Hagens when you asked me to get you the 1953 personnel records from the state hospital I refused. The records obviously had to do with the killer of Clara Reece. You could have asked Jessie, she would have gotten what you wanted, but you didn't ask her. Why?"

Matt held up his hand stopping my interruption. "I was of two minds. I decided you knew Clara Reece was murdered. Then I concluded you were way off base, and the death of Clara Reece was really a suicide as the hospital claimed."

I said, "I didn't know Frances Johnson had worked at the state hospital until the night Mamie shot me. She was the only one who had a reason, other than Mamie, to poison Clara.

"I'm beholden to you, Nick. You protected Jessica, that's all that counts."

Matt would call from Florida when the thermometer dropped out of sight, but I'm still sitting here on my dead rear sipping bourbon and smoking. And I'd call W.D. and Red at Hagens when the mood inspired me. That way I get a twofer. I got the idea that they had slowed up a tad, but as to the current status of the East End, or as a matter of fact Hagens, absolutely nothing had changed. The WWII crowd at the bar had thinned, but otherwise life proceeded at a pace consistent with a snails. Ann hangs onto our old home that is still known as the James place. Kinda ironic when the renters are named Gonzales.

My life hasn't changed outwardly, still having coffee at Ed's, still the constable. Crime is up. I arrested Jimmy Rawling's boy one night trying to make change at Sarah's restaurant register by flashlight. But inwardly I'm at loose ends. I smoke and drink too much. The best friend I have is my Zippo lighter. Without a partner helping me do the work the house redo sort of came to a standstill. And when I brush my hand over my end table I smile. It is still in the barn. I guess it will always remain there.

The doorbell rang.
I opened the door.
It was Ellen.

AFTERWORD

I began this mystery some ten years ago. The initial draft and subsequent rewrites did not develop the story line to my satisfaction. One thing I had right was the setting. What I call the East End in the book is the neighborhood from 43rd street to 55th street, the last street in Moline, Illinois – from 5th avenue and the bluff and woods above it down 48th street that dead ends before the Rock Island railroad tracks. And lastly, the old river road and the Mississippi River that at this stage in its geography runs east to west.

There were no murders or suicides in the East End of my youth. The plot is imaginary and many of the characters are facsimiles of neighbors from an age long gone. Other characters are entirely fictional. I sent the reworked manuscript to Tom Mitz my New York City editor who had brilliantly critiqued my first two books. Once again Tom addressed a number of vexing problems, thus the final rewrite of, *Let The Dead Stay Buried.* I hope you enjoyed it.

Robert R. Glendon